The Garden Of Eve
Book one

By: Flo V.J. Shephard

~ In Gratitude~

To all who have found it in their hearts to
help, coddle, share and teach.

Kari, Kristian, Joyce, Colleen, and Bill,
you gave me notes with much to think about.
Thank you from the bottom of my heart.

Especially to Sue; you were the first to
read the first draft. Your excitement and
encouragement gave me the courage to take the
next step. Thank you for the love.

© Copyright 2017
Published by: Live4once Books
In association with Cajones Productions

1

Artwork by: Robert DuBack
Editing by: Patricia Watkins

Table of Contents

Prologue: In The Beginning

There may be a traditional upbringing,
but I certainly didn't have one. For as long as I
can remember I preferred running around naked
to having to suffer clothing. Didn't make me a
pervert or eccentric at the age of 3, but at any age
after 12 it was often frowned upon. Fortunately
I had very loving and understanding parents.
My Dad; Adam West is a sex educator, sex
therapist, basically a sexologist. My mother
Sylvia is just sexy and as cunning as they come!

The first time my parents brought me to a
nude beach I was 6 years old. When my Mom
brought me into the water, it was like being in a
bathtub only with colder water and it was the
size of the ocean as far as I could tell! It felt good
being able to swim around and not have the
confines of straps either being too tight or falling
off my shoulders every five seconds!

My father taught me to respect my body;
my temple. In turn I was also to respect the
bodies of other people as their temple, not
something to make fun of or gawk at. "All of

God's creatures are beautiful in their own ways"
he would say and he meant ways because
"Human beings are complex multiple
organisms, not just a single cell life form", he
would also say. It took me a few years to
understand how right he was. The complexities
of the human race can be a life time of study all
by itself. So I took to concentrating on women.

By the time I was ten, I had already met
many girls who were very insecure about
themselves, girls who were so self-conscious and
afraid of their own shadow. I just didn't get it.
My mother was a constant reminder of how
beautiful all her children were, how smart they
were. We could do or be anything we wanted. I
did everything I could to show other girls how
wonderful they were, how special they were. I
was often told I was overbearing and too huggy.
I was left so confused. Did the negative attitude
of others discourage me? Hell no! I realized at a
young age I had a mission in life. It was up to
me to show as many girls as possible their
beauty, self-worth, and their wonderment.

Me, I'm Veronica. I was brought up to be comfortable in my own skin, to be happy with who I am no matter what I am dealing with in my life. Don't get me wrong, I am far from perfect, I have my quirks, my insecurities and my faults, but I do my best to keep a happy outlook on life. I also try not to let someone else's misery or drama ruin my day. Let's face it there are sucky times that happen in life, but as the old saying goes

"It's not what happens to you
in life that counts;
it is how you deal with it that does."

It has taken me most of my life to take what I have learned from my father's lessons and from my own life to realize how I could help women in a less clinical surrounding and create a safe comfortable environment for them to discover who they are, who they can be and to know it is okay for them to be who they feel they are, to be who they want to be and to get away from who everyone else thinks they should be. Finding the different *keys* to unlock ones confidence, faith, and knowledge of how

6

wonderful each individual is has been an enlightening and fulfilling experience I am grateful to live. Women are extraordinary beings and most of the time they don't realize how much they effect those around them.

Being the owner operator of the only educational escape resort for women in the USA (as far as I know) is a dream come true. "The Garden" was born after I freed myself from a marriage that I didn't realize was going to be one of convenience for him. It was time for a fresh start, to find a new path to make sure other women had a chance to avoid the misrepresentation that so many of us before have suffered.

It was the untimely death of my Dads' brother; my Uncle Simon that brought about the beginning of the dream. Simon was like a second father to me and he treated me like I was his. He knew I wanted to start The Garden but the money wasn't there. He had no children of his own and knew long before I did how ill he was. He left me a small inheritance and his second home which had a vineyard on a 400 acre property. He had already nurtured 69 of the acres of vines for 4 years with the help of my dear friend Maia Hanlin.

Maia's love of plants, and needing a job when my uncle needed help, made all right with the world. And thus this became the perfect "front" to help build the world I wanted for my resort.

Maia is a striking 6 foot tall Austrian who is free of spirit, full of brains and nurturer of nature. She took over the grounds of my uncles' property and expanded on what he began with varied grape vines she acquired from all over the world. She also began growing whatever other fruits and vegetables would sustain in the environment of central California. We met at a Women's Studies 101 class some 20 odd years ago. Within the first hour of the first class we both knew we were in the wrong place. I don't recall how we noticed each other's disbelief and discomfort with the teachers' lackluster interpretation but we left at the same time and found ourselves drinking margaritas at a local haunt discussing the unfairness of society's views and expectations of the fairer sex. I believe we were both dumbfounded to find someone who felt so strongly as each of us did about the wonder of the creature known as woman. She became a bright ray of sunshine in my life. It was a match made by the goddess' I say.

During the time of my Uncles illness my childhood friend Sienna Praddon; who is a medical Doctor came to help me with my uncle's health needs while Maia continued to nurture the property in readiness for the launch of Hanlin Cellars Wines.

Sienna and I go way back. Her mother had assisted my father with some of the "medical" aspects of his research and the two couples hit it off. Her dad was a Colonel in the military so our parents would often socialize at different functions including the officers' club happy hours. I would babysit Sienna because I am the older one you see. As we got older we just got closer. We have been through every wonderful and terrible emotional event in each other's lives. That is a whole story all in itself, for another rainy day perhaps.

Towards the end of my uncle's illness we all had time to sit and talk. With Simon's guidance and the support of my two dearest friends I was able to bring to light my lifelong dream of a place for women to go to for 'whatever need they may desire'.

Now I am in my 50's by the calendar, but my brain feels I'm not far past my early 20's. As my doctor, Sienna says I am over weight. I say I am "well insulated". My love for sugar, chocolate and carbs is my down fall. If I discover a way to be smaller and still have my addictions I will let you know how it is done.

So, this brings me to sharing a peek into life at The Garden with you. Make up your own mind what you think about what we do. If it's not for you, don't come to visit.

If it is something you can see yourself risking a change in the course of your life for, you will find us.

"The Garden"

The resort is not commonly known. How ever, to those "in the know", it is an oasis of knowledge, pleasure and escape for women. It is a full service Inn, restaurant, spa, school and bordella* all wrapped up in one. The resort is hidden behind the vineyards of our central California winery; "Hanlin Cellars", which has become a prestigious award winning venture for us.

The Garden is a perfect place to live a dream. Our guests range from soul searchers to academics, from aspiring chefs to wanna be astronomers, from 18 year old virgins looking to have the best first experience they can, to women hoping to recapture some semblance of their sexuality they thought was lost forever. Our school provides women with classes in a myriad of subjects including art, equestrian studies, music, horticulture, finance, spiritual practices, the science of wine and so much more!

Château Jardin is where all of our guests check in. The exterior is quaint and from the front it looks smaller than it is. The mansion is very country in style painted yellow and white. The old majestic shutters provide the perfect feeling of seclusion. The main building is where you will find our administration offices, the medical clinic, the florist, some rooms for classes, the coffee lounge and the hotel area for many of our guests.

When you enter through the front door the lobby is made up of an old world wood finish with red velvet drapes. The flooring is slices of wood stumps with stones filling in the gaps. The front desk is right out of an old Victorian post office. You are welcomed by one of many of our handsome men. He will most likely greet you by name; or by the name you have given us, and lead you to the front desk leaving you there in the capable hands of our Obi wan Victor Tanner while your luggage gets taken to your room or to a bungalow.

Victor keeps up with all the guests, schedules, events and classes. He knows who needs what, when, where, how and why. He also keeps an eye out for me/Veronica. Victor is an old friend of the family. I have known him most of my life. My father was Victors mentor. They "studied" together, traveling the world learning about love and sexual practices of as many cultures as they could find.

With a dry intellectual sense of humor Victor is often misread by both the staff and guests. More often than not you will find him with a book in hand. He is a handsome Cambridge scholar and has a love hate relationship with Wall Street. He is always giving the staff tips and they have learned it's a good idea to listen. He took the position at the Garden mainly to be a help to my new venture, but also as an extension of his studies. He is very particular about who he studies with though. It is a very short list.

There are plenty of rooms in the main house for guests. However, there are a number of bungalows dotted around the property for those who desire more privacy and or more fantasy. Some of them are themed including Tarzans tree house, The Gatsby, Camelot, an Arabian tent, and a Parisian flat, to name a few.

As you leave the main house by the back door an oasis awaits you. There are beautiful gardens and paths going off in every direction. Occasionally you can catch a glimpse of either an off road looking golf cart on steroids known as a Polaris ranger or in the distance you may see someone on horseback. There are swimming pools on the property, a few woman made hot tubs and 2 outer buildings in view from the back porch of the house.

To the right is "Pandoras Box" which is the main restaurant with a full service bar which includes patio seating for our beautiful sunny days. The décor is very Steampunk; futuristic, Victorian industrialistic. Go ahead, take your time, and wrap your brain around that. There is dark wood holding up the hammered copper bar. The stools are also made of copper with large leather cushions. The leather booths stained in a variety of colors around the walls are circular with curtains in front of them so the patrons can choose privacy or socializing as they dine and drink. There are no windows to be seen but they are there, just higher up and darkened. When the weather is accommodating the windows are open, but when they are closed it gives a better sense of intimacy and again privacy which is what The Garden is all about.

There are also tables in the middle of the room. Most of them are 2 seaters with a few 4 seaters scattered about. The walls are adorned with clocks, clockworks, octopi, and Steampunk accessories including bustles, goggles and hats.

The bar itself is full of Hanlin Cellar wines of course but we also carry wines from around the world and other inebriating concoctions to satisfy the most timid to the most daring partakers of drink. You can chance a sighting of "*la fée verte*" (the green fairy) with one of our home made Absinthes, or try one of our bartenders' favorite forget tonight tomorrow drinks like "Moon Shadow"; made with coconut rum, and Baileys. If alcohol is not to your liking, we also have virgin concoctions as well. We are sure you will be able to find something that works for you.

As you go further into Pandoras there is an area for live music and dancing. Of course we also have karaoke available. The more you drink the better you sound, or so I've heard. For the hard core singer, we also have the Rock Star Fantasy Weekend and Pandoras is a perfect place to rock the night away. Many a performer has had their 15 minutes of fame last 3 to 6 days! You'd be surprised how many have kept copies of the songs they have recorded and have found some stardom on you tube extending that fame a bit further. We have a few who have actually sold some of their talent. But we are not allowed to say who. Due to the "Privacy Factor" shall we say?

Across from Pandoras a little further back on the left is the gym for those who don't like to miss a workout. There are both machines and free weights to help keep you fit. Then you come to the spa. Here is a place to find quiet, peace and tranquility. Time for you to get pampered to your heart's content. There are body treatments, massages, facials, hair and nail attention, energy work, and make overs to be had. You can achieve as little or as much as you want.

We do not do plastic surgery on the premises but we do supply a private place to recuperate for as long as you need to after the fact. Our Doctor has assisted many guests through the most difficult times after any multitude of medical procedures, cosmetic or otherwise. Our confidentiality is of the utmost importance.

It goes both ways you see.
You don't tell on us; we won't tell on you.

Sienna is the resident "Doc". She is here not only as a Doctor, but also as a teacher. She is very professional, quite serious, and dedicated when it comes to her work and her patients. Little is known about her private life by anyone at The Garden other than her closest friends. She accepted the position here because it gives her anonymity. She still hasn't gotten past the loss of a relationship that ended, and here she can do research without having to answer to anyone.

Being the daughter of a life time military man and a Doctor for a mother, Sienna spent much of her young life making sure she was good enough, and smart enough. She strived to be the best at everything in hopes that one of her parents would notice. Ultimately they divorced and were so involved in their own careers that if it wasn't for the love of her grandmother Sienna may never have come to some realization that she already was the best at whatever she put her mind to.

Most of the staff are a bit intimidated by the tough as nails façade she displays. That is fine with her. Sienna does have a sense of humor. Her wit is sarcastic and sharp; it slices you while you still have a smile on your face. Then it dawns on you, that you were the intended target she just bulls eyed.

Once you get past the spa area you are into the remaining vineyards, the stables, and the tennis courts. Off to one side there is a workout area for the staff. The companions seem to prefer an outdoor gym. I think they hope the guests may hear the clank of weights and conversation while on one of our nature walks and take a peek.

Beyond the vines are trails for walking, biking and horseback riding. There is even a rock climbing wall, a repelling line and there are days you see a hot air balloon floating over the property, or hang gliders piloted by a guest like you, swooshing by at sunrise.

Now you have an idea of what The Garden Resort looks like. Let's take a look at The Garden in action. This is your chance to see the inner workings and lives of the people who work here and the guests that spend time here. Happy voyeurism!

♋

A Day Begins

The sun has barely peeked over the horizon this warm spring morning. The grape vines are still young. They are reaching towards those first rays of nutrition and life. In the distance there is a small trail of dust coming into view. As it gets closer and bigger the figures of two horses and riders take shape. A woman is in front followed closely by her male companion. They come to a stop by an orange flag at the end of a row of grapevine.

Veronica's shorter red hair glistens like copper in the sunlight. The glint in her blue eyes hides nothing and everything. You can see she is full of life. Her riding gear that covers her non petite frame is on the Steampunk bohemian side, full of color.

Her riding companion; Samson is a 6'9" strapping African American man. He is wearing jeans and work boots. The white pullover shirt he has donned this morning has the "The Garden" emblem on the front left breast side. It is worn by most of the staff when doing daily duties so guests feel comfortable about asking a question to the right person. His face is full of complexity. When he is smiling, you just want to hug him like a teddy bear, but when he is serious, you don't want to be on his bad side.

Samson is pulling a divining rod off the back of his saddle. This y shaped stick is believed to have the capability of locating water. Today they are using it to test the water levels in the area so they know how much sprinkler time the vines may need.

Veronica is squatting near the flag touching the ground. "I wish Maia was here, she reads dirt much better than I do." Samson hands her the divining rod.

"You'll be fine Madam. Miss Hanlin wouldn't let you near her babies if she didn't have faith in you."

"From your lips my man" Veronica begins to walk down the row with the divining rod in her hands. She has tried using this antiquated form of farming before and has yet to understand Maia's rationale behind it. "What's the weather supposed to be this week?" She yells to Samson.

"No rain if that's what you mean."

"Hm". Veronica continues to walk the row as Samson hangs with the horses talking to them so they don't get too bored waiting for the slow walking water reader.

Veronica isn't one to get frustrated so easily, but she has more important things to tend to and Maia could have found a better way to make her point regarding how she works her magic on the vines. 'Who am I kidding? I have no fucking clue how to use this thing.' "Samson!" Veronica calls across the vines. "I think we need to water for a few hours today."

"Sounds good to me." Samson yells as he holds the horses' reigns patiently as Veronica returns handing him the divining rod. "Let's not make me do this again shall we?" Samson just grins as he helps Veronica get onto her horse and they head back towards the rising sun.

Samson works closely with Maia in the horticulture department. He does have other duties, but the grounds are his main focus most of the time. Samson has had a love of plants for as long as he can remember. Growing up in the city did not make it easy. His mother thought he was crazy when he begged to go to an agricultural high school outside of his schooling district. He was so adamant about it; his Mom made it happen.

He got hooked up with The Garden by a friend who heard a winery was looking for help. When Samson found out what other possibilities were available he was hesitant at first, but once he got through the training he never looked back.

As Veronica and Samson get to the stables Houston is waiting for them. He is sitting on the fence with a steaming cup of joe in his hand. Houston looks like a living Marlboro advertisement. He is rugged yet pleasing to the eye. As he steps down from the fence his gait is one of a man who has been riding horses all his life. His white shirt is long sleeve and rolled up past his elbows. The ornate snaps on the front of the shirt catch the sunlight. His jeans are faded, and his boots reflect his dedication to his work.

When Veronica dismounts he is ready to take the horse from her. He tilts his head and with a smile, he greets the Madam. "Mornin' sunshine"

"Good morning Houston" she replies with honest affection. As she dismounts from her horse Veronica is rubbing his neck. Her feisty ride snuggles his head into her chest. She hands the reigns to Houston. "Solo was a little fragile this morning, mind checking his hooves for me?"

"He just knows he has you wrapped around those hooves of his, but yes I will take a gander at all four after I undress the bastard." Houston takes over the neck rubbing of the frisky young one who seems to know they are talking about him.

"Thank you." Veronica replies as she walks towards the buildings in the distance.

She turns back to look at Houston and Samson who are taking the tack off the horses. 'I am one lucky human being'. She thinks to herself. She is finally in the life she always wanted, a beautiful property for her business of women's growth, great people working with her to obtain her goals and a good horse ride in the morning. "Thank you gentlemen" She says softly but loud enough for them to catch her sincerity.

She hears in stereo "Your welcome" from Houston and Samson as she turns back to continue on.

At a decent pace the walk from the stables to Veronica's bungalow is ten minutes. Veronica has time for a quick shower before facing the crunching of numbers with Will. Veronica's bungalow is not huge but it is "comfortable" as she puts it.

There is a porch that runs the length of it. Once inside, the sitting area is all funky and fun. There is a small kitchen to the right past the sitting area. It has a petite white gothic look. The bathroom is all stone with a tub big enough and deep enough for 2 to soak in. The rain shower over head has 2 heads that can work together or separately. The bedroom is the largest room in the place. The walls look like cream limestone. The curtains and bedding are deep purple. The bed has a thick wood frame stained in dark red. The head and foot boards are ornate with gothic shaped holes scattered along the trim.

As Veronica enters her personal castle the clothes already start coming off. By the time she reaches the bathroom she is naked. She turns on a stereo and "Get Down On It" by Kool and the Gang begins to play. She is in and out of the shower before the song ends.

She walks into the bedroom and begins the search for clothes. This is her least favorite chore of the day. Veronica feels she is not very fashion savvy. She knows what she likes, but what she likes isn't usually in the pages of Vogue or Elle or even People magazine for that matter. Does she care? Not really. She lives in her world and if people don't like what she has on, so be it.

Today she is in the mood for a corset tank top. She pulls out a deep green one. She has the need to feel her colon pressed against her ribs for a few hours to remind her to be healthier, maybe some leggings to continue the reminder. Then add her favorite steam punk boots to offset the misery of being suffocated by the rest of her clothing.

Once all of that is done she can quickly blow out the hair, put on a tad bit o' make up and off to the coffee lounge for something to bring back to her desk and eat while she works. She throws on a knee length jacket, just in case the wind picks up.

In less than 20 minutes Veronica is back outdoors heading for the main house. As she walks through the back door Will Chambers just happens to be walking in her direction. He usually wears dress pants, good shoes and a button down dress shirt open at the first few buttons. "You look like you are ready to squuuueeeze the daylights out of the ol' books today missy!"

"Thank you?" Veronica replies knowing that Will is aware of her aversion to math. She starts to head for the coffee lounge. "I'm going to grab an egg spinach and cheese croissant first." Will puts his arm between Veronica's arm and her side.

"Already at your desk"

"You sly man Friday you!" Veronica responds as they about face to walk towards their offices. Will is Veronica's right hand man. He is a whiz kid on the computer, a numbers man who makes sure Veronica's lack of math compatibility is backed up to the nth degree. He looks like an adult Harry Potter. Will has his nerdish geeky side, but there is a sexiness to him that he has no idea is there. He does fancy himself a ladies' man but seems to have trouble opening his mouth around women he doesn't know.

As they come to Veronica's office, Will steps back to let Veronica enter first. There is already a steaming cup of water with lemon and maple syrup sitting on the single cup hot plate on her desk. The croissant is sitting next to it. The computer is on and there is a small pile of papers next to it. "William, thank you for the set up."

He grins. "My pleasure Madam, now get started and I will be in to bother you in about an hour."

Veronica takes in a deep breath "O.K." Will leaves Veronica as she is walking towards her desk. She places her breakfast sandwich near the computer. The walls of Veronica's office are Venetian plaster in white, with splashes of orange, red, and yellow, and a few dashes of green and purple scattered here and there. Her desk faces the door way, it is beautifully done in a stained wood and painted metal with 2 identical statues of naked men crouched with their hands palms up looking like they are holding the desk in place. The art work on the walls are mostly of naked human forms but there is a sign over the door that no one would see until they were on their way out of the office that reads;

"Sex is the most beautiful
natural thing money can buy."

Maia bought the loose version of a Tom Clancy quote for Veronica as a joke but Veronica had to put it up. She does not take gifts lightly and has a hard time letting go of any of them.

And this one just seemed fitting for her office. There is a huge window to the side of her desk that is tinted on the outside so you can't see in, but Veronica can look out at the back gardens, the vines and the beautiful morning sun. There is a sitting area to the left of the desk with a deep garnet sofa and a chair in view of an old style looking pot belly stove which is actually a working gas heater.

'At least an hour has gone by' Veronica thinks as she looks at the dragon clock on the wall. Sadly only 20 minutes has passed. She continues comparing paperwork to computer screen while biting into her croissant sandwich and popping grapes into her mouth that Will so thoughtfully left on her desk as well. She stops to see a group of women walking over to Pandoras. "Must be Maia's spirit of the full moon group, they are looking chipper after their morning meditation." She says as if someone who is interested is actually listening, but there is no one but the totally slow and uninterested dragon clock mocking her and her poor math skills.

There is a light knock at Veronica's open door. She looks up to see who it is. "Good morning Si!" Veronica is glad for the interruption. Sienna walks in and sits down. She is wearing a gray pencil skirt. Under her clinic jacket; there is a hint of a black shirt peeking out at her bust line. Her kitten pumps are deep purple. "Hey, sorry to bother you"

"No bother, what's up?"

"I'm in the middle of physicals and was just wondering when the new pony is arriving so I know for sure when I need to have lessons prepared."

Veronica is a little confused and her look shows it. Sienna is always on top of these things. Why would she be asking? "Sienna, he arrives today."
Sienna is surprised. She thought she had a few more days to get ready. "Today?"
"Yeah, didn't we just talk about this? You're first meeting with him is tomorrow morning."
Veronica is going through the schedule in her head trying to figure out how she can change things around and give Sienna more time.

"Look, I can switch you out with Maia's time if…"

"NO! No, it'll be fine." Sienna still seems distracted.

"What's going on?" Veronica asks with a little concern.

Sienna lets out an exasperated sigh leaning back into the chair. "You should be wearing my shoes with that corset."

"What?"

"I'm just having a little trouble focusing lately."

"Are you sleeping?"

"Some."

"Eating?"

"Does chocolate count?"

"No. Getting laid?"

"What?"

Veronica tilted her head. "You heard me."

"What does that have to do with anything?"

"Sienna, if you aren't getting any, are you at least taking care of yourself?"

"I don't have time. There's too much going on. Physicals, lessons, research…"

"We make time for what's important right?" Veronica is giving Sienna a look of I'm about to tell you so. Sienna see's where this is going and responds quietly head down. "Yes." Veronica has barely taken a breath, "…*Or we bury ourselves in other things when we don't want to face something*." Veronica looks at Sienna like a mother waiting for her child to get the point.

Sienna stands up to leave. Veronica knows her too well and she doesn't even know why she is fuzzy so she isn't ready to talk about it. "I have to go, seeing as I have pony lessons to prepare."
Veronica can't help herself. "This isn't over young lady."
Sienna just shakes her head. "How was your ride this morning?" Sienna asks, because she is jealous she hasn't had time to ride and because she is probing to see who accompanied Veronica on her venture this morning.

"Can't call it much of a ride, but I think Samson got a kick out of my inadequacy in the use of a divining rod." Veronica switches back to what she feels should be the topic at hand. "Who's on your exam list today?"
Sienna looks up thinking and starts counting on her fingers. "Let's see, Dugan, Trent, Peter and Samson."

"Samson?" Veronica looks encouraged. Sienna is in no mood to go where her friend is insinuating she go. "Shut up"

Veronica leans back in her chair trying to be nonchalant about it. "Just sayin'"
Sienna is at the door. "Shut-up" she says putting her hand up in defense before Veronica can continue her lecture. Sienna leaves and Veronica sits back in thought then sees the papers that are still sitting on her desk, waiting for solutions. "Uh."

On her way out Sienna passes Will. "Have a good day doctor." he gets out before she slips by. "You too William" and Sienna is off like a shot. As Sienna disappears in the hallway Chevalier is heading towards Will's desk. "Is the madam in?" He asks hopefully. Will looks up from his papers.

"She's crunching numbers, so I'm sure she will be glad to see you." Chevalier gives Will an off handed salute and knocks on Veronica's office door.

"Come in," slips lightly from her lips. As she sees Chevalier peek his head in the room before opening the door all the way and entering, she smiles. "Good timing Chev, she's on her way." He brings his tall British frame into her office and plants himself comfortably in the chair in front of her desk. His British accent along with his charming demeanor pulls you in right away. "Mornin' love. So why did you want to meet here first?"

Veronica finds a folder on her desk and opens it. "I know I usually meet the guests at the lobby when they arrive, but today I want you with your alluring French accent to sweep Ms. Julia Bishop off her feet." He leans forward. This is an unusual occurrence at The Garden. "What's the occasion?" He asks because he can't think of any reason she wouldn't meet the guest first.

"After reading her questionnaire and her comments, I feel she will need you to be her one and only focus."

"I can live with that." Chevalier leans back in the chair.

"Chevy, she is going to be nervous. Kid gloves ok?"

Chevalier stands up. He bows and begins speaking with a French accent. "Madame, Ms. Bishop will be safe with me. Do not worry your pretty little head one moment more."

Veronica is looking in the folder again. "Good thing she likes a hairy chest and French accents hey?" Chevalier gives her a grin, "I believe I fit all of her criteria quite well." He takes a deep breath and heads for the door. "Curtains up Madame!" He leaves with his usual flourish, leaving Veronica feeling better about the day ahead.

Will gets up to head into Veronica's office after Chevalier is clear of the area. He picks up a few files from his desk to take with him. As he nears the door he hears Veronica talking to herself. This is not an unusual occurrence. Talking aloud while alone is a habit Veronica picked up from her grandmother who used to say it was a sign of "Intelligence" to talk to oneself. So Veronica started doing so at a young age because who doesn't want to be intelligent? He eaves drops for only a moment.

"Now if I could only get this math to come out the same way TAH WIIIICE!" she growls as she calculates on her computer. Will walks into the office shaking his head. Veronica is staring at the screen with her chin in her hand. He puts his hands on her shoulders and looks at her screen. "All right, maybe I can help."

"William, I would like to get through one day, just one without you saving my ass."

"But I like saving it!" Will retorts with a matter of fact attitude.
She glances up in his direction. "Cute, not funny, but cute."

"Here, let me see what you're doing." Will puts his arms around Veronica reaching for the keyboard, much like a teacher with a student. "Are you sure you have these numbers right?" he asks knowing the answer.

"Of course… not." She replies with a hint of sarcasm.

"Roni, send what you've done over to my computer. I will look at it while you go through these, deal?" He hands her the new pile of paper work.

"Yes boss", comes her softer sarcastic remark.

The phone rings before Will leaves so he fights off Veronica as she tries to pick it up first. He gets hold of the receiver and answers, "Veronica West's office this is Chambers, may I help you? Hmm. Let me see if she is available, hold on please." Will puts the call on hold. "Do you want to speak to Mr. Shipton?"
Veronica has been looking at Will the whole time. "Do you always answer the phone like that?"

"Comes with the territory *boss*."
Veronica reaches for the receiver as Will holds it back. Yes Chambers, I will take it thank you."
Will reluctantly, teasingly hands her the phone.

As Veronica takes the receiver she releases the hold button and waves at Will "Toodle loo!" Will whispers "I love how you brush me off." He walks out wearing a grin. He loves the fact that he enjoys his boss's company and that he can tease her without fear of losing his job. He knows he is lucky on many levels to work and live amongst the people he does.

"Jonathan! How was your flight?" Veronica asks into the receiver as she turns her chair away from the task she was hoping for yet another distraction to get away from the dreaded math. Their discussion is short but Veronica is excited about the possibility of a new staff member.

Joseph our dandy of a mature gentleman who is ever so respectful and pleasant is hoping he isn't late. His latest charge Mrs. Julia Bishop should be arriving at the train station anytime now. He glances at the passenger seat making sure the sign that reads "Rose Willow" is still there. This is Julia's code name so she knows who her ride is. Joseph turns his remarkably unremarkable looking sedan into the station lot just before the train arrives. He gets out of the car and makes sure his suit is straight and his cap is on his head leaning a touch to the right and forward. He grabs his sign and heads for the landing where visitors will be entering the building.

It's been a long night of no sleep on the train for Julia Bishop. She still can't believe she actually left her daughter in charge of her life for a few days so she could have this escape. She places her hand on her head of faded red hair in need of a touch up and scratches it in thought then she notices the porter has already taken exit with her luggage so she realizes she better get a move on so she doesn't miss her stop and end up God knows where instead. She catches sight of her floral upholstery luggage getting smaller in the distance. Julia slowly gets her 60 something, I have sat at a desk for over 30 years frame down the steps of the train. In her attempt to catch up to her luggage she walks by Joseph and his sign without even noticing them.

When the porter finally stops at the other end of the building Julia hands him a couple of dollar bills. "Thank you so much young man." She smiles at him and begins looking around for *the sign* that is supposed to mark the beginning of her adventure. The porter looks at the two dollars, shrugs his shoulders and stuffs the money in his pocket before heading back to the train. Julia is looking around her. There aren't many people here; it shouldn't be hard to find a sign. She reaches into her purse to look for her paper with her notes and the name she's supposed to look for. She knows it was a flower and a tree. 'Rose something, it is Rose. Aha!' She finds her paper with the name Rose Willow written on it. Just as she does a nice looking man wearing a suit and tweed cap walks up to her with the sign in hand. "Excuse me Miss, are you waiting for a ride?"

Julia blurts out "Yes! Rose Willow!"

"Blimey" he exclaims, "I thought I met the wrong train! You walked right by me so I was lookin' and didn't see one other person that matched your description."

"I walked by you? Oh, I am so sorry."
Julia pats his hand with hers. Joseph holds onto
her hand. "Oh no, please don't apologize."

"But I should have seen you. I was so
busy chasing my suitcase!" Her statement
causes Joseph to drop her hand and reach for the
luggage. Before his hand reaches the bags he
stops because he realizes he hasn't properly
introduced himself. He tugs on his cap and
slightly bows, "Joseph at your service Miss. I am
the one who should apologize for not noticing
you right away! Follow me and off we will go."
He picks up her bag and takes her smaller bag
from her shoulder before he heads back to the
parking lot.

As they are walking Joseph is filling Julia
in on the ride ahead. "The windows are tinted
in back so you can enjoy a book or a movie or
you can nap for a while before we get to our
destination." Julia is thinking a nap may be in
order after that train ride.
Joseph opens the back door of the vehicle and
leads a hand for Julia to follow.

"Thank you" Julia climbs in noticing a small cooler on the floor of the other side of the car. It is a sizable back seat area. Joseph leans in and begins pointing out all the amenities at Julia's disposal. "If you need me or have a question, please feel free to press the intercom here." He demonstrates how to use it. Julia nods her head in understanding. He then opens the cooler. "Hanlin Cellars is a very good local wine if you choose to unwind with a beverage." He points out where the books and magazines are. Then he shows Julia how to lean her seat back into a reclined position for comfort. Julia is amazed at this. "I didn't know a car like this existed!"

"We want you ta be as comfortable as possible Miss. Any questions before I get yer luggage?" Julia is so excited she just giggles and nods her head no.

Joseph shuts her door then puts the luggage in the trunk. When he gets in the driver's seat. He looks back to Julia, "I will be closing the window between us. We should arrive at The Garden in about an hour. Call me if you have need of me." He closes the tinted pane between them leaving Julia to her thoughts. 'Well, I better get some shut eye so I don't look a total mess when I arrive' she tells herself trying to be distracted from her reasons for taking this little trip.

Yearly Exams

As Sienna is heading towards her office she notices her nurse; Michael Cox is at the front desk talking with Victor. Michael was brought up in Ireland and moved to California to go to nursing school while learning how to surf. At the moment, Michael and Victor have their heads together over the financial section of the Wall Street Journal. Michaels Irish accent is very apparent when he speaks. "Do yew rrrreally believe it's gonna turn so quickly Victor?"

"Michael, I would bet my mother's life on it."

"But your matha's dead."

"Ah, there you have it then."

"Victor. Aye, I'll give it a wee look." As Michael turns to head back to the clinic Sienna is standing right behind him.

He jumps back a step before reprimanding his boss. "You scared the daylights outta me woman!"

"Out for a breather already are we Nurse Cox?" Sienna is soft but stern.

"Ackchewlly I'm jes' gettin' in ya see." He proudly responds.

"Just…." Sienna turns on her heel and heads for the clinic. 'Just what I need today, more of what will Nurse Cox do next to annoy me'. She doesn't understand how someone so dedicated can also be so lackadaisical about their job.

Michael turns back to Victor. "Better get me arse in gear." Victor smiles and says "Before yer arse is in a sling." Michael slowly meanders in Sienna's direction keeping a safe distance in case she has any more surprises up her sleeve. Victor looks back to the paper and writes a few notes on his pad on the counter.

When Michael reaches the exam room Sienna is going through chart folders trying not to let her irritation get the best of her. "Dugan, Trent, Peter…" She doesn't see him at the door and yells "COX! Where is Samson's file?" Michael steps into the room.

"In a bit of a tizzy are we?" He is leaning in the doorway.

"Tizzy, we have three days to finish these exams and you call my question a tizzy?"

"Well?" Michael asks in what Sienna refers to as his cocky attitude.

"Well?" She responds right back. Michael breaks, he never seems to be able to hold up against Sienna for long.

"Rrright, the file is behind ya."

"Whe-" Sienna starts, then she sees the file on the counter. She sighs in exasperation then continues not wanting to admit she missed it or that Michael may be on top of it. "Send him in please."

"I'll text the big guy then." Michael leaves the room with a smile. Just knowing he got one over on the Doc with Samson's file sitting right there, this will be a good day!

♋

Samson is sitting in the coffee lounge reading the paper on one of the six computers in the back. The lounge is a buzz with women who are getting ready for classes. One of which will be held in the lounge in an hour. His phone rings with the song "Mr. Big Stuff" by Jean

Knight. He looks at the screen and see's it is Nurse Cox texting him to come in for his exam. Some of the women notice the ring tone and giggle. Samson is mentally trying to prepare himself. He gets up and turns around suddenly realizing how crowded it is. He acknowledges a group of women sitting around a circular fire pit as he exits. "Good morning ladies" a chorus of

"Good mornings" follow him. As he gets close to the door the young man behind the coffee bar raises his hand. "Good luck buddy!"

"Yeah" Samson replies.

He is taking his time to get around the corner to the clinic. He is very "fond" of Dr. Praddon. Being prodded by her in an exam room just doesn't seem right. The first time he met the doctor he was instantly taken by her strong demeanor in such a petite frame. She didn't take shit from anybody. But somehow he still feels the need to protect her from the world and now he was going to be anally violated by his paramour in the sterile setting of an exam room. How was he going to get past this emotional cluster fuck?

"Hey!" Nurse Cox's voice startles Samson back to reality and the fact that he didn't even realize he has already reached his destination. "Hey." Samson mumbles.

"Are you ready?" Michael asks. Samson nods in response. "Good, she is *patiently* waiting for you." Both men know Sienna is anything but patient. She is prompt, organized and practical.

It is so quiet in the exam room when Samson enters he can hear the clock on the far wall ticking the seconds away to his doom of awkwardness. Sienna is standing by the counter looking down at his file. He begins to say good morning and is cut off by Sienna's "How's your hand doing?" Samson had forgotten about his hand injury that occurred when Toby; the youngest Garden apprentice dropped a new 80 pound terra cotta planter on his hand and it broke into pieces lacerating his hand across the palm.

Because of his training Samson took off his shirt and wrapped his hand immediately. Poor Toby was mortified. He thought Samson was super human and not capable of mere human bloodletting. He took off running to get help. Fortunately, he left the Polaris sitting there so Samson could drive himself back to the main house and get to the clinic.

Nurse Cox saw him coming and paged the Dr. who was teaching a class. As Samson was relaying to Michael what that "dumb ass punk" did Sienna was there. Sienna and Michael were getting Samson prepped for stitches. Sienna told Samson how lucky he was that the slice didn't go through a tendon as Michael gave him a shot to numb the area. Sienna let Michael know she could handle the stitches so he could go back to whatever he was doing.

As Sienna was stitching Samson's hand he began to perspire at the brow. "Are you feeling pain?" she asks with concern.

"No"

"Why are you sweating?" She looks at him with concern. Samson could feel the heat of a blush on his face. Sienna's face was so close to his. His heart was going a hundred miles a minute, not because of his hand but because

Sienna smelled so good! She was clean and fresh. She was holding his arm with her small, cool fragile looking hand while she prepared for the next stitch.

Samson's voice came out softly "I, ah"

"Samson, I need to know if you are ok so I can continue." Samson put his other hand on Sienna's arm.

The penny has dropped. She can see his eyes have dilated a bit. Sienna is totally caught by surprise. She has always liked Samson and his protective attitude towards her, but she didn't expect him to react like this, then she noticed the touch of his hand on her arm and the timber of his voice causing her heart to speed up. They found themselves coming closer face to face. When their lips meet the temperature in the room seemed to rise immediately. Samson pulled Sienna to him pressing his hand across her mid back. She responded to his kiss with such passion it took him by surprise. He pulls her even closer. Then the syringe on the side table topples to the floor bringing Sienna back to business.

"Damn it!" she turns to see where the syringe is. Her hands are a little shaky. "I need to finish this."

Samson begins to apologize. "I'm sorry, I"

"No." Sienna looks him in the eyes. "Please, don't be." As she goes back to stitching his hand Samson leans back closing his eyes to relive what just happened. Sienna is trying to keep focused on the matter at hand but she is a little unsteady first thinking 'What the fuck just happened?' Then she began berating herself for being unprofessional then she looks at the smile on Samson's face and her mind switches gears. This may be a distraction she needs.

That very night Samson and Sienna copulated (as she puts it) for the first time, and now he was in her exam room wanting to be anywhere but here. He replies to her question. "It's fine. You didn't even mess up my hand so I could have a scar to brag about."

"Good, good. I'll step out so you can undress."

Samson gives her a smile. "You don't need to."

"Yes, I do." There is a hint of a chuckle in enna's voice. Samson understands she doesn't want "their business" to be anyone else's business. Samson takes his shirt off then reaches for the laces of his boots. All the while he is thinking of that first night.

Sienna had finished stitching his hand up and wrapped it up nicely. Every movement she made within a few inches of him had him rise and stiffen, there were moments he even felt his head swimming. He was worried he may pass out. Sienna handed him a small cup of orange juice as if she had read his mind. "Here, drink this" she paused to think about what she was about to say, but decides if she doesn't then nothing will happen. "If you are up to it, come to my bungalow at 8." Samson looked at the Dr. in disbelief. 'Did she just say what I thought?' She then asked, "Is 8 ok with you?"

"Uh, fine, fine." One of the things Sienna likes about Samson; he is a man of few words.

When he showed up at her bungalow he had an indoor potted plant in hand. In case someone noticed where he was, he had a reason for being there. He couldn't believe how nervous he was. When Sienna opened the door he noticed her hair was down. Samson barely got out "Your hair looks good that way." Before Sienna pulled him in the door, helped him put the plant down and brought his face to hers. They kissed as she held his shirt collar in her hands and led him to her bedroom. He didn't even get a chance to see where he was going. He just followed her lead.

The bedroom was very simple and basic, but there were a few candles lit. The music softly playing in the background was bang your head metal which Samson didn't expect.

When Sienna got him to the bed she walked back onto the bed and began taking Samson's shirt off. Samson went to help and she stopped, looking him in the eyes once again and shaking her head no. She wanted to enjoy every bit of the strip. Samson let her finish what she started. Methodically Sienna took each piece of his clothing off and folded it placing each one onto a chair.

Every time she came back she would stroke the newly naked area of his "beautiful brownness" as she called it. When she got to his bandaged hand she paused., "Are you sure you are up for this?" Samson put his bandaged hand to her face. He gruffly whispers "Trying to back out already?"

Sienna put her fists on her hips without even realizing it then she began taking her own clothes off and Samson stopped her. It was his turn. As he disrobed Sienna he kissed and or suckled each area of her petite body. Her soft moans made it difficult for him to stay focused at times, but he is a well trained Garden man after all and he "muscled" through it.

Once they were naked in the candle light; Sienna on the bed Samson standing at the foot of it. Sienna made a sound like a soldier going into battle. She grabbed Samson's arms put a foot under his torso and threw him to the bed. He landed on his back and before he knew it she had her hands and mouth wrapped around his already hard penis. She was so forceful he had to pull her back a few times so he wouldn't lose control. He pulled her to him biting and sucking at her neck, then down to her breasts.

Out of nowhere he felt the condom go on and she mounted him. Sienna rode him like a wild stallion. She pushed herself along his torso feeling the sensation of his pubic hair on her clit raising her excitement to new levels. Samson tried to slow her down so it wouldn't end too soon, but Sienna kept going. She had her hands on his shoulders pulling her body even further down on him and moving faster to the music playing softly in the air.

Then Sienna paused. She placed Samson's hands at her hips asking him to put downward pressure on them as she moved. He was afraid of his size in her, but she never looked or sounded uncomfortable. Sienna seemed to know when he could take no more and they came crashing at the same time.

She lay on top of him as their chests heaved in breath for a few minutes. Then quietly Sienna slid off him and removed the condom. She went into the bathroom leaving Samson wondering what he should do next.

As he lay waiting he was thinking how quickly his nervousness escaped his mind and how very few women have actually ever asked him to do something specific. They are often too shy or don't know what to ask for. It was refreshing not having to guess. When she came back, Sienna had a washcloth in her hand. She stroked Samson's shaft and cleaned all around it. The first touch set a new shock wave through his body, the warmth of the cloth and the tenderness of the act only make him ache for more. He was ready for another round.

Before he could recall their second round of love making the exam room door opens suddenly bringing Samson back to the present and his reality standing in the Doctors exam room and the impending humiliation. Sienna can see Samson in all his glory sporting a woody. He hadn't put the craptacular paper hospital gown on. Sienna is grateful for the sight. She smiles, enters the room and closes the door.

♋

Grounds Keepers

The green houses are not far from the
main house. This is where Maia keeps starter
plants and a few plants she can't dream of
growing outdoors. Her office is also here so she
can be close to her new babies, should they need
her attention. Her office is all of about a
hundred and ten square feet. There are books
about plants on one whole wall. Her "desk" is
an old planting table with shelves attached to it
with holes in them for pots to sit. An old wall
phone is next to the desk.

There are some extra gloves and tools
scattered about, and a poster of a peace sign on
the far wall. As you get a closer look, the peace
sign is a photo of a naked couple lying down.
The woman is on the bottom lying on her back
with her legs spread. The man is on top of the
woman with his legs together. They are
encircled by a wreath of flowers.

Maia walks into her office wearing her
uniform of khaki shorts, a Garden tank top, and
work boots and today she has a rainbow head

band holding her hair back from her face. The manager of her team; Peter Mossin is right behind her. He sometimes forgets who is boss. He is following her as they enter the office. "I don't understand why you have to continue with this."

She turns to face him as she responds. Maia's exasperation of explaining herself to Peter again is apparent in her demeanor. "Of course you don't Peter, you have never had an illness where the only escape from the pain you have is a few hits of a doobie in the morning." She turns to look for something among the wall of books she has just reached.

"I'm not opposed to people needing it. I just don't understand why you have to grow it."

"I grow it because the Madam allows me to and the local clinic needs it, end of story."

The real reason Maia is growing is, it is the one thing that makes her feel like she didn't totally mess up when her twin brother Luca was ill. Marijuana was the only thing that helped him. It was the only relief from many symptoms, and later the only ease of pain giving him at least some semblance of normalcy.

Luca was Maia's partner in everything when they were young. They played together, read together, they went skiing, hiking, swimming and any other outdoor sport together. They had their own language and most of the time didn't have to speak a word. When Maia decided to move to the U.S., Luca moved with her. Although his work brought him around the world, she was his home base. She used to call him Meio so they could be Meio Maia. He hated it when they were kids, but he saw the humor in it as they got older and appreciated his two minute older sisters affectionate nick name for him.

If it wasn't for her brothers' encourage ment Maia never would have gone to school for horticulture. He even talked her into taking the women's studies class which fatefully introduced her to Veronica. She still thanks him for that.

When he got ill Maia's life changed forever. When he died Maia wanted to die.

After a year of hiding she decided she better find some kind of life again or her brother would continue finding ways to haunt her. Maia was not a very religious person, but after the death of her brother and the communication she still felt she had with him, her search for a more spiritual life began and that is the one other thing she feels she can share with the women who come to The Garden in search of 'something' they can't put their finger on.

Maia continues looking for "A desk reference to Nature's medicine" by: S. Foster and R Johnson. "Aha! Here it is." Maia exclaims. "I want to start some new medicinal herbs in the hot house spaces where the poppies were that we just planted on the front lawn."

"Medicinal herbs?" Peter repeats rather sarcastically.

"You have a problem with that Mr. Mossin?" Maia asks not even looking up from the book. Peter knows there are at least 50 other pertinent things they could be planting. His frustration with Maia is building. "Of all the things we could be planting, an herb with no sufficient evidence of having any healing properties is not what I think we need."

"Well, it's a good thing it's my responsibility to decide what we need then isn't it?" Peter turns away from Maia, the frustration heating him up. He begins to exit. Maia reminds him though, "Don't forget we have a meeting in fifteen minutes." Peter can't even respond. He leaves the office. He dons his "Terminator" sunglasses as he stomps away.

Maia's logic is no logic at all to Peter, but somehow she is 90% right with all of her choices regarding the plants and what should go where and be used for what.

"Herbs, we already grow basil, thyme, scallions and there's fucking lavender everywhere!" He is thinking as he is making his way to sanity away from Maia. "The women seem to like that lavender shit in their tea, in a soak, in massage oil. What medicinal herb other than her freakin' pot is going to be worth growing?" He is exasperated.

Peter heads for Pandoras because it is closer than the coffee lounge and much quieter this time of day. Hopefully Dominic is there with a readymade pot of coffee to help him change focus before the meeting starts. 'I used to run the show where I was, what made me blow it all and take orders from a tyrant?' Peters' good cop bad cop conscience is toying with him.

'Because you saw blonde hair, blue eyes and a kick ass 6 foot tall woman with legs that go on forever and the rest of her ain't too shabby either.' 'Yes, she's got the brains too; I just don't understand how hers work most of the time.'

Peter did run the show at his family's nursery until his brothers had enough and fired him for never listening to anyone else's ideas. It was his way, or no way. He was a task master and never had any time for breaks, lunches or a life period. He was all work all the time. His seriousness lost sight of the enjoyment of the business.

Peter has yet to realize Maia isn't as rough on him as he was on his brothers.

Apparently his karma is yet to be settled. He is exactly where he needs to be. Feeling a bit defeated Peter walks his six foot two frame with tousled brown curly hair and serious brown eyes into Pandoras. Only a few dim lights are on but the windows above are open streaming God light into the morning mist of the bar area. Dominic is behind the bar just pouring himself his first cup of coffee.

Dominic is all New York, from his accent to the Yankees emblem on his t-shirt. He looks up from mixing his sugar into his black wake up call to see Peter coming up to the bar. "Ready for some mawnin' brewski?" "Double what you're having." Peter mumbles. "Ah, the Awestrian under yer skin again?" Peter takes a seat at the end of the bar where Dominic is pouring him a cup. "What did I do to deserve this?"

"Hey, yew got it made Mossin. I been here tew years longer than yew and they still don't train me. Dew I lewk like chop liveh?"

"No, but you sound like fuckin' chop liver."
They both have a chuckle over this and clink
their Garden coffee mugs that read;

"The Garden
a place to remember
the night before
the morning after"

As they finish their first sip a sigh of
appreciation comes from both men. "Look
Peteh, women are a whole different animule.
You just ave ta come ta terms with the fact that
yew will never figure them out. Just treat em'
nice and they will dew the same fer yew." Peter
stands, he raises his mug to Dominic again. "Eh,
nice huh?"

"Nice"

"Thanks Dom. Off to the meeting of the
horticultural minds."

"Lucky man." Dominic says with envy as
Peter leaves the dim darkness of Pandoras for
the bright light outside. Dominic returns to his

coffee and the New York times before he gets ready for the day.

As Peter returns to the sunlight he once again places his Terminators over his eyes for privacy more than anything. When he gets to the picnic table area Toby, Hawk, and Bull are already there, they all exchange hello's. Peter notices Samson is missing.

"Where is Samson?" Bull is the first to reluctantly respond "His turn for the yearly inspection." They all feel Samson's pain. They don't know about the situation between he and the doctor as of yet, so they can only share part of his misery today. None of the men enjoy the yearly exam, even with the doctors' petite fingers.

Maia makes her way over to the picnic area. Most of the time she has a beaming smile that just lights up wherever she is. Lucky for Peter he didn't ruin that for the rest of the men today by disagreeing with her. As he watches her arrival it seems she hasn't given it a second thought. Maybe he needs to do the same. "Think nice" he tells himself.

"Good morning my lovelies." Maia greets her crew as she gets closer to them. As they did with Peter; they all exchange good mornings and hellos. Peter says nothing but is wearing an uncharacteristic grin on his face. Maia turns to him, "Are you all right Peter?"

"Yes" he says still smiling. "Ok then" she smirks and carries on with the meeting. "The Madam and Samson went to the far end of the vines this morning to check for water levels. Her recommendations are for a few hours of watering so we will do two today and see about tomorrow o.k.?" Hawk speaks up. "You really sent her out there with a divining rod?" The men share a laugh.

"She questioned my wine practices, so she got to get up bright and early on a busy day."

"How did you get her to ride out and check water levels?" Peter is surprised he hadn't heard about anything.

Looking right at Peter, Maia shares, "I'm more influential than you know." Then she scans a view of all her men. "You should all take heed." Maia is playfully secretive. "Come on,

there is work to be done. Hawk, Bull you two
head for sector 4 to set the water please." They
nod and head out. "Toby darlin' would you be
so kind to find Jake or Trent and have them help
you take care of the indoor plants in the main
house?"

"Yes miss." Toby stumbles down the
picnic table he was sitting on. He is always
excited when Maia lets him do something he
feels is important. To Toby the main house is
important.

Peter asks Maia, "And what do you have
in mind for me today?" still wearing that
ridiculous grin on his face.

"Peter, you must be high! So I'm not sure
you should be doing anything strenuous today."
She walks away from him and he is not sure
what to say to that. He follows her. "I am not
high. What do you want me to do?"

"Just keep an eye on Toby at the main
house for me this morning o.k.?" She continues
to walk away.

"Baby sitter, she wants me to be a fucking babysitter."   He stomps in the direction of the main house.

The Arrival of Julia Bishop

Julia is startled awake by Joseph's voice over the intercom. "We are about 15 minutes away from The Garden Miss. I thought you may want to freshen up a little." Julia looks for the intercom button. After a few attempts she finds it. "Uh, yes thank you."

"Would you like a little verbal tour before we arrive?" He asks in hopes of a yes.

"That would be wonderful!" Julia responds glad for the distraction before arriving. Joseph clears his throat in preparation of his well rehearsed litany about the place he calls home. "The Garden is on 400 acres of land. Approximately 69 of those acres grow some of the best wine grapes in California. When we pull into the drive you will see it mirrored on both sides by beautiful California oak trees hovering their canopy to welcome you. The first building you will see is a huge old barn. Inside that old looking behemoth is our grand hall. We have all kinds of events in that place."

Julia has her eyes closed again as she imagines what Joseph is talking about over the speaker. He continues. "While you are here we have the 'Full moon 'event happening. It's a hum dinger of a dance. Some dress in 1800's formal wear, some come as all types of mythological and fantasy characters, there are even robed druids prancing to the rhythmic beating of the music." Julia is relieved she cannot see her driver and vice versa for her mouth is wide open to the floor thinking how crazy it all sounds. She looks for the intercom button and speaks a bit loud and stiffly, "That sounds very interesting."

"And that's not the most popular evening at the hall! It seems the Pirate's Lair gets the most attendee's yo hoed with their bottles of rum!"

"Pirates?" Julia exclaims.

"Yee be right about that Miss! Pirates, pirate lass's, wenches, a rowdy night. My favorite though is the Jumpin' jive jubilee. There is a live big band, many people dress in 1940's clothing and many of the men are in military uniforms. Some of the dancing is tremendous! There is even an amazing Frank Sinatra sound alike." Joseph begins to sing "That Old Black Magic, has me in a spell… He stops to clear his throat again. Oh, sorry Miss, I'm no Sinatra."

Julia is enjoying his tour. "Don't stop on my account."

"The local favorite event at the hall is the hoe down. Lots of cowboys and country ladies two stepping and line dancing to some of the best country music!

As Joseph turns onto the property, there is a parking area and a 2000 square foot wine tasting and gift shop building with a sign reading "Award winning Hanlin Cellars". Julia does not see this building for Joseph hasn't turned down the tints yet. Once past the entry Joseph lowers the tints so Julia can see the landscape. She sees the canopy of trees surrounding the drive and the barn in the distance. "This is beautiful!" She exclaims to Joseph as he lowers the window between them.

At the end of the road is a circular drive that goes past the main house. Julia Bishop has arrived at The Garden. She can feel her stomach begin to knot up, her pulse is racing and her mouth goes cotton dry. She doesn't know if she can go through with this. How could she let her daughter Angela talk her into it? A whore house for women, what was she thinking? 'I am old enough to be the mother of these men. So, I haven't had an intimate encounter with my husband of 40 years in more than 7 years. That's life, it happens, Alzheimer's happens. How can I betray him? How can I be so selfish?' Before she could say anything more in her head, the car door opens and Joseph's hand is reaching for her.

"Welcome to The Garden Miss." Joseph barely gets the words out as he is getting her out of the vehicle when another gentleman slips one arm behind Julia's back and reaches for her hand as Joseph releases her from his grip. "Good morning Mon Cherie. I will take it from here Joseph, thank you."

Chevalier leads Julia to the front door. "I feel az though I know you already mademoiselle. Ow waz your journay?" Julia is a bit taken aback by this handsome French man; who is exactly what she had asked for by the way. The knots in her stomach are turning into butterflies as she blushes under his gaze and his gentle but firm touch.

The cotton mouth has taken over however and Julia is not sure how to answer. She giggles lightly out of pure nervousness. "To be honest with you, I could use a stiff drink and a hot bath right now." She quickly puts her hand over her mouth not believing she just blurted that out. "By zee time you check in zee tub will be ready, and iz it zee rrrrob rrrroy you desire or a bottle of our best champagne?"

"What? Ah, let's go with Rob Roy kiddo! Now let's get me checked in so I can soak in that hot bath!"

"Az you wish." Chevalier leads Julia to the lobby.

Victor is patiently waiting for Julia's French date for the weekend to bring her inside. "Chevy" as his friends call him ooozes charm, wit, or intelligence as needed. Victor thinks Chevaliers charm is smarmy to say the least, but the women seem to fall for him "hook line and sinker every time." Victor realizes it takes all kinds but Chevy really gets under his skin and Chevalier knows it and uses it to his advantage whenever possible.

Giving way to Julia, Chevalier walks in behind her. He presents her to Victor as if he is introducing the queen. "Mr. Tanner, Mademoiselle Bishop az arrived." Victor does everything in his power not to roll his eyes. "Good morning Mrs. Bishop."

"Julia please." She whispers quickly as if she is afraid someone is going to know her here. "Of course, Miss Julia. As you can see Chevalier has been waiting like a lost puppy for you to arrive. He will show you to your room." Chevalier snaps his fingers at Victor "Victor, please ave Dominic send someone to ze room with a rrrob rrrroy, twist of orange rind no lemawn."

"Of course." Victor says tight lipped staring Chevy down as he leads Julia out from the lobby to the wing of the mansion where the rooms are. Julia chose a room instead of a bungalow because she didn't know if she was just going to hide in a room the whole time or take a class or "what", but she didn't want to waste money on a bungalow that wouldn't get used properly.

There is one flight of stairs to Julia's room. When you reach the second floor the hallway is along the front of the house where all the windows are. These guarantees' the guests' privacy from the front driveway. Her room is the first one at the top of the stairs so she has less walking to do. When Chevalier opens the door you can hear the tub water running. There is a path of flower petals leading to the bathroom. Julia follows the trail with her eyes passing her luggage that is already in the room and into the steamy bathroom.

Julia looks to Chevaliers smiling face. "How did you get this started already?"

"You are at zee Garden mon cherie. We do our best to accommodate our guests. "Now," He leads her to put her purse down on the oversized down comforter covered bed and takes her coat off. "You get yourself into zee bath and I will wait for your drink and bring it to you." Julia stops in her tracks like a frightened rabbit. "Bring it to me?"

"Julia, I am here to serve. This is your partay no? We will only do what you wish to do. You are in control. But surely, having a man servant bathe you while you enjoy a cocktail in zee steam and bubbles of your bath will not hurt anyone oui?"

Hoping her nervousness doesn't show through like sweaty armpits in a silk shirt, Julia calculates how to respond without putting this handsome man off. "Leh, let me get in the tub, then that drink, then we'll see, ok?"

"Az you wish" Chevalier squeezes her hand gently and turns towards the door while Julia heads for the bathroom. The beautiful multicolored flower petals go from the floor to the tub to floating on the bubbles. There are enough candles lit to bring a warm glow to the closed curtain room.

She closes the door and leans against it. "What the hell am I doing?" She whispers to herself, and then she takes a deep breath. "OK, he said it, I'm in control. It's just a bath." She begins taking her clothes off. Julia is in her early 60's. She dresses very Midwest grandma style with elasticized pants that go to her upper rib cage. The shirt she is taking off is a flower print blouse she has owned since the 80's.

There is a knock at the room door. "Zat will be room service cherie, I will bring it in momentarily."

"Give me two minutes to get into the tub Chev" she whispers to herself "Chevalier right?" then louder "Chevalier."

"No worries mademoiselle." He answers from behind the bathroom door. Julia slowly sinks into the hot water with whispers of ooo's and ah's. She is still nervous but as she moves the bubbles with her hands they seem to camouflage her well enough.
Music begins to play from the speaker in the ceiling. It conveys a beautiful mood lightening ambiance. Julia can't believe she is going to speak first. "You can bring that drink in now."

Chevalier enters the bathroom with the drink in hand, a towel over his arm and no shirt to be seen. Julia looks up to his hairy chest as he bends to give her the drink. She just wants to reach up and touch that chest of tight beauty. It is all she can do to keep her hands off. She is afraid she is going to make a fool of herself by hyper ventilating and passing out. "Thank you" she whispers as he hands her the glass. "You are welcome mon cherie." He notices her staring at his chest. "If you do allow me to bathe you, I did not wish to get zee shirt wet, no?"

"We wouldn't want to do that now would we?" she says after swallowing half of her drink a little quicker than she had anticipated. "Maybe you should order me another one of these before…"

"I have a carafe in zee room just in case." Julia finishes the drink and puts her hand out with the glass. "Let's have some more. Will you join me?"

"In a drink or in zee bath?" Chevalier responds with a clever smile on his face.

"A drink" Julia quips back. Reprimanding herself for speaking without thinking. Chevalier takes the glass and turns to go into the room. "I will join you, in zee drink." He winks and leaves the bathroom.

Julia closes her eyes. She can already feel the effects of the alcohol as it begins to course through her veins. She is slipping into a comfort zone. The relaxing has begun. She hears Chevalier whisper "Do not open your eyes." She almost does but then she squeezes them shut like she did when she was a little girl about to blow the candles out on her birthday cake. She even takes a deep breath. Then it happens. She feels a warm wet cloth caressing her shoulder. She stiffens at first, so Chevalier stops. Julia is nervous, but this is why she is here. It is happening so fast, but if it doesn't happen fast, it won't happen at all. "Don't stop." is her whispered recommendation. He continues on.

"Relax your closed eyes mon cherie." She didn't realize she was still squeezing them so tight. In relaxing her eyes she is also able to allow her breath to release and her shoulders drop almost 3 whole inches!

The cloth continues down her arm. When it gets to her hand under the water's surface Chevalier gives each finger personal attention. He brings the cloth back up the arm to the side of the neck. He lightly brings the cloth to the top of her jaw, under her ear then firmly brings it down her neck over her shoulder and across her chest. He rubs the cloth against the fragrant lavender/vanilla soap and dunks it in the water again before bringing it back and forth across her chest. Then he brings it to her other arm and hand, and again across a third time. With each stroke Julia lets out a soft gasp of appreciation. Her mind is racing from one thing to another in rapid secession. 'Should I let him continue? Smell that lavender and vanilla, I mentioned I like that aroma. He looks and sounds even better than I could have imagined!'

Before he brings the cloth down to her chest again Chevalier softly states "I am your sehrvant. I will stop when you ask." Julia inhales deeply but says nothing so Chevalier soaps the cloth again and proceeds to engulf her breast in the warm aromatic cloth. Julia feels the strongest tingling sensation. She almost slides further into the water, but Chevaliers hold of her breast keeps her where she is.

He slowly continues to her other breast circling it lightly at the nipple at first causing Julia to moan. She was already having an out of body experience and now she feels like she is in a dream. The aroma is intoxicating. It fills her nostrils into her head and through her body.

She is afraid to open her eyes now for fear that it will end. The cloth continues its search reaching around her waist then pulling back lifting her slightly from the water which instantly brings her nipples to attention from the cooler but not cold temperature of the bathroom. As Chevalier relaxes his grip and Julia eases back into the water, again she feels the sensation of the warmth of the depths making her body tingle once more.

The cloth makes its way to clockwise circles around her abdomen then over to the other side of her waist lifting her ever so slightly again. As she comes back into the water Julia's moans grow stronger. Chevalier makes sure he gives her legs and feet the same attention he has given to her upper body. He sweeps the warm soaped cloth under Julia's bottom. Once again he lifts her slightly out of the water. Julia is anticipating Chevaliers next move.

He pulls the cloth between her legs and rubs up against her vaginal opening. Julia actually quivers. He pauses with his hand in her bush, waiting for her to signal whether he should continue or not. She softly says "O.K." The soft cloth with the strength of his hand beneath it slowly opens her legs. He then slowly and firmly begins moving the cloth along her womanhood. The friction of the cloth moving along her clit causes her to pulse with desire. Both of her nipples wake up stiffening and Julia can feel them pulsing with desire.

As Chevalier continues stroking Julia he brings his other hand to her breast lifting it out of the water so he can suckle the nipple. When his mouth covers her nipple and he begins sucking and swirling his tongue along the tip, Julia knows she is in heaven. Chevalier begins twisting Julia's clit with the cloth between his fingers sending jolts of electricity through her body once again.

While caressing the same breast he was sucking on, he continues to manipulate Julia's genital area. Chevalier lets the cloth fall away so he can use his fingers more efficiently and slip a finger up inside her. Julia feels she is about to explode. He goes back to vigorously tonguing and suckling her breast while continuing to be just as attentive below.

Julia cannot help her moans of 'oh' and 'oh goodness' as the orgasms flow through her. She had never had an experience like this. Her whole body is quivering. She has to stop Chevalier as the shocks through her body continue. She isn't sure she can take any more.

She puts her hands over his. They are both panting. Chevalier stops but does not take his hands away. He holds her between the legs and behind the neck, putting his forehead to hers. Julia still has her eyes closed. Neither says a word.

In all her years of marriage she had never had an experience like this. You just didn't do these things. What the hell? She was missing this? Why didn't anyone ever tell her this could be so amazing?!

When she feels Chevaliers' warm breath on her shoulder she knows it is real. She slowly opens her eyes. She leans her head into Chevaliers. "Thank you" she whispers.

"I am here for you mon fleur" he whispers back then kisses the top of her head. They sit in silence for a few minutes more before Julia suddenly feels the chill of a long bath past its prime. She softly asks her partner, "May I have a robe, and maybe that drink?" They share a chuckle and Chevalier gets up. He hands her the drink that was waiting by the tub, then he goes to fetch a robe for his lady.

The New Pony Arrives

     Sienna is in her office writing notes after the morning's exams. Michael pokes his head in the doorway. "The new pony is here." He is gone with a flash. Sienna methodically puts down her pen straightens up her paperwork and heads out the door.

     Maia is potting plants in the green house. She has dirt on her cheek and sweat on her brow. Peter walks in. "Found some herbs to plant?"

     "Are you just going to stand there, or are you going to help?"

     "I think I'll take over for a bit, the new pony has arrived." Maia looks up from her plants smiling. Peter wipes at the dirt on her face with his hand. "Tisk, tisk, don't want you to be all dirty in case he see's you."

     "Thank you, Peter! You are so sweet." Maia takes off her gloves and wipes her hands on her shorts to swipe away any excess dirt. As she leaves the green house Peter continues on with the work she has started still smiling like an idiot. "You're welcome." he says softly knowing Maia does appreciate this gesture. It actually feels good for him too.

Victor looks up from his book that he is reading as he stands behind the front desk. He knows Jonathan Shipton is arriving soon and hopes he has a few moments alone with the man before the Madam shows up. It must be his lucky day because he catches a glimpse of Joseph's car coming down the drive.

As the car comes to a stop Victor puts his book under the desk then grabs a bottle of water from below taking a few sips. Leandro; one of the companions on bellman duty today comes walking into the front entry area. "Getting ready for your pep talk?"

"Whatever do you mean?"

"Right, want me to get his bags while you drill him old man?"

"Old man my ass, but yes, please do." Leandro heads out and holds the door as Mr. Shipton walks in. "Hello" Leandro cheerfully conveys to the new arrival. He gets a "Hello" from Jonathan who is a little unsure how he should respond. His mind is already wondering if this man is competition or not. Sizing him up in a matter of seconds, he decides the good looking olive skinned man seems easy going, not a threat.

Jonathan Shipton is and looks cunning. He is someone you don't want to cross, however his classic good looks and charm out shine the cunning when he wants them to. He found out about The Garden from a woman he would escort to social events who has been here.

He was brought up in the best private schools, went to West Point and served 7 years in the army. He spent time in the Special Forces. Somehow none of it fascinated him as much as women did. He was amazed at the softness of their skin, the smell of their bodies and the difference in the way they thought and acted opposed to men. While in his 5th year in the military a general's assistant told him about male escorts.

It had never occurred to him before but he thought he would try it before giving the rest of his life to the military. He had followed his father's wishes all his young life. Then he met Louisa Treadmill who is a regular at The Garden. She gave him the phone number to Madam West as she called her and now he was on an adventure he never expected.

Jonathan walks into the old world lobby. He sees the man behind the counter as he comes around to the front looking all kinds of serious. He notices the expensive embossed jacket. The ascot is a bit of a surprise, but it seems to fit the man. Victor starts the conversation "Nice to see you made it Mr. Shipton, I'm Victor Tanner." The men shake hands. "Thank you Mr. Tanner. I already get the feeling you run a tight ship around here."

"As tight as it needs to be, but, there is always breathing room." This brings a slight smile to Jonathans face. "Good to know." Victor turns to head back behind the desk. "So, you are a military man?"

"I was, yes." Jonathan is wondering where this is going to lead.

"This is an interesting choice for a career change Mr. Shipton." Victor is being as non chalant as he can be.

"Ah yes, well, the military was my father's idea. This is mine."

Victor nods his head as if he understands where Jonathan is coming from. "Hm, the effect of parental direction, it affects us in many forms does it not?" It takes a moment for Jonathan to take in what was just said. He nods his head as the understanding sinks in. He had never thought about it quite like that before. He wasn't sure what to say but he does now have some food for thought.

Victor offers Jonathan a small bottle of water from below the counter. As he does Sienna and Maia are standing across the lobby behind a curtain that leads to a sitting area with a huge fireplace in it. The two women are looking through the curtain so as not to be seen checking out the new arrival. "I love training days." Sienna whispers.

Maia grins, "Me too. Where is the Madam?"

"Watch, like clockwork." As Sienna's words come out Veronica walks into the lobby from the back.

"How does she do that?" Maia whispers in wonder.

"I think she waits in the shadows, like we do." The two women silently giggle. They listen to the beginning of the ensuing conversation. Maia whispers. "He looks like he will be an easy one to adapt to our family."

"I've heard that before." Sienna snorts and begins to leave. Maia follows her asking "Up for lunch today?"

"Wish I could, these exams are kicking my ass Mai, maybe tomorrow?"

"OK"

Sienna heads back towards her office leaving Maia alone. She pouts for a second wondering why her friend is so evasive today. Then she catches sight of the sun outdoors it beckons to her like a flame to a moth she heads for the glow.

Back at the front desk Veronica and Jonathan are already done with the pleasantries of a meet and greet. "Jonathan, before I show you the grounds and begin your training, would you mind coming to my office?"

"You're the boss." He quips.

"That my man, she is." Victor's velvety voice softly confirms.

Jonathan walks towards Veronica. When he reaches her she turns to walk with him out the back of the lobby. Jonathan puts his elbow out to her. "Madam". His chivalry actually catches Veronica by surprise, but she smiles and accepts his gentle offer of assistance.

As they walk Veronica is pointing out areas of the mansion. "To the left is the clinic and Dr. Pardons' office. To the right is the gift shop. Although we don't allow guests to take photos of their time at The Garden, they are allowed to bring home telltale signs of their visit. Coffee mugs, key chains, clothing, oddly our highest selling item is journals."

"Really?" Jonathan is surprised.

"Writing down memories of life experiences in long hand seems to mean more, especially when it comes from one of our pens in one of our journals. A personal memoir so to speak."

They walk a little further revealing the expanse of the mansion that isn't noticeable from the front. "On the right here is the coffee lounge. You can also get some light food and snacks here. We conduct some of our smaller classes in there. It's usually very busy in the morning, then again between 3 and 4 in the afternoon. Otherwise it's a nice quiet area to read, do computer research and have some remarkably average coffee."

As Veronica is giving Jonathan the tour he is watching her every move. She walks with a quiet confidence that could easily go unnoticed. He could see the excitement in her face as she speaks of this place she obviously cares deeply about. She often puts her hand on his shoulder or touches his elbow almost in a reassuring manner to make him more comfortable. There are many layers to this woman. He is already looking forward to his final days of training.

At the end of a hall they enter what looks like a suite. Will is at his desk but on the phone so Veronica gets his attention by tipping the Star Wars travel mug on his desk. His reflex catches it before he realizes how it got knocked over. He looks up initially in annoyance but once he sees who it is he smiles and waves her off. He puts his hand on the speaker of the phone and mouths the word "Treadwell". Veronica nods her head in understanding. Apparently Louisa is checking to see if Jonathan has progressed to make it to the Garden. Veronica points to Jonathan while looking at Will and mouths "No calls." Will smiles and nods and gives her the thumbs up.

It is early afternoon. Veronica's office window is large enough to let a good amount of filtered light thru the tinted glass. When she gets to her desk she picks up a remote causing deep purple drapes a foot higher than the window to close, cutting the daylight back to a dim glow. Veronica steps away from Jonathan to sit at her desk and motions for Jonathan to sit across from her. Once they are seated she begins talking. Her tone is suddenly formal.

"You've come this far Jonathan. It would pain me to lose you at this juncture. However, I need you to be blatantly honest with yourself and with me. Do you truly believe you are up for the task of becoming a Garden Man?" Jonathan's mind is searching for the proper answer. Is this a test? Is it a riddle? Or is it a simple concern? He leans forward a little.

"Miss West, I am at your command."

Veronica feels she has been holding her breath for minutes. She releases a sigh of relief. "That is music to my ears." Veronica slowly stands up. She begins to clear a few things off her desk. Jonathan takes this as a hint. He takes a large weighted art piece from her and places it on the chair he was just sitting on. He slips his hand around her waist. "How may I be of service Madam?" he asks. Veronica gently places her hand on his chest. "You can start by not calling me Madam in a situation like this. Hmmm your strength is good. Finesse is important. But, you need to be able to sense a woman's comfort zone."

She gently pushes Jonathan back. "Is she hesitant, does she seem nervous? What do you do?" Jonathan loosens his grip and puts a slight distance between their bodies. "Or" Veronica continues. She pulls him close again and begins to unbutton his shirt. "Is she playing right along with you?" Jonathan smiles and leans in. "I have been waiting for this moment." They are about to kiss when a voice comes from a hand held walkie talkie on a side table. It is Victor trying to keep his voice calm. "Madam wolf sighting in the front drive." Before their lips meet Veronica stops cold. She stiffens like she has seen a ghost. She goes to the radio and picks it up and talks into it.

"Thank you Victor. I'm on my way." She recovers her composure and looks at Jonathan with disappoint in her demeanor. "I am so sorry! I have to take care of this. I will explain later."

Veronica is heading out the door. She turns back to see the man looking absolutely lost. Why would she be so concerned about a wolf? She walks back to him and gives him a passionate kiss on the lips. As she is leaving she tells him "Bungalow #4 in an hour. Ask Victor, he will direct you."

Maia is coming into the suite carrying a plant catalog as Veronica is walking out.

"Oh, good I caught you!" She notices Jonathan coming out of the office. Then she catches up with Veronica in the hall. "Looks like the new one is eager!" Veronica responds in a distracted way. "I'd say there's definite promise with this one."

"Good!" Maia raises her book to show Veronica a page. "I wanted your input regarding this flora."

"Maia, I would love to, but can we discuss it later?" Maia stops walking and Veronica disappears down the hall. "Did I do something wrong? What is it today?" Maia cups her hand over her mouth and breathes. "Nope". She then lifts her arm and sniffs "nope not that!" She is about to head back out when she see's Jonathan coming down the hall.

"Excuse me" he asks her. "Do you know how to get back to the lobby? I am supposed to talk to Victor." Maia smiles, "Are you now?" Maia figures now is the best time to get acquainted with their new arrival. "We can have a little chat along the way." Jonathan is instantly aware of Maia's shine and confident presence. She is taller than he is and she is only wearing worn out work boots.

"I am glad you made it Mr. Shipton, I am Maia Hanlin."

"Hanlin Cellars Hanlin?" Jonathan saw the sign when they drove in. He wasn't sure how the two were related. The puzzle is just beginning to piece together. Maia's grin of pride makes Jonathan smile. Maia just gave this new one a point for observation. "Ahhhh, you notice things. That is an important asset to be successful in this job, and yes, the winery is my baby, although I can only take a portion of the credit. I have an amazing team." Maia puts her arm in his and leads him down the hallway. Let's get you to your destination, but maybe some coffee first." Maia takes a slight detour to the coffee lounge.

When Past and Present Collide

The head of security is standing at the front door looking out at the scene unfolding in front of him. Anders has been security at The Garden since it opened four years ago. He considered himself lucky to get such an easy and rewarding gig after years of abuse in the military then being a stunt man in the entertainment industry and just not able to do it anymore.

Veronica is the best boss he has ever had, his crew is respectable and reliable and he has learned more about women and humans in general than he ever knew was possible. Needless to say he is very protective of his adopted family, especially Veronica. So seeing the Madams obnoxious, arrogant, entitled ex-husband standing in the drive way arguing with Reggie who is his second in command and Leandro who just happened to get bellman duty today, is not his idea of a good time.

It will be only moments before Veronica shows up at the door. Anders does not envy the argumentative and clueless asshole he is forced to look at when she does arrive. At the same time a hundred scenarios are going through his head of how this man found this place. Anders is not amused.

Erik Lockhart is yelling as he tries to get past Reggie and Leandro. "What are you doing? I work here!" The two men holding him back are actually enjoying themselves. It's similar to when two cats are teasing the mouse who thinks he is going to get by the predators before him. "Hey Leo, ever see a dog like this working here?"

"No one this fugly Reg."

"I am not ugly!" Erik is not in as good shape as the wall of men in front of him. He is dressed in cheap polyester dress pants and his version of a Garden shirt. Leandro looks at Lockhart's clothes. "I said fugly. You are not worthy to wear a shirt that is even close to ours."

"I have every right to be here!" He struggles a bit more. "Where is my wife?!"

"That is ex-wife Mr. Lockhart." Veronica yells back. She heard him yelling as she got to

the front door. She steps out to stand next to
Anders.

There is a pause in the three-man shuffle
as Erik steps back so he can see Veronica. He
grins as he rearranges his shirt. "Hey baby, miss
me?"

"Almost as much as I miss my period
when I don't have it." There is nothing like
talking about the female bleeding cycle to make
men feel awkward.

"Well ain't that sweet?" Erik knows he
has already struck a nerve.

Veronica's façade is that of boredom, but
underneath she feels a combination of anger and
betrayal. How the hell did he find her? Why
now? Things have been going so well and now
she has to deal with the man who left her with
nothing and wants everything. Veronica
touches Anders shoulder. "Anders, will you do
me a favor and take out the trash?" Anders
smiles and is glad for the permission to kick this
douche bag off the property. "Yes, Madam"
comes his reply with the lilt of an accent that is
hard to place. He gives a hand signal. Reggie

and Leandro lift Erik to bring him back to his car.

Erik begins yelling again. "Trash? Me trash? Look who's talking Miss Madam! You are going to pay for this Veronica! You owe me!" Veronica turns to Anders. "Thank you Anders." She leans in standing on her tippy toes. She looks to make sure Erik can see and as she did moments before with Jonathan, she kisses Anders with passion.

"How dare you! He's, he's, he's a foreigner!" Erik is still yelling as Reggie and Leandro put him back in his car.

Once he is in, Reggie leans in forcing Erik to lean away from him. The threat in his voice is not unnoticed by Erik. "If you ever step foot on this property again, I will shoot you and make you fertilizer for the lavender plants. Understood?" Erik gives him a halfhearted defiant look, but decides leaving is the best choice 'for now'. He peels out forcing Reggie to step back quickly.

The men hadn't even realized that Veronica wasn't there anymore. She had walked back into the lobby. Victor was standing, waiting, in case he needed to call 911. He comes to Veronica as she sits on the settee in the sitting room. "Veronica"

"I'm o.k. Victor. Thank you. Go back to business oh wise one." She utters. Victor is clearly worried. "I will have Anders tighten security immediately." Veronica gets up and nods her head in agreement. She walks away from Victor. As she reaches the doorway to the back exit, Anders comes in from the front. He goes to follow her but Victor stops him. "Give her a minute."

Anders is a man of few words and more action. He feels it was his fault Lockhart got onto the property at all. Getting to the bottom of this as soon as possible so it doesn't happen again is imperative. He feels as though he has let Veronica down. The idea of not being able to do anything to fix it right now is killing him.

There are a multitude of paths to walk along in the back yard of The Garden. Veronica finds she isn't going anywhere in particular so she stops at a bench. She puts her head down placing her face in her hands. She is shaking a little. She is making the noises of almost crying as her frustration is building. The cascade of emotions are flowing.

"Shake it off West. Don't give him the power! Fuck! How did he find me?" In her head she is thinking, 'What does it matter? It was only a matter of time. Seven years of not having to see that face or hear that voice was not enough.' In the back of her head she is still thinking 'Why now? What had made him desperate enough to look for her?' She stands up to psychologically wipe the dust off and continue on with the day suddenly remembering Jonathan. She looks at her watch. "Shit!" She heads towards her bungalow to prepare. Her walk now has purpose.

What a few seconds and a change of thought
can do to get you back to your senses.
And having a goal; something to look forward
to makes ALL the difference in the world.

♋

Victor and Anders are standing towards the back of the lobby. "What I want to know is how did he get past the grand hall?" Victor is beyond agitated and Anders can't blame him. "I don't know Victor."

"That's not good enough. Anders." Victor is staring Anders down.

"I know, let me get this sorted and I will let you and the Madam know what happened." Victor nods and heads back towards the front desk. As he stands there shuffling papers thoughtlessly because his mind is anywhere but there, Sienna walks in. She is a woman on a mission. "What happened?" Victor looks up but has no response.

"Lockhart shows up and no one calls me or Maia?"

"It happened so fast doctor."

"Someone needs to call me or Maia. Where is she?"

"She is getting ready for her first lesson with Mr. Shipton."

"O.K." Sienna doesn't know if she should go talk her out of it, but thinking on it she knows

Veronica would ignore her advice anyway. "Do you know when she will be done?"

Victor gives the doctor his look. "It all depends on how well the student is doing I believe."

Sienna sighs. "True enough. I want every staff member to have a picture of this asshole. We can't let him slip in again."

"Yes doctor, I believe that will be first on Anders list."

"First should have been keeping this from happening in the first place. Just call me when you see her emerge."

"Yes doctor." Victor reassures her.

Sienna is out of sight by the time Maia and Jonathan arrive at the front desk. Maia hands Jonathan over to Victor. "I believe the gentleman has some inquiries Victor." She notices the look on Victors face. "Are you O.K.?"

"Fine, yes fine. If you stay for a moment after I help Mr. Shipton I would appreciate it."

"Alright."

Victor looks to Jonathan. "What can I help you with Mr. Shipton?"

"I need to get to bungalow #4."

"Ah, let me mark the map for you."
Victor pulls out the property map. It shows all
of the bungalows and the outer buildings and
how to find almost anywhere you need to go on
the resort. Victor pulls out a pink highlighter.
"You are here, and here is where you need to go.
Feel free to use the shower when you arrive.

"Thank you. See you later Miss Hanlin?"

"I'm sure you will!" Maia smiles.

Jonathan tries to hear their conversation
as he leaves, but the whispers are too low. He is
curious as to what maybe going on, but to no
avail they guard their words carefully.

Into The Afternoon

After being snubbed by both Veronica and Sienna today and upon the unexpected visit from Erik Lockhart, Maia is in need of a distraction. She decides to walk to the center of the property where her marijuana plants are growing. Many of the younglings are new to the field and need some extra attention.

The most difficult part of growing these plants is not the early fragility, not the fact she has so many state rules to follow and not the harvesting, but that she cannot help but think of her brother Luca every time she is doing anything in connection with these plants.

Luca died of AIDS. Can it really be 15 years ago already? Maia is doing the math in her head. No one should be getting this horrific disease anymore. People should be aware and be more fucking responsible, but no! How can people put their heads in the sand and live in such denial?

Thinking it will never happen to you will most certainly make it happen to you.

Was all she could hear in her head.

Luca worked for a medical charity organization. He was working at a makeshift clinic in Africa that was overrun by the government militia. He was put in prison for treason. Before they could execute him Maia had found out what had happened. Fortunately she was able to rely on some influential people she had met over the years. A few of her 'connections' made it clear to the General who was in charge of the attack on the clinic that he would never have a sound sleep again if Luca was killed. It took months to get him back to the states. It cost her everything she had.

When he returned he was malnourished and a changed man. He never spoke of how he contracted the disease. He didn't have to. One could only imagine the possibilities being held as a prisoner for so long. He never recovered mentally, physically or emotionally.

He couldn't gain his weight back, and he was sick all the time. When he finally went to the Doctor he was diagnosed with AIDS. He was too far along to do much of anything for him other than make him as comfortable as possible.

When a friend told Maia the benefits of marijuana for pain, nausea and anxiety, she had to fight with Luca to get him to try it. When he finally did she was relieved to see his body actually relax. It was only for short amounts of time, but that was something. He slept better and they could actually have conversations without her losing him to those horrific past events every time he tried to participate in life.

Before the disease took him, Luca took his own life. It only took one bullet to the head; his beautiful head. Maia had gone to get groceries. The last thing he had said to her before she left was "Don't forget love."

She said "What?"

"Don't forget love." He repeated smiling at her. She smiled at him, walked back to give him a kiss on the head and tousle his shaggy blonde hair. Then headed out the door thinking he must be high or just teasing her like he used to, teasing would actually be nice for a change.

She returned less than an hour later. Luca was sitting under the tree in the back yard which he was prone to do when the sun was out. She was saying something about the stupid traffic as she went to greet him. Maia noticed his left hand was palm up on the ground. She immediately ran to the trunk of the willow tree. The gun was still in his right hand. The blood was already clogging in the mass of his blonde hair.

Immediately Maia checked the wound and felt for a pulse. It was too late. First she touched his cheek. On the surface it was warm but just below he was already cold. She pulled her brothers lifeless body to her. She could feel the anger well up inside her, but she didn't expect the warriess* cries that came from the depth of her soul as she verbally berated him for leaving her, for not telling her goodbye, for not giving her more time. She held him closely to her chest hoping there would be a response, some warmth, something living.

All she heard was the cry of a hawk in attack mode. Telling its' prey he was about to strike and there was nothing the poor little animal he was after could do about it. Maia felt like that little animal at that moment. She was being taken over by the numbness of shock. She didn't even notice the tears that were cleaning her now bloodied cheek that she was resting her brothers injured head upon.

Veronica was the first to find Maia in the yard with her brother still in her arms. Maia was now brushing the hair from his face sobbing and telling him she was sorry for being angry. "I know you were dead inside long before today, but why didn't you give me a chance to say goodbye?" As Veronica got closer Maia was speaking in German. It sounded like a sing song lullaby. Veronica touched Maia's shoulder with her hand, so she would know she wasn't alone. Bringing herself down to sit with her arms lightly around her friend, she began to hum Maia's song letting her tears fall as well before taking care of the practical business at hand.

♋

Maia now standing in the middle of the marijuana fields takes a deep breath and raises her face to the sun. Feeling that warmth with the energy sinking in always helps bring her calm back to where it belongs. She returns them to the matters at hand. The plants are doing well. She should have a new crop for the clinic soon. 'Ah, this is where your train of thought should be young lady' she thinks to herself.

She continues to walk through the plants letting her fingers run across the leaves. This is her reward for her efforts. This is the one thing she can do to help her deal with her loss. As if on cue, she hears the cry of a hawk but can't see one anywhere. To her, this is Luca saying he feels her thinking of him and he is letting her know he is always with her.

Suddenly Maia realizes she has lost track of time and needs to head back to the main compound. There will be a full moon tonight and she has an active meditation* to get ready for! She blows a kiss to the heavens saying "See you later" to her brother.

♋

Mon petite fleur Julia is still wearing her robe. Chevalier has put his shirt back on but has left it unbuttoned. He wants to make sure he keeps Julia interested. They are sitting at a small table in Julia's room enjoying each other's company.

Julia is tipsy, but not drunk. "You are so sweet fawning over me, calling me such wonderful frenchy names. I have no idea what they mean, but they sound beautiful!"

"You are beautiful, mon cherie".

"Oh, maybe once, but I'm old."

"There is beauty at any age and your bright spirit iz what helps to bring yours to zee surface." Chevaliers' voice is sincere. "You allowed yourself mere moments of pleasure and zee beauty that emerged was breathtaking."

Julia guffaws "I thought I was going to have a stroke! You know you shouldn't be allowed to do that to an old woman!"

"Julia, no matter how old we are we all want to feel alive eh? I think you need a little more life!"

Julia smiles at Chevalier then the reality

seems to hit her. The tears begin to fall. She is trying to hold them back. "This is all wrong Chevalier. I shouldn't be here. I shouldn't have let you..." She bows her head in shame putting her hands over her face beginning to let the crying flow. "What was I thinking?"

Chevalier puts his arms around Julia letting her have a minute before he tells her "Come now. Dry those tears. Julia, do you know how many women never take zee step you have? How many people let misery and fear take over zer lives? No, I will not let zee ignorawnce of society make you feel guilty. You are brave to come here and give yourself a chance to feel again. I for one am honored you gave me zee opportunity to spend time with you." Julia cries even harder. Chevalier hands her a hanky from his shirt pocket. Trying not to let the crying make her totally inaudible Julia gets out a gasping "Thank you"

"No, mon fleur, if you are crying my job is not complete. Maybe if you get some of what you are thinking of off your chest it will help." Julia grabs a tissue from the table top. She wipes her eyes and blows her nose. "I've been married to the same man for over 40 years. He is the love of my life Chevalier. Yet his mind and his body have been lost to me for 7 years now. Roger used to do everything. Oh, I had my share of responsibility, but he took care of me.

Although it was slow at first, he started to forget things, bills didn't get paid, and he'd get lost walking in our own neighborhood. We've lived there over 30 years. I didn't even notice the loneliness at first, but Roger and I were a very hands on couple you see. We loved the attention and affection we got from each other, even if it was just holding hands while shopping for groceries. I just miss him sooo much." Julia begins to tear up again. "He rarely recognizes me anymore. Most of the time he thinks I'm his flippin' mother! What a kick in the teeth that is! She was always a witch, especially to me. Anyway, my daughter and I had more than one conversation about me just needing someone to pay attention to me. She didn't want me finding some old fart; as she said it, that I would have to take care of. But she did understand my dilemma. When she found out about this place, it took her months to convince me. I just wasn't brought up this way. Til death do us part, in sickness and in health. I'm sorry, I'm just going on and on."

Chevalier doesn't speak at first. He is weighing the possibilities of what to do next. He makes his choice and he begins. "I am going to tell you a story. When I was very young I always asked questions. Many of zee answers were, 'Because that is how it is, or that is how God wants it.' No one could give me any answers zat made sense to me. This got me into trouble many times as a young boy, let me tell you. Zen I met my mothers' friend; her name was Clara Luna, or Clara Moon in English."

As he is telling his story he stands Julia up and leads her to the bed. He pulls the covers back and puts her under the covers robe and all. He nudges her over so he can sit beside her putting one arm around her. "Clara was zee most beautiful woman I had ever seen. She was very smart and very funny. She used to make me and my brother laugh until our sides hurt!

One day I came home early from playing with friends because I had gotten into a fight. One of zee other boys said that Clara Luna was a whore who got paid to have sex with men. I was outraged and protective so when I called him a liar he punched me, I punched him. We pretty much stopped there because we were both bleeding and it hurt! So we both ran home.

When I told my mother what happened she sat me down and explained that zee boys' story was true. I was devastated, I yelled, "How could my angel be a whore?" My mother corrected me. "She is a prostitute, not a whore."

"What is zee difference?" I cried in anger. My mother told me Clara should not be judged by anyone but God. We are often told we should do what we love in life. Clara loved being with men.

"But if she slept with married men..." Julia asks

"Do you know how many marriages Clara saved? More than she ruined I tell you! Some men do not know how to keep it in their pants, and with zee added guilt" he nudges Julia "zey do not wish to bother their spouse too often for they feel bad about wanting it all zee time. We as a society are too quick to judge others mon cherie. Ah, but back to my story."

"Of course years later I understood what Clara loved but in my own way. My place is to be with women. They so often put themselves last on zee list of importahnce.

Women have been told for centuries that they are zee second class citizen. Women are told sex is only for producing offspring. Make your man appy. What poppy cock! Sex is beautiful. It can be raw. It is rarely pretty, but it is a connection between two beings. You have done nothing wrong Julia, nothing. I still have zee rest of today to show you. I will let you take a cat nap with this in mind." Chevalier kisses her on the forehead as he begins to stand. Julia snuggles down into the bed. She pops her head up. "How do I find you?"

"I am a phone call away mon cherie. Rest a bit and we will dine when you are ready! Oui?"

"O.K." Julia replies as she sighs herself into the covers. As Chevalier is closing the door he whispers "Dream of me mon fleur." He can only hope his story made some sense to Julia. He isn't even sure if it made sense to him.

♋

The First Lesson

Jonathan is pacing like a tiger in a cage in the sitting area of bungalow #4. This is not a themed bungalow but it is tastefully decorated and furnished. He doesn't seem to notice any of it. He is sure his first sex test is going to be today. As he is trying to mentally prepare himself, he finds it frustrating that he felt he was dropped like a hot potato, and for what, a wolf? 'This must be part of the training.' He reassures himself. 'This is testing my patience. I'm not doing very well with it am I? If I stop walking I will explode!' Just as all of this is racing through his mind he hears a knock at the door. He walks over and opens it.

Veronica is standing there. She is wearing a long coat and he catches the slightest scent of what he can't place, but he is instantly aroused. "May I come in?" Veronica asks. "Oh, of course" he now feels stupid because he let too much time pass and didn't ask her in first.

When Veronica enters she begins apologizing immediately. "I am so sorry. I have never left a new arrival hanging like that. You must think I am a total flake." Flake? That hadn't even crossed his mind. "No, no, I'm just a bit confused to be honest with you."

"I don't blame you." Veronica sits on the couch and pats the cushion for Jonathan to join her. "It's a long story I'd rather not bother you with." She admits, "But I will give you a summary. I divorced quite a few years ago. It was messy. He isn't supposed to know where I am. Well, he found me today, and I just had to deal with it quickly." Veronica shrugs her shoulders.

"Wolf sighting." It is suddenly making sense to Jonathan.

"I know, it's silly."

"No, not at all, are you all right? Should we wait?" He asks hoping she won't, but understanding if she would.

Veronica is taken back by his concern. "No such luck for you Mr. Shipton. I need the distraction of working you til you can't walk for a week!"

"Really," Jonathan smiles, he then takes Veronica by the hand and stands up.

"Well, almost." She accepts his invitation standing as well. "Have you scoped the place out while you were waiting?"

"You did give me plenty of time." He slightly berates her as he leads her into the bedroom. Veronica can't help herself. "Patience not one of your strong suits eh?" Jonathan bows his head. " I'm working on that one."

Veronica stops. She turns him to face her. The look on her face is of concern. "It's the most important trait most of the time here. We can't afford tempers and no patience. We deal with very fragile human beings who need all of our support and attention. Understood? " Jonathan nods and whispers "Yes I do." as he leads Veronica towards the darkness ahead.

They enter the bedroom. It is dark aside from two small bedside lamps that give a glow to only the bed. Veronica takes off her coat revealing a long dark purple robe. "Today we will start with the art of multiple orgasms without ejaculation. Shall we?"

Jonathan has been practicing this technique since he read about it in his training manual. He had never heard of it before and was fascinated to find out it is actually possible. This being his first time with the Madam made him wonder if he could pull it off. He couldn't remember the last time he was this nervous about making love. As if Veronica could read his mind she began. "Don't be nervous. I am going to be your easiest prospect at The Garden. Consider me your training wheels before you can ride on your own." It dawns on Jonathan that she has just broken the tension with that silly little analogy. He chuckles and feels a little less self-conscious now.

Veronica's voice turns into teaching mode as she stops him a few steps away from the bed and she walks to it. "You will have many partners much younger and much more beautiful than I am, but many won't have the confidence or experience I do. Then, you will have partners who are even less appealing than I am. You have to connect to each and every one of them as if they are the most fascinating person you have ever met, without coming off as a fake."

Veronica asks him to slowly take off his clothes while she watches. "There are some guests who enjoy a bit of voyeurism." She wants to see how he handles it. Jonathan is confident he'll have no trouble with this. He enjoys the "tease". It often seems to excite the women he has been with before. He is unbuttoning his shirt when he hears "Slower". He instantly thinks "Am I fucking this up already?" then he hears Veronica's "mmmmmm". He takes off his shoes heel to toe and places them at the end of the bed. Again he hears Veronica's voice "Nice".

When he undoes his belt he places it over his shoulder. He brings his pants down and takes them off with his socks at the same time. "Bravo" she applauds, he smiles. He decides to take a chance and now naked aside from his shouldered belt he begins to walk towards Veronica. When he gets to her he opens her robe and slips his belt around her waist and brings her towards the bed.

"Nice and slow." Veronica whispers. "Time to get the crock-pot known as woman heated up."

"Right" Jonathan knows exactly what she means. He lets his belt slip away as he brings his other hand behind her head. He reaches his fingers up through her hair grabbing hold, but not pulling. He presses his body against hers and his belt hand comes to rest across the small of her back, bringing her tighter against him.

There is nowhere else to go but the kiss. He is surprised at the agility of her tongue as she seems to pull his tongue further into her mouth. Veronica has one hand on his ass and the other already with a firm grip on his stiff pulsing shaft. He decides to lead her to the bed one step at a time. With each step bringing his excitement higher as her tongue is circling his. Her grip on him is moving up and down slow and firm. He is trying to do what he thinks is right while paying attention to what she is doing so he can remember what to do in the future. Veronica can feel the change in his attention.

"Don't over think it. I will stop you if I need to."

Jonathan turns Veronica onto the bed. He leads her down on her back. He begins to suckle on the side of her neck. She moans for the first time. It's a good sign. At the same time he reaches for her breast covering it with his hand. He lightly pulls it towards him then gets a better grip. He repeats this while continuing to suckle and bite her neck. Not in a manner that will leave marks. That would be a number one mistake for any Garden Man. There is never a mark to be left, unless it is requested. This is another lesson that is repeated time and time again in studying.

Jonathan brings his mouth to her breast and his hand reaches between her thighs. When he sucks on her nipple there is little response, but when he moves his mouth to the flesh area of her breast another moan greets him. Before he puts his hand to her vaginal area he reaches for the lube on the bedside table remembering lubrication is of the utmost importance. He knows this from experience, but also from the many reminders from page after page of the training manuals he has labored over. He reaches back between her legs then begins to stimulate her clit putting moving pressure up and down between the top of her tulip. He hears a sigh.

After making sure both breasts have had attention Jonathan brings his mouth between Veronica's legs. He starts at her taint. He brings his tongue full on along from the bottom to the top of her vaginal area. When he reaches it, he immediately begins suckling and tonguing her clitoris. Veronica gasps. As he continues his oral fixation between her legs, Veronica is gripping her hands into the sheets. After a few moments she puts her hands to his head and begins a rhythmic movement of her hips. Her moans just charge Jonathan up more. After a while he notices she has stopped moving and her hands are pulling his head up towards her torso.

"It's time." She says with the hoarseness of sexual pleasure in her voice. She continues to pull him up. She reaches to the lamp table for a condom. "So sad we have to do this." She claims, even if she says it only to make him feel better. Condoms are another golden rule of The Garden. She uses a small amount of lube and strokes his penis before placing the condom over his already sensitive member. He feels the tightness of its grip. "Now remember, you need to mentally pull yourself back when you feel you are close to ejaculation. Then stop inside like you are retracting at the base of your penis. Jonathan nods his head. He brushes lube along Veronicas' warm wetness. When he finds his way inside her she meets him from his first plunge lifting her hips in rhythm with him already. He feels her nails on his back creating even more sensation below his skin, making him push into her even harder and faster.

He starts to kiss her to distract himself from the swelling he feels beginning. She turns her head away. "No cheating" she says softly, almost teasingly. Jonathan grunts then Veronica says "hold it, but keep moving. Pull back inside, but keep moving." Jonathan lets out a primeval growl but begins to laugh when he realizes he just had an orgasm without ejaculating. "Fuck!" He blurts out. Veronica giggles. "Uhm, hello, I am a guest right now! Remember no cursing please."

"I'm sorry, I didn't mean to"

"I know, just reminding you. There are guests who request cursing."

"Really?"

"It takes all kinds Mr. Shipton."

Obviously there is now a break in the rhythm so Veronica takes the opportunity to switch things up. "Slowly pull out, if you are still hard enough I will turn over. You will take me from behind." Jonathan nods again. He is ready. As Veronica turns over she lifts her robe so he can only see her from mid back to her round full ass. He immediately rises strongly to the occasion. Veronica grabs hold of the head rest with both hands. Jonathan checks her moistness with his hand to see if she needs more lubrication. She has no need of any.

When Jonathan enters her, she is swollen from their first encounter so the tightness around him is even better than before. Again Veronica is moving with him perfectly, even when he slows. He is taken by surprise again as she leans her body onto one elbow and takes her other hand palm up to brush against his balls. The sensation is almost more than he can take. Her voice whispers again. "Hold it, keep moving, but hold... back." Jonathan growls again and stops movement. "If your partner isn't done angel, you have to keep moving."

"What if I can't?"

"Concentrate. You can. Meanwhile, bring my back to you so you can move in, and manipulate my clit. It will distract you while you continue to pleasure your partner." Jonathan puts his arm around Veronica's sternum and pulls her to him. He begins moving his hips again as he brings his hand down to feel her swollen and excited womanhood. Veronica has one hand holding onto his muscled thigh rather enjoying the moment herself. Her other hand reaches behind his head with her fingers entwined in his hair. "If your partner is shy or not involved, you can show her where to place her hands or talk her through it. Just ask her if it's ok for you to show or ask." Jonathan is concentrating on not cumming but still grunts an acknowledgment of what his trainer has just said. He puts more attention on Veronica to keep his mind off of his movements.

Veronica was so busy schooling Jonathan she didn't expect to find herself in the throes of orgasm. Their guttural responses happened simultaneously and Jonathan had yet to ejaculate. This may be one of her best trainee's yet. Jonathan slowly leads Veronica down, letting her knee's straighten onto the bed surface. He rolls her over onto her back and lies down next to her. "How many was that?" He asks.

"I believe that was three Mr. Shipton."

"I haven't been able to handle it this well before. What did you do?" He is totally fascinated with the outcome.

"Me?" Veronica rolls over on top of him. He is still hard and she is not about to finish a lesson until her trainee is completely depleted. "It's all you. I just put in the occasional pause so you can regroup."

"No, it's more than that. You do some" …as Veronica once more places him inside her… "thing. I don't know what it is yet, but I have to figure it out so I can keep doing this" …Veronica starts slowly sliding herself along his pelvic area… "right."

"You will be just fine." Veronica begins to speed up her pace. She continues to slide along his shaft putting pressure on his shoulders with her fore arms so she can bring herself lower and move quicker. Jonathan finally can take no more. Every movement she makes has him contracting inside, constricting his abdomen in the best kind of work out he would prefer to endure on a daily basis. When he climaxes it explodes with a force he hasn't felt before.

Veronica is now slightly perspiring. She is satisfied that her new pony will be a working stallion much sooner than many who came before him. As she lies back next to Jonathan her robe gently brushes over his mid-section, causing him to once again jump slightly with sensitivity.

"Do you play poker?" Veronica asks. Jonathan finds this an odd question to ask at this time, but he responds. "Occasionally"

"How good are you at finding anothers tell?"

"I do O.K., watching the man who confidently leans back in his chair when he has a good hand, or the one twitching his finger on his cards, not sure whether or not to place the next bet."

"In love making we need to find and take advantage of our partners tells." As she is talking Veronica gently strokes Jonathan's chest. She reaches a nipple and pinches lightly which causes him to gasp. "The difference between poker tells and sexual tells, is when you are making love you want to see what pleases, what brings euphoria. You want to take your partner to new levels of passion. In poker you're looking for signs of weakness and nervousness to defeat."

Jonathan turns on his side to face Veronica. She has peaked his interest. "You need to keep in mind different people have different tells, some may be similar, but they aren't always the same. We've been together for a short time. Do you know what any of my tells are?" She asks innocently.

Jonathan grins. "Hmmm, let me see, you…"

"Shhh, no, no, don't tell me, show me." Jonathan brings himself over Veronica facing her. "O.K., would you mind closing your eyes Madam for full affect?" Veronica does as she is asked.

First Jonathan uses his head to move Veronica's head to one side. He begins lightly tonguing and suckling her neck then gets more aggressive. "That's one" she says.

As Jonathan moves himself down her body he holds her right hand in his left above her head causing her breast to stretch a little which enhances the sensitivity. When he covers the flesh area of her breast with his mouth again

Veronica instantly gasps and finds a way to
breathe "Two". He lingers at her breast long
enough to hear her moan some more. Then he
releases her hand and once again brings his face
between her legs. He is so adept at sucking and
almost chewing on her that Veronica arches her
back experiencing almost instant orgasm. The
word three is in Jonathans head, but it is not
spoken as Veronica holds onto his head between
her widely spread legs.

Veronica has never had such an intense
experience with a trainee before. He is still
between her legs causing jolts of electricity to
run through her body time and time again. She
gets her wits about her and takes a deep breath.
She leads his head towards hers. As his face gets
closer she can still see the intensity in him. He
slides along her torso and brings the intensity
from his lips to hers and enters her one more
time. This is clearly not part of the training.
Jonathan is now in control. He takes her hands
in his and places them over her head. They are
pulling back and slamming back into each other,
both vocalizing each breath from the back of

their throats. It's a symphony of body slams and guttural sounds.

Veronica is orgasming again and again.

Jonathan cums and he rolls to her side. When they stop they both lay quietly with their own thoughts.

Veronica is thinking 'Shit! What the hell did I just do? How the fuck did I just let that happen?'

Jonathan is thinking 'Did that really just happen? That was amazing! How did I do that?' The silence becomes awkward because Jonathan is waiting for Veronica to say something and Veronica doesn't know what to say just yet. She looks at Jonathan and softly smiles. "Nice work Mr. Shipton. You will be running with the herd sooner than you think." Before he can respond she is leaving the bed and heading for the bathroom. She closes the door behind her.

Jonathan is feeling that confusion once again. She sounded like it was good, but her body language didn't make him feel confident about it. 'Damn! Did I go too far? She would have stopped me, right?'

Leaning against the door in the bathroom Veronica is taking in what just transpired. Did this feel so amazing because she was shaken up from her encounter with Erik? Is she just not on top of things because of that? Should she have waited a day or two? Or was it really that good? "God damn it woman! Wash up and get on with it!" Her self-reprimand running in her head as she pees and washes up brings her senses back. She calls to her trainee so he doesn't think she passed out or something.

"Jonathan, relax, I will be out in a minute."

"O.K. Is there anything I should be doing?"

"No, just relax."

Jonathan does as he is told lying on his back bringing his arms behind his head. His eyes are closed as he is recording everything in his head that had passed in the last few hours for safe keeping. He hears a door open. He opens his eyes as Veronica steps out. Her hair is still a bit of a mess but he can tell she washed her face and her cheeks are still flushed. She has no makeup on. He is immediately aroused… again.

'You look beautiful'. Thank God he just said that in his head and not out loud. He also can't believe he is ready for more. He sits up pulling the pillow from behind his head onto his lap. "What are you wearing?" he asks trying to make conversation and change the subject in his head. "Ah, it's one of our fragrances, loaded with pheromones. You like?"

"It's very persuasive."

Veronica walks over to the bed and sits on the opposite edge from Jonathan.

"That is the point. If one wants to attract a partner, one cannot get enough assistance."

"You hardly need assistance." Jonathan comments hoping he doesn't sound like a complete idiot. Veronica can feel the heat of a blush rising. It's very uncharacteristic of her. She stands and turns her face slightly hoping he won't notice. "Thank you." She says sounding much more matter of fact than she meant to. "I will leave you to shower and get settled in.

Victor will have someone show you to your accommodations and give you a better tour of your new second home." She begins putting on her coat.

"When do we meet to continue training?" he asks trying not to sound too eager. Veronica smiles "Tomorrow. You will first meet with Ms. Hanlin for some physical training and some focus training, then you will meet with Dr. Praddon for some practical no nonsense science."

"Then I will work with you again?"

"Yes." She replies as she heads for the front door. "I hate to tell you, it gets harder from here."

"Harder?"

"You'll see. Enjoy getting acquainted with your new surroundings." Veronica leaves.

Jonathan realizes he never got out of the bed. He should have gotten up, opened the door. "Shit". He gets up and heads for the shower wondering what lay ahead.

♋

The Evening Begins

It's 5 o'clock in the afternoon. Julia is putting on her bright pink lipstick to cap off her outfit for the evening because she can't find the one Chauncey left for her that he called copper zing. Her experience in the bathtub earlier comes to mind and her hand begins to tremble a little. "Don't mess up the make-up old lady!" she says to herself. She puts the lipstick into her small hand bag.

When she woke from her nap there was a note slipped under her door. It read *Call extension 707 to have your evening outfit brought up to your room. Please specify your shoe size to the tailor.* Julia called and had a wonderful conversation with Chauncey who was so excited about her outfit that he offered to help her if she had trouble figuring it out. She did, so he came up and when he was finished Julia looked like a Grecian goddess ready to face her court! She is draped in soft layers of lime green, olive green and dark green to accent her beautiful eyes and her newly Chauncey rejuvenated red hair.

Just as she looks in the mirror to check for pink smudging on her lips there is a knock on her door. She knows it is Chevalier. Why does she feel so nervous? She begins feeling those butterflies in her stomach again. "This is soo silly!" she whispers.

"Coming!" she says louder as she goes to the door. As she opens it a dozen pink roses enter the room. Julia inhales a gasp of surprise. She smiles as Chevalier enters attached to the bouquet. She feels giddy once again and has no clue why. "Les fleurs for mon petite fleur. Oui?"

" Merci Chevalier."

"Aha you speak ze language of love?"

"No not really, occasionally a word comes to mind. I took French in High school; a hundred years ago."

Chevalier places the flowers in the top of the carafe from earlier. He takes Julia's hand and kisses it. He steps back and pauses with a flourish as he takes in Julia's new look.

"You look fantastique!"

Julia's blush is bright as a crimson rose, but Chevalier pretends not to notice. Shall we?"

"I am rather hungry."

"As you should be." Chevy winks as he puts his elbow out for Julia to escort her to Pandoras for dinner.

It's not a far walk to the restaurant. Julia is enjoying Chevalier telling her the history of the property and of how The Garden began. She is looking at his dress pants, and the open dress shirt he has on so she can see his chest peeking out from underneath. His shoes are well shined. Then she is watching the expressions on his handsome face. She is totally enamored with this man.

Then she realizes Chevalier is trying to persuade her into going for a horse ride in the morning. Having never been on a horse in her life Julia replies, "I don't think that is such a good idea. I wouldn't know the first thing about riding a horse."

"It is not unlike when you ride your husband." Chevalier says assuming Julia would know exactly what he is talking about.

"Uhhh, there you go making me blush again, like a June bride. We were brought up in a small town, nothing like yours. Sex is practical, it's functional. It's not supposed to be fun or crazy!" Julia can't believe she is saying these things out loud.

"Have you not ridden your husband?" Chevalier asks, honestly believing she will say yes. She only nods with a no. "You will just have to practeese on moi." Chevalier says very matter of factly.

"What?" Julia can feel the blood rising to her cheeks.

"Practice? Are you trying to give me a heart attack Mr.?"

"No mon fleur" Chevalier leans in towards Julia and whispers "I just want to make sure you want to come back to Zee Garden one day."

They have just reached the entrance to Pandoras. Young Toby meets them as they walk in. "Hello Miss. Table for two this evening?" Julia looks to Chevalier for guidance. He takes over. "Is there a booth available Toby?"

"As a matter of fact there is, follow me please." Toby seats them and hands them each a menu. "Would you like something to drink?" He asks looking at Julia. She clears her throat. "Yes, I think we need a little champagne to celebrate."

"O.K." Toby leaves to get the drinks while they look at the menu.

"What are we celebrating?" Chevalier asks. Julia leans in and puts her hand by her mouth to whisper. "My first orgasm at the grand old age of 63."

"Your first….." Chevalier blurts out, but Julia cuts him off. "Shhhh sh sh. You couldn't tell?"

"I do not think one can tell zese things Julia. Hm, so I am your first. Well, I am one lucky man." He says as he puts his hand on hers.

"Well-schooled maybe, but I am the lucky one. There is only one problem."

"Oui."

Julia looks around the room to be sure no one is paying attention. "Now, I do want more." The grin on Chevy's face reflects his enjoyment at Julia's statement. "Zat my dear is not a problem." Then he opens Julia's menu and hands it to her. "Come now. You will need your strength." Julia blushes again and chuckles.

"You are a devil."

"Angel love, angel." Chevalier smiles softly at his pash.

♋

By the time Veronica gets back to her bungalow Sienna is already waiting on the porch. Sienna looks her over. "Guess I shouldn't have worried. You look fine."

"Fine? Heh, I am many things, I don't know if fine is one of them." Veronica opens her door and nods to Sienna to enter behind her. Veronica goes straight for the kitchen and gets a bottled water from the fridge. "Want one?"

"No thanks." Sienna is watching as Veronica guzzles down half the bottle. "Good session I take it."

Veronica pauses. "We'll get to that. Obviously you heard about Erik."

"Obviously. You could have put Mr. Shipton off for a day. I think he would have understood."

"Sienna, I needed to put my mind anywhere but on Erik." There is a tap on the door and Maia sticks her head in.

"You too?" Veronica asks and waves Maia in.

"Are you ok Roni?" Maia walks in wearing a very colorful caftan and a concerned look.

"Full moon tonight huh?" Veronica says noticing Maia's attire.

"Yes, are you going to the event in the grand hall while I am with my ladies?" Maia finds herself a seat next to Sienna.

"I'm a little wiped today. Maybe that's why I'm off kilter; the moon is pulling me."

"You off kilter?" Sienna is now watching Veronica with more concern.

Maia throws her hands in the air. "It's got my mind wandering all over the place. I was planting herbs today. Herbs, like I didn't know better that there are other things I need to be planting. Peter called me on it and I still didn't budge."

"Peter calls you out on everything." Sienna quips.
Maia lets Sienna's words hang for a moment while she considers them. Then she decides to share her thoughts. "He's being odd today." Sienna looks at her. "Peter being odd, now that's an oxymoron."

"He's got this stupid grin on his face and he's being... nice."
Veronica pipes in. "Maybe he's finally having an epiphany. Realizing you're not his enemy."

Veronica taps Maia's shoulder. "By the way, thanks for the easy morning missy." She gives Maia a sarcastic smile.

"My pleasure. No more second guessing me regarding my grapes?"

"You know how short my memory is. It may happen again."

Sienna turns her attention back to Veronica. "So, why are you feeling off today?"

Veronica is standing with her arms crossed across her chest. "This new guy, he's good."

"Really." Maia is eager to hear. Veronica is shaking her head.

"He read me like a book he's read a hundred times. He read over his favorite parts more than once. He brushed his finger along the page when something caught his attention and made sure I was aware of it. He is a quick learner. We were there three hours before he finally came."

"Three hours, and you're still walking?" Maia is impressed.

"I am the trainer you know." Veronica sarcastically responds.

"No wonder you're fuzzy in the head." Sienna remarks. Veronica cocks her head and raises a brow. "Hmmm, ladies, this could be a great thing or a catastrophe. I just haven't figured out which one yet."

"I vote for great thing." Maia raises her hand.

"I second that." Sienna raises her hand. They all chuckle, but Veronica is still trying to make sense of her new pony. "If nothing else, I think you will both enjoy your time with him."

"Good! O.K. now, regarding Erik." Sienna puts her hand on Veronica's arm.

"Yes, Erik. God damn mother fucking Erik. I just don't understand why he is here now?"
Maia looks up at Veronica thinking about what she just said about the new pony.

"Because, with every good there's bad right? Every dark, some light. Etc, etc. You have a wonderful new pupil, but the universe doesn't want you getting too comfortable."

Sienna looks at Maia trying to figure out what planet she comes from. "Nah, that's not it." Sienna is very cynical of Maia's universe speak. "It was only a matter of time before he found out where you were honey."

"Yeah, that's what I told myself, but he was extra smarmy today." Veronica recalls. Sienna doesn't like the sound of Veronica's voice. "What do you mean?

Veronica shakes it off. "I don't know, he is a user and a manipulator, but today he seemed almost... desperate."

Sienna continues watching for a sign from Veronica's body language, her voice...

Sienna is trying to be light. "He probably sent someone to check the place out and then planned his stupid grand entrance. He just wants attention."

Veronica shrugs her shoulders. "Yeah, did Victor tell you he had made his own Garden staff shirt?"

"What?" Maia and Sienna ask in stereo.

"I know right? Dumb ass." Veronica heads for the kitchen. "Anybody want a drink? I need a drink."

"Yes." Both ladies answer. Veronica is shuffling around in the kitchen so Sienna and Maia begin a discussion in whispers.

Sienna leans towards Maia. "Did you see her face?"

"Yah, she looks good."

"No she doesn't, she's glowing." They hear a cork pop in the kitchen.

"That's not good?"

"Lockhart shows up and now she's glowing?"

"Si, she just had sex for three hours. Remember what that is like?" Sienna is about to respond when Veronica walks in with three wine glasses and a bottle of "Sticky Fingers" Red from Hanlin Cellars sensual line.

"Just a short one for me, please." Maia says off handedly. She knows she is still technically on duty. Veronica is pouring. "You can have a full one. It will help open your senses to the goddess within!"

"I have to worry about my clan. They can't have a drunk guide bringing them to the enlightenment of their inner goddess."

"I'll drink to that." Sienna raises her glass. The other two follow suit.

"Probst" Maia toasts.

"L'caim!" Veronica adds in. They all chuckle and take their first sip. "Ah, a little slice of heaven." Veronica takes another sip before Sienna's gentle jibe. "Are you talking about the wine or our new trainee?"

"Hm, could be both, but right now, the wine just tastes good."

"Of course it does Madame. I would not allow anything less." Maia defends her efforts. "And what is going on with you today?" Maia asks Sienna.

"Just trying to get through these yearly exams. Trying to get the men to show up on time or show up at all. Michael is more interested in his portfolio these days rather than being a nurse."

Veronica decides to pick up their conversation from the morning. "How was Samson today?"

"Ooo, you had hunk o burnin' love today?" Maia chimes in and smiles.

"I never should have told you two anything. I examined him today."

"Bet he wasn't lovin' that." Maia continues.

"Why not?" Sienna takes a sip of her wine.

Veronica shakes her head. "Put yourself in his shoes Si, would you want him being all clinical up your ass?"

Sienna snorts almost losing her wine. "I didn't think of that."

"Of course you didn't. When you're working you are working, bet you didn't let that exam get all animal either did you?" Veronica asks.

"Noooo! Of course not. Oh" Sienna is catching on to the looks on her friends faces. "You're saying I should have."

"Ding, give the doctor ten points." Maia is laughing now.

"This is why I don't tell you guys anything."

"Come on." Veronica raises her glass. "That is why we do tell each other everything. We laugh at each other, we cry with each other, we're here for each other."

All three ladies raise their glasses and are all teary eyed for a moment. Each one lost in their own thoughts from the day.

♋

When Jonathan stepped into the hot shower he looked down and saw the condom was still intact, hanging from his now less than massive dick. He waited until the water poured over him for a minute before pulling it off. He was surprised to feel he was still sensitive.

His mind kept going over every detail he thought would be important from his time with Veronica. Did he miss anything, did he forget anything? What he did know; if he actually gets the job when all this is over, he was definitely in the right place.

As he walks out the door of bungalow #4 Leandro is there to meet him. "Hey man, Come on, I'll show you around. I'm Leandro." Jonathan walks up to him and they shake hands. "Jonathan." Leandro takes the lead. They head for the staff work out area. It's a short walk but long enough to have a conversation. Leandro begins, "So, how'd it go today?" Jonathan is taken off guard. He did not expect Leandro to ask such a personal question.

"Good, I think."

"Not ready to run away just yet, huh?" Leandro elbows Jonathan's side lightly.

"Run away, no, no I don't think so." Jonathan pulls up his chest a bit. The cock is ruffling his feathers to show his strength and he doesn't even know he's doing it.

"Easy man, for some, all it takes is an hour with the Madam and we never hear from them again."

"An hour?" Jonathan repeats. "I thought everyone had to be up for three or more." Leandro laughs. "Three?" No wonder you're feeling no pain." He gently pushes Jonathan who easily stumbles.

As they approach the work out area Samson is on his way out. Leandro catches him to make introductions. "Hey Samson, meet our new arrival; Mr. Shipton."

"Hey" Samson puts out his gigantic hand to shake Jonathans. Jonathan puts out his hand thinking 'Holy shit! What does he do?' As if he can hear him Samson says,

"I'm with the horticultural team."

"Right, remind me not to step on any plants when you're looking."

Samson smiles, his tough demeanor lightens a bit.

"Get through exam day ok Sam?"

"RRRrrr. It was fine."

"It's time for yearly physicals." Leandro explains to Jonathan's quizzical expression. "I have the pleasure of Dr. Praddons attentions tomorrow, maybe I should paint glitter on my ass and throw the good old doc off a bit." Samson pats Leandro on the shoulder as he leaves. "You do that Leo, and everyone will know about it by the end of the gay, oh, I mean day." Leandro shakes his head in disbelief that Samson would actually say something like that, and be so quick of wit, but basically ignores the rub and carries on.

After giving Jonathan the rundown of where everything is in the work out area Leandro asks, "Hungry?"

"Starving"

"No wonder, three hours? Dude!"

"Three hours plus." Jonathan reminds him, casually of course.
Come on, let's hit Pandoras" Leandro leads the way.

It's early in the evening but Pandoras is already a buzz with guests and staff. Leandro brings Jonathan to the bar to save the tables for guests. There is a group of six women at the bar. They are dressed in similar caftans to the one Maia is wearing tonight. They are sipping the recommended absinthe through a sugar cube from snifters before they head to the tree grove with Maia. The men can't help but over hear the conversation next to them.

"We are going to catch a death of a cold being out there tonight."

"Why do you think she wants us to have a couple of drinks before we head out?"

"Oh, come on. We are here to find something in ourselves right?"

"Like one of those two hunks who just walked in?"

"Tammy! They will hear you!"
Leandro and Jonathans beers had just arrived so they both turn and hold their glasses up to the ladies who fall into fits of giggles.
Leandro turns to Jonathan. "And so it begins."

♋

In spite of the continuous growth in numbers of people arriving for dinner, Chevalier is totally focused on Julia. He doesn't go too far, so he doesn't make her feel uncomfortable, yet he pushes her just enough for her to make up her own mind to feel better about her decision to come to the Garden.

The meal is fabulous as always. Chef Benoit can make toast taste incredible. Julia chose Chevaliers recommendation of the beef bourguignon with egg noodles in Florentine cream sauce. He had an herb chicken with broccoli and rice. They shared the dinners quite evenly just taking from one anothers plate until both plates were sponged empty with the last pieces of dark molasses bread. Fortunately Toby had brought a bottle of champagne to accompany their dinner. Julia said she was "Too full for dessert, just yet." So they put that off.

Chevalier excuses himself from the table to go freshen up. On his way back from the restroom Julia notices him speaking with Toby who disappears from view as Chevalier makes his way back to the table.

As he arrives he puts his hand out to Julia. The music has changed from the wordless undescriptive* sort, to her favorite; vintage jazz.

"May I ave this dance Mon cherie?"

Julia looks to what she believes is the dance floor. It is empty. She looks up at Chevalier "but, no one else is dancing."

"So?"

Julia takes in a deep breath to work up the courage. "Alright, I would be delighted sir." She puts her hand in his and they go to the back dance area. Chevalier is very respectful of his partner putting her in a proper dance hold to begin with.

"Ah, you ave done this before oui?"

"Roger and I have won our share of dance competitions I'll have you know."

"Ah." Chevalier turns Julia ever so gracefully so he can watch her flowing dress move. "I love ze way your dress accents your body just so." Julia smiles.

"Thank you, it is amazing isn't it?"

"Oui." Chevalier says softer and pulls Julia a bit closer. "A beautiful woman deserves beautiful things."
Julia smiles again bringing Chevalier closer to her so she can rest her head on his shoulder hoping he won't notice her blushing yet again.

They continue to dance. By now a few more couples are on or approaching the floor; each as awkward as the last until they get through a song or two. At the end of the third song Julia asks "Can we take a break? This old girl isn't used to such excitement."

"Of course." Chevalier leads her back to their table.

"Would you like some coffee or an after dinner drink?" Toby asks as the pair take to their seats.

"Not for me Toby, mademoiselle?"

"No thank you, I don't want to be up all night or fall asleep too soon." Toby smiles and leaves them.

"Are you sure?" Chevalier asks teasingly.

"Oh, you are absolutely incorrigible." Julia replies feigning a reprimand.

"Moi? Nevair!"

♋

Leandro and Jonathan have finished eating. Jonathan is relieved that they could have a conversation without there being any competition or tension between them. Leandro seems like a nice laid back guy. He hopes he has as much luck with the rest of "The Garden Men" as Leandro calls them.

They head out thanking Dominic who waves his hand without taking his visual attention away from the guest he is listening to at the moment. Leandro leads Jonathan past the work out area to a two story building you would never notice hiding behind growth. Jonathan can hear water running in the dark. "Is that a stream?" he asks Leandro.

"Yeah, Ms Hanlin found a spring on the property and had it fed as a creek to this end. It has a nice calming quality doesn't it?" Jonathan only nods as he is already paying attention to the building.

When they walk in Jonathan notices a sign on the wall that reads

"Only Stallions live in these stables."

Leandro chuckles. "That's Houston's idea of a joke. He is our resident cowboy although you may have to play that role at some point."

"I don't think I fit cowboy criteria."

"Better talk to Houston then, maybe time for some horseback riding lessons. For some reason there are quite a few cowboy fantasies. You don't want to miss out." Leandro walks over to a door by the stairs. He opens it to a lounge area. "That's odd, there's usually a few guys hanging out in here. Maybe they are all working the full moon event in the grand hall." He walks in and Jonathan follows.

The room is large. There are two pool tables, a few dart boards, a long desk on one wall with 3 computers, a small kitchenette area and two big screen TV's with video game set ups.

"Cowboys are popular?" Jonathan is surprised once again.

"Oh yeah, you'd be amazed at the popular requests." Leandro walks over towards the computers. "Some women request to be dueled over. Some are looking for the American Gigolo. Then there are the unique requests, like the woman who wanted to be with Napoleon."

"Really?"

"You can look at the list of requests here after I show you the schedules. You will see there is someone for everyone."

Leandro turns on one of the computers, showing Jonathan how to find the schedule.

"Our schedules are sent to us individually, but the full schedules are in these computers. In case you want to switch a job with someone else."

"What do you mean switch jobs?"

"When we aren't with guests we have other duties I guess you would say. One day you could work behind the counter at the coffee bar or wait tables at Pandoras. There is always work with Miss Hanlin's crew. If you have any special skills you can train either guests or staff in those skills."

"Never a dull moment, I like that." Jonathan is looking at the schedules on the screen. "Is everyone trained in massage?" Leandro starts to walk out of the room. "It's another good plus to have. Remember, we are a profit sharing company, so we all do what we can to keep the ship afloat. If everyone works for the team, the end of the year bonuses are worthwhile."

Leandro heads for the stairs to the second floor. Being the new guy, Jonathan gets the unit at the far end. Leandro unlocks the door, turns on the light and lets Jonathan enter first. The living quarters for the staff are not shabby.

Each unit is roughly 800 square feet. There is a nice size living room, a small kitchen area, a bedroom, a second room that can be used as a den or an office and a full bathroom. Once a new staff member is hired there is a four month probation period. If all goes well they are signed into a contract for a year at a time and they are allowed to paint and or decorate their space any way they please.

Right now Jonathan's unit is bland in navajo white, just waiting to be brought back to life. "Here ya go." Leandro hands him the key.

"Thanks" Jonathan looks around. He walks into the kitchen. When he opens the fridge it is stocked with the basics. "Hmm." He turns back to Leandro. "So, how long have you been here?"

"Four years, into my fifth."

"and how long do you plan on staying?"

"As long as I can man. Even when I'm too old to be desirable, I will take whatever job I am offered. Unless I get hit with the love bug or something, then I'm fucked, cuz I don't know what I could do in the real world."

"What did you do before this?"

Leandro lifts his hands for Jonathan to see. They are smooth and well-manicured. "I was a grease monkey. Look at these hands, how could I go back to that? What did you do?"

Jonathan walks over and sits on the couch. "Special Forces." He is interested to see Leandro's reaction.

"fuck me!" Leandro is surprised. He walks over and sits on the chair next to the couch. "You're military?"

"Ex-military."

"No one is ever ex-military. Dude, why this?"

"Whadiya mean?"

"How does one make the switch from special forces to fucking and role playing for a living?"

"The same way a mechanic does it I guess."

"Touché. But seriously Special Forces to this? I see you bored in less than three months."

Leandro eases back into the sofa to a lounging position with beer in hand. Jonathan leans forward and puts his hand out to Leandro.

"I'll take that bet."

Leandro moves forward to grasp Jonathans hand in wager. "Let's be nice and make it one bill, good luck man."

Both men are thinking this will be easy money.

The Spirit of The Full Moon

It is a cool night, but as the colorfully caftaned ladies make their way to the grove of trees under the gorgeous light of the full moon, they see a bonfire burning in the center of their meeting place. They are here for a full moon ceremony to discover self. There is already native Indian music being played coming from somewhere. Drums are beating at a steady pace. The wooden flute tones float in then away into the night sky. Incense is burning adding to the already intoxicating smell of the smoke from the fire.

The ladies are still chatty from their walk until Maia appears from behind the bon fire. Her golden hair has a glow to it. Silence falls for a mere moment until the next snap sounds from a piece of wood feeling the heat of the flames licking between its cracks.

"Good evening ladies." Maia lightly takes hold of each woman's hands as she walks through them. "Tonight is about re-centering yourself, rejuvenating your soul. Discovering something about yourself you never knew existed before."

Maia places each woman to a specific spot around the fire. Even though they can see one another if they look, they are far enough apart to have privacy during the 'active meditation'*. "Keep in mind the work you have already done to get to this evening. Be patient with yourself. You want to enjoy the experience, the moment." Maia has already worked with these women. They have shared guided meditations, facing their inner demons while looking inward for who they know they can be.

"The goddess of the full moon welcomes you to her light. She is known as Luna or sometimes as Diana. Her energy makes us yearn for something we can't always put our finger on. She makes some of us a little crazy sometimes. But she always affects us, which is why we are here on this night." Her statement makes all the women look up to the bright yellowish white circle in the sky looking down on them with her positive glow of encouragement.

"To begin with I ask you all to close your eyes." She watches as each woman, some of them nervously doing as they are asked. "Now, listen to the beat of the drum. Let your body sway with it. Nice and easy" As she speaks the ladies are in various states of movement. Some are still a bit shy while others have decided to just let go and be in the moment. They are paying attention to the feel of the drum beat each time they move with it.

Maia is walking around the fire while she is speaking, outlining each person with her hands without touching them. She is giving them energy and confidence that she is near as her voice travels around the fire.

"Picture yourself hundreds of years back in time. Imagine the earth is new. The air is fresh. Allow it to fill your lungs." All the ladies instinctively take a deep breath. The incense is even more intoxicating. "Now, let the music fill the rest of you."

"Move with it." She moves the hips of one of the shyer girls, helping her find her rhythm. "Let it take you."

Maia continues giving personal attention to each participant. She speaks slowly with intent behind each statement. "You are strong in spirit, strong in mind and strong in body. Embrace your strengths."

"We are all equal in our strengths,
equal in our vulnerabilities,
and equal in the beauty of nature."

Maia is noticing many of the women are struggling with opening up to movement. She needs to encourage them more. "Don't hesitate to turn your back to the flames. Turn as you feel so inclined, but be careful not to get too close." With permission many of the women seem to be a bit freer with their movements. Some are still a little hesitant, yet all are trying.

Maia stands at one end of the fire taking in the progress of her new clan. "Now feel the warmth of "your" energy as it moves through your body. Again, feel the warmth within you. See the white glow of energy in your minds eye." The ladies are now engulfed in dance. Their bodies moving like the flames they surround, glowing in the amber light.

Maia lifts her hands then says "Lift your hands in the air and let the energy of the earth rise through you. Sway, move, feel the heat rising in you." Some of the women are now touching themselves, running their hands along their bodies, around their waist, up to their heads through their hair and into the air. It is a beautiful sight to see.

The music changes to a faster tempo a more urgent song coming from the flute. Some women are moaning, some are sighing. "Enjoy feeling that freedom, your freedom. Freedom of movement, freedom from restriction." The dancing is more intense.

There is a crunch of branches under a foot. Obviously someone else knows this is a sight to see. The ladies are too involved in the process to notice, yet Maia does notice, she looks into the darkness of the trees and she lets the intruders know she is aware of their presence. "There is NO ONE here to impress." She says louder than anything else she has spoken yet. "Dig deeper, Breathe life into your new discovery"

"Feel the music as it fills you. Allow the drum to pulse with the beat of your heart!"

You are a goddess. You are a fighter.

You are a lover.

And remember, you are beautiful!"

The women are in a frenzied state moving to the even faster pace of the drums. Maia is back at one end of the group taking it all in. She has a hold of her caftan and is beginning to remove it from her body. "Now ladies, keep your energy moving and let your trappings go, remove your bonds of society's expectations." Maia barely has the words out of her mouth and the women are stripping themselves of their colorful bonds of clothing.

The naked women continue their dance to the intense rhythmic intonations. As the music begins to slow, the women slow their swaying. Most of them are in a trance like state. Some are heaving from the exertion. Some have tears rolling down their face. As the music gets quieter they seem to come back to themselves. The beauty of all of them and their individual expression always brings tears to Maia's eyes.

"There is no age difference here. Intellect is irrelevant. There is no comparison of weight or size. This is all about acceptance and encouraging personal growth."

Maia continues her rounds giving each close eyed woman her personal attention, sharing love, acceptance and understanding. There is laughter, there is some crying. Maia picks up a pile of thick hooded robes and begins wrapping them around each woman as she goes around the clan one more time. "That was breathtaking ladies." As she places the last robe she invites. "Now anyone who would like to sit and talk about this experience while it is fresh, come sit by the fire. If you prefer to recall it in solitude, you are welcome to make your way back to your room."

All of the women find a log to sit on by the fire. Maia takes a seat in the middle of them all. "First, breathe in this crisp air again. Take a moment to remember these feelings. Find your center. Ground your being right to your solar plexus. You have just opened a door to a new you." Again there are sounds of giggles and some sniffles in the group.

"Would anyone like to share?" Maia suspects it will be difficult to get the first person to talk when suddenly she hears

"That was amazing! It was like out of body, I really think I was out of my body! and I think I orgasmed!" This brings a round of laughter from the group and the conversation is now open.

"Of course you did Tam. I don't know about the last part, but I definitely felt like I was watching everything happen from above. I could see everyone dancing like the ya ya sisterhood or something."

Then another voice is heard. "At first I felt small and ugly like this was wrong. Then when I took a few more deep breaths and really listened to my body and let the music move me, not me forcing movement, I felt so good, so light."

The next voice responds. "I just cried through the whole thing, but by letting myself cry, I did feel the weight of the world leaving my shoulders. I have no rhythm either, but when I stopped paying attention to trying to be in sync with the music, I just was."

A younger girl sitting next to Maia speaks up softly "I'm not sure what I felt. My head got kind of fuzzy and everything in my brain was all jumbled up. Nothing made sense. I guess I just didn't get it." Maia puts her hand on the woman's leg. "This isn't for everyone you know, or maybe you just need another try."

"Once I got into the groove of what you were saying Miss Hanlin, I was engulfed in colors. I felt like I could do anything! I felt better than any time I can remember." There were nods of relating. Maia could see that more than half of the women concurred with that experience.

"Anything else?"

"Yeah, now that we've stopped moving I'm freezing my ass off! Can we hit the sitting room and sit by the fire with a nightcap?"

Maia smiles and stands. "Miss Jenkins" she says looking at Tammy. "I think that is a smashing idea!" The ladies follow Maia in pairs, huddling for warmth on the walk back to the main house.

By the time the ladies leave the grove the voyeurs' who happened to enjoy the show had already skee daddled back to the safety of Pandoras, but they knew they were going to be in hot water with Maia at some point.

♋

Rekindling The Burning Embers

The moon is now high and the clouds are few, so walking along the pathways of The Garden is relatively easy, even without a light. Chevalier has lead Julia back to the main house. They can hear voices from the coffee lounge and the front sitting area as guests are enjoying their evenings.

Julia feels that nervousness coming and she is not sure how to handle it. Chevalier squeezes her hand lightly as if he can read her mind and he is telling her it is going to be o.k. They take the back steps to the second floor. They pass a pair of women coming down the stairs dressed like fairies. They exchange pleasantries in passing. "Don't they look adorable?" Julia is enjoying the many new experiences of The Garden.

"Zay are heading back to zee full moon partay in zee Grand hall. Would you like to go see?"

"No, that's ok. I'd rather just be with you."

Chevalier grins broadly. They continue up the stairs to Julia's room. Chevalier opens the door to let Julia in.

Once they are in the room Julia asks "Give me a minute, oky doky?" He smiles and gives a slight bow as she heads into the bathroom. Chevalier lights a few candles and puts on music while Julia is in the bathroom. He can hear the sink water running as she tries to camouflage that fact that she is peeing, he can hear that as well and just smiles again. "Julia! Do you mind if I burn incense?" he asks loudly.

"I don't know! I've never tried it!"

"Zen we will try!"

"O.K."

He remembers to turn the thermostat up so the temperature is warm enough for Julia should they end up naked.

Julia is so nervous about not smelling good, about the fact that he wants her to be 'on top'. She has never been on top! Is she really going to have sex? She keeps the water running while she brushes her teeth. God forbid she should have terrible breath tonight!

Finally, she makes up her mind. How could she have lived all these years and never even tried burning incense? "Darn it! I have this one opportunity and I may never have another one. I can do this!"

Julia opens the door. She can see that Chevalier has moved the flowers to the bedside table. The room is dimly lit with a few candles. The aroma of the incense is a new intoxication. There is one rose on the turned down sheet of the bed. Julia's heart is beating a mile a minute.

When Chevalier hears the door open he turns to see Julia. He watches her as she takes everything in. Suddenly she looks white as a ghost. Chevalier knows what is going to happen next and only hopes he reaches her in time. Julia passes out and her body goes limp. 'By the grace of God' Chevalier is thinking as he catches her in his arms before gently bringing her to the floor.

It is only a matter of seconds before Julia's eyes flutter open. She doesn't understand how Chevalier talked her into lying on the floor or when he did. "Why are we on the floor?" She whispers in a fog.

"You fainted mon cherie."

"I what?"

"It is O.K. Stay here for a moment. Then we will get you to ze bed." Julia takes a deep breath. She brings her head back to look at Chevalier. 'Even upside down he is handsome' she thinks to herself. Then she lets out a huge sigh. "I'm sorry honey, too much excitement for the old lady."

"Too much excitement por moi!" They both start giggling.

Their giggles turn into laughter as they both recognize the absurdity of them sitting on the floor hearts a pitter patter from anything but a romantic tryst. After a few minutes they gather their wits and Julia starts to get herself up. Chevalier is quick to help her finish the challenging task. More giggling ensues when she gets tangled in her 'fancy shmancy dress' as she calls it.

They get to the bed and Julia picks up the single rose, placing it on the bedside table. She turns to sit on the edge of the bed. "Guess I wasn't ready for incense just yet."

"Pah, you ave had a busy day young lady." He sits next to Julia and takes her by the hand. He can see Julia's shoulders are folded forward; her head is down, she feels deflated, defeated. He cups her chin in his hand and slowly brings his lips to hers.

Julia didn't expect a kiss. She thought nothing was going to happen because she fainted and ruined everything. She felt bad that she had messed up Chevaliers' night. He could be off with one of those young fairies right now! But no, here he is… putting his minty fresh tongue masterfully into my mouth searching for, oh! Searching for mine! He is looking for me to respond. 'Thank goodness I just brushed my teeth! Go with it old lady! Go with it, stop thinking!' Julia's tongue awakens. She returns Chevaliers kiss, trying not to be over zealous and just let it happen. 'This is sooo exciting! I am sucking face with a hot Frenchman!'

Julia can feel the tingling in her body go straight to her va jay jay* as she has heard is the

184

latest word for it. Julia is wondering how he got his breath so fresh when suddenly she feels his tongue playing with hers and a small mint is rolling between them. 'Aha!' flashes through her mind. Chevalier continues the play of mint tongue soccer going until the candy melts away.

Chevalier is concentrating on what he is doing, on Julia's reactions and making sure she is o.k. He stops the kissing but only takes his mouth from hers and leans his forehead on hers. "May I undress you mon fleur?" He asks with such a sexy whisper Julia has no other response. "Please Monsieur" she whispers back. She can feel her heart racing again and the heat of yet another blush.

The flowing gown she is wearing is made of several pieces of silk. As Chevalier pulls each strip away Julia enjoys the sensation of them gliding along her body. After a slow steady stream of enticement Julia feels like her whole body is a buzz with sensitivity.

Chevalier steps back to undress himself. Julia begins to sit up. "No, angel, you relax." She sits back and watches.

He picks something up from the table. He presses it with his thumb and it begins to vibrate. Julia is thinking 'why would he need a pager right now?' He puts lube on the small vibrator and walks over putting his hand between her legs lubing her crotch as well. He works the vibrator between her legs down between the lips of her vagina, so it rests on her clit. Julia jumps with startled exclamations following. "Oh my! Oh!"
With his hand still between her legs Chevalier whispers.. "Something to warm you up while I undress."

He slowly takes his hand away and starts to unbutton his shirt while kissing Julia again. He brings her hand to his chest. She loves the feel of the hair on it as she moves her fingers across. He steps back to take off his shirt. He kicks off his shoes while undoing his pants. It all comes off with one bend and swipe.

Chevalier moves towards Julia. He gently takes hold of her legs and slides her to a laying position. He climbs over her always keeping in mind 'gentle' 'caring'. When he has met her torso to torso one hand reaches between her legs again. She gasps then reaches her hand for his penis. "Julia, you don't... " Julia shushes Chevalier as she begins to caress and encourage him to rise to the occasion. "I want to be an active participant thank you." He gratefully allows her to do so. She is surprised to find it didn't take much for him to get excited.

They are kissing as they continue foreplay. Chevalier wants to make sure he can feel the swelling of her labia and then he reaches for the lube again. He knows after a certain age women need more lubrication, and this woman hasn't had any sex in years. He doesn't want to hurt her. When he is sure he has them both ready he asks Julia, "Are you certain? He doesn't want any regrets. She looks him in the eyes.

"Yes." She says breathlessly.

Chevalier puts on a condom without Julia even noticing. He enters her slowly swinging his hips to and fro. 'A little at a time' he is telling himself. Julia is feeling an explosion of sensation. She feels like she is tightly wrapped around him because she must be an old born again virgin after all this time!

The heat of his body so close to hers feels amazing! His breathe in her ear with each forward motion is warm. Each pump into her feels better than the last. Every few times he brushes his chest against her breasts. She knows she is saying "Oh, God" almost every time he moves, but she can't help herself.

Chevalier is moving a little faster now. Julia places her hands on his back just to have a better connection to him. She can feel the muscles in his back working with each movement. Enjoying herself as she is, Julia realizes her legs can't hold up this way much longer. She has to say "Chevalier."

"Oui."

"My legs."

"Oui?"

"I can't."

"Ah, o.k." He slows down then stops. Julia looks at his face and he is looking at her with such genuine concern. He is in this moment

188

with her. Again she feels like she is a disappointment.

"Julia, we can stop, or you can lay on your side and we can try again."

"We can?" She asks hopefully.

"Oui, we can try."

Julia turns to face Chevalier. He chuckles, "Try zee other way mon fleur."

"Oh, O.K." Her heart is in her throat, she doesn't want to mess things up anymore. She turns away from him. Chevalier takes one of the pillows from the bed. He folds it in half. He brings it to the front of Julia's knees and places it on the bed, leading her top knee to rest on the pillow. "This will help you stay comfortable." Chevalier's heart goes out to this woman who spends all her time worrying about everyone else and not seeing she deserves so much more, and not just sexually. "If it is still too much, you tell me, oui?"

"O.K." Julia doesn't want to be a disappointment. She feels she is making it difficult for her partner who is amazingly hot, sexy and understanding. She sighs as Chevalier enters from behind her now.

"Are you O.K.?" he asks.

She sighs, "Another first to thank you for." She softly responds as she is holding onto the pillow under her head loving this new position.

Chevalier has one arm wrapped around Julia's waist. He brings his hand down to work her clit area with his fingers. His other arm is under his head holding onto the head board for leverage. He can tell by Julia's breathing and the rapid vocalizations of 'Oh God', that she has orgasmed. He thrusts a few more times and finishes with an explosion of his own. Julia pulls his arm tighter around her waist, holding onto his hand within her grasp. He kisses the back of her head.

"Merci mon cherie."

"Merci, and mercy mercy me!" she quips. Again they share a bit of a chuckle.

"I will stay until you fall asleep oui?"

"Thank you." Julia falls asleep almost immediately.

Chevalier lies with her for about 10 minutes until her steady breathing is accompanied by light snores. He looks at her sleeping face, so sweet, so gentle. He is glad he was the one who was chosen to be with this lovely woman. He feels it is a shame how people put such restrictions on their lives without even realizing they are doing so, and so many live their life in a lie of sanctity. He quietly gets up and makes sure she is covered with blankets before getting dressed. Then he turns on the night light in the bathroom and blows out the candles and heads to his own bed for some much needed shut eye.

A New Day Breaks

Sienna got to her office early this morning. The room looks like a corner in an old library at Yale University. The walls are mostly wooden book cases. They are very old world looking. The oak stain has a hint of black finish to encourage the antique atmosphere. Anywhere you can see wall it is white, except for the wall behind her desk. That one is deep burgundy. Veronica picked out her desk, so it is a little more ornate than she would have picked out, but it is beautifully made of oak.

There are only three exam appointments today. That should give her time to look at some of the results from her latest round of tests on her natural healing studies; as she calls it. 'Damn!'
She forgot she also meets with Mr. Shipton today. "What's his first name? Ah yes, Jonathan. Veronica was very distracted yesterday. I hope she isn't wrong about this guy. If he is as good as she thinks, it may be good for business."

Sienna is now just tapping her pen on her desk, lost in her thoughts. Tap tap tap tap.

Michael comes to the door noticing she is distracted in thought. How can he resist? He loudly surprises her with "Still in a bit of a tizzy are we?"

"Michael Cox, I will tizzy you if you startle me like that again!"

"Good morning Doc."

"Humph!"

"Leandro asked if it was O.K. for him to come in a little early this morning."

"Early?"

"Yeah, he is going to help Samson with some work in the vines since there are no new arrivals today."

Sienna really doesn't want anyone to know she is having sex with Samson so she hopes she hasn't done anything to betray where her thoughts just went. "Fine, fine. I'll take him when he is ready." Michael nods in compliance and heads out the door.

"Back to reality." Sienna sighs as she begins looking for the men's medical folders, and then she realizes they are in the exam room. "Why am I so brainless lately?" She then looks for the books she will be giving Jonathan to read from. He has already done most of the required reading and worksheets in his early training before ever coming here. There are just a few things Sienna likes to make sure all trainees have an understanding of before she approves them as part of the staff. "Hope he is as fast a learner with the books as he was in the bedroom."

It isn't long before Michael calls Sienna letting her know that Leandro is on his way down for his appointment. She finds it a little odd that he is so eager to come in, but maybe he just wants to get it over with.

By the time Sienna gets herself together and heads for the exam room Michael stops her. "He is already undressed, gowned up and ready. Didn't think you wanted to walk in and be caught off guard."

"Thanks Michael." Sienna goes into the exam room.

Leandro is sitting on the exam table watching his legs as he swings them back and forth in front of him. "Mornin' Doc." Leandro gives her a big smile.

"Good morning, busy day ahead Leo?" Sienna walks over to her little mobile station of accessories. She pulls it up to Leandro's side. "I just promised Samson I'd help him with a few things for Miss Hanlin today."
Sienna is taking his blood pressure. "Anything interesting?"

"No."

Sienna puts a temperature meter on his forehead. "How are you feeling?"

"You know me Doc, always ready to rock n roll!" Comes Leandro's affirmative response. She is looking in his ears with her 'white light' as the men refer to it. "Looks good Leo."

"See I told you!!"

Sienna makes some notes on her clip board. "O.K., you can get off the table."

Leandro jumps off the table like he is in a long jump competition. Sienna jumps back. "Woah there champ! No need for gymnastics!"

"Just want to make sure you see I'm in tip top shape!"

Leandro stands to the side of the table and leans onto it. "Man this floor is cold!"

"We do have slippers you know." Sienna is putting on a latex glove. "And before you bend over let me look into your mouth will you?"

"Sure!" Leandro spins around to face her.

"Are you on speed this morning?" Sienna pokes her light into his mouth now. She presses her tongue depressor in his mouth. "You know the drill."

"Aaaaaaahhhhhh. Aaaaahhhhh. Aaaah. Aaaaah."

"O.K. you can turn around now." Leandro obliges.

Sienna puts some ky jelly on her glove and on Leandro's back door entrance. As she pulls her glove up she notices something shiny. "What the...?" She looks closer at the glove.

"What's the matter Doc.?" Leandro asks with concern.

"It seems as though your ass is full of glitter cha cha, care to explain?"

Leandro feigns surprise. "Full of what?" He turns around to look at Sienna's glove hand. "Oh my God, how the hell did that get there?!"

Sienna spins him around again and pushes him forward. "Just for that, it is going up to put sparkle in your bowel movements for the next few days!"

"You don't have to... do oo that Doc!" Leandro stands on his tippy toes. Sienna can't help but smile at Leandro's making of her day. She doesn't often admit it, but she does love her job.

♋

Julia wakes up feeling amazingly refreshed and vibrant! She looks at her surroundings and can still smell a hint of the incense from the evening before. She rolls onto her back remembering every single tid bit of the day before. She begins giggling. Then it occurs to her; she never got on top! 'Thank goodness!' She thinks to herself. What a nightmare that could have turned out to be.

She notices the pieces of her dress strewn all over the bed. She looks under the covers and retrieves the pillow that was between her legs. "This was a life saver." The pink roses look beautiful in the carafe from the night before, and next to them lies the vibrator Chevalier left. 'Hmmm' she thinks to herself. She picks up the vibrator and pushes the button. "I had no idea" she says aloud. Turning off the vibrator and putting it back on the table she realizes' Oh, no! I am supposed to go home today.' How was she going to change that? She needed more time. She had so many questions and a few more 'things' she wanted to do before leaving.

Julia goes to get up and the reality of her arthritis, the champagne and her active day yesterday hit. "Holy moly!" she exclaims as she lies back down. Her phone rings. She leans over to pick up the receiver feeling the effort it takes causing a few ohs, of aches. "Hello?"

"Good morning Miss Julia, this is Mr. Tanner at the front desk, when would you like someone to get your luggage?"

"I am so glad you called. Is there any possible way I could stay another night?"

"I would certainly love to say yes." Victor sounds a bit surprised.

Julia is holding her breathe anticipating a negative follow through. "Will you allow me a minute to look at the schedule and call you back?"

"That would be wonderful, thank you Mr. Tanner." Julia hangs up. She is hopeful now, so she will suffer through a little soreness to get ready for the day.

First she must locate all of her dress and her shoes to be sent back to Chauncey with a tip and a note. By then Mr. Tanner should call back and she can shower and continue her day.

The phone rings before she can finish her first task. "Hello?"

"Yes, Miss Julia, you can even stay in the room you currently reside in if you prefer."

"That would be marvelous!"

"The only change unfortunately is Chevalier is not available after midday."

"Oh, that is too bad."

"However, depending on what activities you are looking for there may be someone else who can assist you, and Chevalier is available tomorrow morning."

"Thank you Mr. Tanner I will take that into consideration." Julia hangs up, gets her dress and shoes together on the chair by the door and heads into the bathroom for a long hot soak so her body can recover enough to enjoy another day at The Garden.

Change Your Mind Change Your Life

There is a group of women sitting around the lit fire pit in the coffee lounge this morning. They are all equipped with a Garden pen and a Garden journal. They arrived yesterday at the request of Veronica. She wanted them to experience the full moon event in the Grand Hall before they started their 'Change your mind, change your life' sessions with her today.

More often than not this event gives one the feeling of being at an adult Goth version of a Hogwarts dance from the Harry Potter stories. There are druids, witch and wizard types, goddess', fairies, and vampires afoot, to name a few. The euphoric aromas that fill the room are heady and memory erasing. It's an evening everyone should experience once in a lifetime.

Apparently everyone had a good time. The chatter by the fire is loud and boisterous! "Did you see those women who were only wearing body paint?"

"I know! How could they do that? I can't wear a tight shirt, forget no clothes and just paint something on me!"

"If I wasn't so fat I would have loved to have been one of those fairies. Those outfits were great!"

"Seriously, a fairy?"

"You have a problem with that?"

"Whatever floats your boat."

"At least some of us went to Chauncey for an outfit."

"Well, not all of us can afford such a luxury."

Trent is bringing them a fruit and vegetable tray which includes some Garden made oat clusters and root chips. They are already enjoying their first cup of coffee or tea when he asks "Would anyone like a refill?" There is a mixed chorus of "yes's" and "no's" he is just trying to get a head count of who wants what.

"Excuse me Trent, when will Miss West arrive?"

Trent looks over his shoulder. "What time are you supposed to start?"

"10."

"She'll be here by then." He heads off to get refills.

As if on cue; Veronica enters the coffee lounge at 9:55 A.M. She is wearing many layers of colors. They are flowing all around her as she walks over to meet her students.

"Good morning ladies!" Her voice is warm and immediately makes one comfortable.

The women respond in kind with harmonic tones of "Good morning!" Trent comes back with coffee in one pot and hot water in another. Will is behind him with a mug of tea and a glass of ice water with lemon for Veronica. She smiles and nods her appreciation to Will. "Before you go; ladies, this is my assistant Mr. Chambers. If you can't find me he can, so ask Victor at the front desk to connect you with him."

"Morning ladies." Will smiles as they all chorus "Good morning Mr. Chambers." He bows as he backs away to go to the counter for a break.

Veronica takes a sip of her tea taking a mental count of her group. "Before we begin, please introduce yourselves so I hear your name. Please do not take it personally if I ask for it again. I am great at faces and I suck at names." The ladies chuckle at Veronica's self-awareness. Some of them voice how they can relate.

"Hi, I'm Penny."

"I'm Carla"

"I'm Virginia"

"Mary"

"I'm Stephanie" Then there is a lag of silence hanging in the air.

"Oh, who are we missing?" Veronica asks as she looks at her notes.
Stephanie can't resist. "That would be Jen. I think she had a little too much fun last night."

"Ah, yes, Jen. No worries we will catch her up right?"

As Veronica is talking a commotion of fluttering woman comes running into the lounge.

"I am sooo sorry. I forgot to set my alarm. Fortunately Mr. Tanner called my room to make sure I was O.K. when he didn't see me come down this morning." She looks accusingly at her roommate Stephanie.

"Hey, I'm not your keeper Jen." Stephanie feeling a little put upon by the look.

"Come join us Jen, better late than never." Veronica is ready to start things in motion. "So, what did we all think of the full moon gathering in the Grand Hall?"

"Jen, had a good time." Stephanie's snotty remark was just the ammunition Veronica needed to get the ball rolling.

"I want to hear what your experience was. Not what you perceive someone else's was. Ladies,

You have to start with you.
Not what someone else's idea of a good time is. Not what someone else thinks you should be doing or saying, or wearing for that matter. Understand?"

Everyone shifts uncomfortably. This is why they are here. To make some changes in their lives, "but we all know

Change rarely comes easily"

And now they know this isn't going to be a walk in the park.

"Let's try this again." Veronica is not accusational, just letting everyone know they are not off the hook. "Penny, tell me what you thought about last night."

Penny shifts in her seat. "It was something I have never seen before; men and women in all manner of dress... or lack thereof. Most people were very friendly, talkative, and kind of touchy."

"Touchy?" Veronica asks.

"Yes, they acted as if they'd known me all their lives, putting their hand on my shoulder or my knee while talking to me. You know that kind of thing."

"Did this make you uncomfortable?" Veronica wants her to continue.

"At first it did, but when I realized it was just part of the way some people communicated

I was o.k. with it. No one was suggestive or anything."

"Anything else?"

"The dancing, it was, well, it was wild!" This hits a note with Del. "The dancing was crazy!"

Veronica looks to Del. "Did you dance?"

"No way! I can't dance like that?"

"Have you tried?"

"I just don't dance."

"Ladies, during the next couple of days you are all going to be trying things for the first time."

"Some things will fit you, some won't, but until you try,

Until you give something a chance,
You won't know."

Virginia looks like she is trying to hide herself so no one will notice she is even there. So of course Veronica asks her next. "Virginia I know we've talked about it, but would you mind sharing with everyone why you are here?" Virginia seems almost relieved. "You don't want to know what I thought about last night?"

"No, but will you share your story?"

"O.K." Virginia has to think about it first to organize her thoughts. While she is doing so, the other women are all running through their minds why they are here and what they thought of last night, thinking, 'Oh God is she going to ask me that?' Everyone seems to be in motion, grabbing for some food or a sip of a drink before Virginia starts.

Virginia clears her throat then takes a sip of coffee hoping she won't choke on her words. "I've been shy all of my life. I am always afraid I am doing or saying something wrong. When I do speak up it almost always comes out nothing like I heard in my head. So I don't speak up very often. I hate conflict, so I go with what everyone else says so I don't offend anyone. Also so I don't have to decide, that way I can't be wrong. I am 55 years old and I don't know who 'I am.' That is why I'm here."

Veronica looks at the ladies seated around her. "Can anyone relate?" The women nod their heads, all except for Stephanie. Virginia is a little shaken up so the women next to her; Carla and Mary are patting her on the knees and whispering words of encouragement.

"Carla and Mary are a perfect example right now of how wonderful most women are, and they don't even realize it." Veronica takes a sip of her tea then stands up to drive her point home.

"Most women easily encourage others,
easily support others,
easily show love and consideration to others.
What we often forget, is how to do
the same for ourselves."

"Then there are those who think they can only feel good about themselves if they are cutting someone else down. I am sure most of us have been on either side of this proverbial fence before." Veronica sits back down feeling her points have been made. "I am not judging anyone."

"I just want you to <u>be honest with yourself</u>
about where you are coming from,
so you can make
the appropriate changes to benefit <u>your life</u>
and move forward."

Most of the women are taking this in and writing notes in their journals they just remembered they have with them. "I will give you a moment to write and reflect." Veronica gets up from the table with her tea in hand. She walks over to the counter and sits next to Will.

"How's it goin' guru girl?" He teases.

"See that one, second from the end to your right?" Veronica asks without looking at the group.

"Yeeeessss." Will says trying not to be obvious looking out of the corner of his eye.

"That is Stephanie." Veronica sighs. "She is going to be the biggest challenge of this group."

Will nudges his shoulder into hers. "Gotta have at least one right?"

Veronica smiles. "I could go one class without one, but, the one on the end next to her is Jen. She is a sweetie. I think she will benefit most from her time here. Are they done writing?"

Will takes another look. "Yep." Veronica puts her hand on Wills. "Thanks" She takes another sip of her tea and she is on her way back to her session.

The ladies have had a chance to eat more from the platter and discuss a little before Veronica comes back to join them. Meanwhile Veronica notices Jen looking at Will. She makes a mental note of it. Stephanie is the first to ask about what Veronica just said. "Miss West, how do we know what type we are if we don't know who we are?"

"If you don't know what side of the fence you fall in at this time, I will ask you a few questions. I don't want any of you to answer out loud. Just put a y for yes in your book or an n for no." All of the women are pen ready to open journals.

"You may have to think a bit about some of these things before you write an answer, because we aren't always honest with ourselves, it's not easy. We don't always pay attention nor do we always consciously realize what is going on in our own lives. So if I go too fast or you need me to repeat please don't hesitate to let me know. Ready?" Veronica pauses to let the women prepare for concentration.

"Do you feel anger more often than you feel sadness?" Veronica is looking to see their reactions.

"Do you have trouble keeping friendships?" The ladies are quietly writing.

"Are you better at talking than listening?" Some of the ladies are rolling their eyes in understanding.

"Do you go out of your way to tell someone when you think they are doing something wrong?"

As the ladies are listening and answering the questions you can see the light bulb moment or that aha moment as they occur to each one of them. Veronica hasn't even given them a hint as to which personality side of the fence they are in yet and most of them know by now. Veronica can see this and decides she need not ask any more questions.

"If you have answered yes to three or more of these questions, you need to stop blaming everyone else for the unhappiness in your life, for everything that goes wrong. It is time to step up and accept responsibility. You need to recognize that you are responsible for the 'choices' you make."

"If you answered no to three or more of these questions you need to learn to stand up for yourself more. You also need to take responsibility for your choices or your lack of making choices. You need to say shit once in a while!"

The ladies chuckle and begin writing again. Stephanie's writing is hard on the book and slightly on the angry side. It doesn't go unnoticed by anyone.

"Does anyone have two and two?" No one raises a hand. "Thank goodness, If you were perfect you wouldn't feel the need to be here."

"And if you are here today, you feel you need reassurance that you are ok. That's why I live here. I need that support every day." Again the ladies laugh. This also helps the women realize Veronica needs help too. "This is not a three day fix for anyone. This can be a jump start. The first few baby steps, but you will have to continue to…

> *"Work on yourself for yourself first,*
> *And then for those whom you love."*

Virginia raises her hand. Veronica looks in her direction and smiles. With a nod of her head giving Virginia the floor. "Are you telling me in order to be happy with myself I have to run around half naked and dance like I've just been hit by a jolt of electricity?" Everyone can't help but outright laugh at her analogy.

"No, the reason I wanted you all to go to the full moon event, was to experience something you most likely never have. To be exposed to something different but to realize in its difference it's not bad, it's not wrong. Just different than what you are used to. Does that make sense?"

Del pipes up. "Actually it's a relief. I thought you were going to make me dance around in a fairy costume." More chuckles ensue.

"Who said I'm not going to?" Veronica winks.

"So, is that your answer to our problems? Pretend to be someone we aren't?" Stephanie retorts.

Veronica pauses she sees Del fidgeting and decides to let her respond. "Can anyone else answer that?" Veronica looks among the ladies. Del raises her hand. "I don't know if I have the answer, but I for one didn't take what Miss West said as anything about pretending. But maybe we have to

Act like who we want to be in order to reach and be the person we want to be,

and maybe we will find out we have to try something else if that doesn't fit."

Many of the women clap for Del's bravery and her enlightened understanding. Many write down notes again. Stephanie is now openly pouting because she thought she 'had' West for a moment and she was outdone by an old bitty.

"Thank you Del, I couldn't have said it better. Ladies, it's time to step out of your comfort zone." Veronica begins handing out papers. "You know that feeling you get in the pit of your stomach?" There are "Mmmmmm's" and head nods around the group. "Sometimes your gut is telling you do this! Go for it! Other times it's telling you no, don't even think about it honey. What I want you to think about today while you are each doing your own challenge is, what is your gut telling you? Is it a true warning or is it something else inside, that fear factor. Your ego saying, I don't like change. Why would you want to do this? Listen carefully, your gut knows." As she finishes her last sentence Veronica's mind wanders to Jonathan, then Erik. In her head she hears 'So what is your gut telling you West?'

The ladies are looking at the list Veronica has handed out. Virginia is shaking her head no. "It would be easier to jump out of a plane then do anything on your list here Miss West."

"Come on Virginia, you just spilled your guts, so doing anything on this list should be a breeze!" Mary is looking at the list while she is speaking.

*"The first step is always the most difficult,
but once you start walking each step gets easier"*

"Enjoy your endeavors ladies. Don't forget your appointments with Chauncey. He will lock you out if you are late! See you tomorrow!"

The list of possible choices for the ladies is as follows...

The Change Your Mind to do list

Only do something on this list that you haven't done before and are nervous about doing. Remember if you are not honest with yourself nothing will change. See Mr. Tanner at the front desk. He will guide you to a time and place for whatever 'to do' you pick!

1. Get a massage
2. Bungee jump
3. Speak for 5 minutes in front of a crowd

4. Work with a teacher to paint a scene

5. Do 2 minutes of stand up at Pandoras

6. Take a singing lesson

7. Target shoot lesson with a gun

8. Take a dance lesson

9. Train with a whip master

10. At 1pm walk around Pandoras. Introduce yourself to each patron. Ask them each a different question about themselves. Listen. Above all, have fun!

See you tomorrow!

V.W.

Finding Focus

Maia is sitting on the top of the picnic table where she meets with her crew every morning. It is early afternoon. She has a bowl with grapes and strawberries in it. There is a bottle of champagne chilling in its' own silver holder. She has classical music playing from a small speaker that is also on the table. Now all she needs is her student to arrive.

Jonathan walks up to the picnic area. Maia doesn't say a word. She is waiting to see how he approaches her first. "I wasn't sure if I was in the right place. Good to see you again Miss Hanlin." He puts out his hand. Maia takes it putting her other hand on his shoulder.

"Good, good, you are on time and polite." Now, shall we begin? Have a seat Mr. Shipton."

"Please, you can call me Jonathan."

"O.K. First I want to talk a little about your fitness regimen. Women love to look and appreciate just as much as men do, although most of us just don't admit it. So, we need you to be in good shape. Not unlike a Michelangelo sculpture."

Maia walks over to a grassy area near the table. "Will you be so kind as to indulge me by doing some push-ups?"
Jonathan joins her on the grass and begins doing push-ups. As he does so Maia gets on her knees and puts her hands on his back to give him a little more resistance. "Just keep in mind physical strength translates to sexual endurance later." She doesn't tell him to stop. He has done about 40 pushups by now, Jonathan waivers. "Oops! Here, let me lighten up a bit." Maia doesn't lean so hard. "Just a few more. We will talk about your usual routine as well. I think that will do for now thank you."

Jonathan refuses to look weak so he doesn't lie on the ground as he would love to at this moment. He gets himself up and follows Maia back to the table praying he doesn't throw up.

She hands him a damp cloth to wipe his face and neck. "Cool down while you listen to this music. This can transport you anywhere you want it to. Remember that line for your guests. 'This music or this moment can transport you anywhere', but remember to only use it for first timers. It is a well-used phrase to help a guest get to the next level of whatever they are experiencing." Jonathan is repeating what she just said in his head, hoping to remember this and whatever else comes up.

Maia has barely taken a breath. "The right piece of music can reduce fear or stress, it can reduce apprehension, make one happy or sad, and it can also encourage confidence. A potential guest fills out an extensive form of information. You want to know everything you can about them to fulfill their wants and needs to the best of your ability. Their music preferences are a large section."

Maia walks up to Jonathan. She puts her left hand on his shoulder and takes his left hand in her right. She leads him to a dance to the music playing. While she is talking Jonathan is paying attention to where his feet are going. He is not used to someone else leading and every time he tries to take over Maia doesn't let him.

"At the next event we have, pay attention to how the music playing affects each person differently. I don't know exactly how men always react, but there is at least one song for every woman that throws her into tears. We want to stay away from those while they are a guest here."

"Now, moving on." Maia breaks up the dance and goes to sit at the picnic table motioning him to do the same across from her. "You have a very strong masculine vibration. Don't misunderstand me, this is a wonderful asset for many of our guests, but some of our visitors either have no experience around men or little at best. So we have to teach you how to dial down that animal magnetism. O.K.?"

"Thank you, I think. I didn't know I needed dialing down." Jonathan is glad she thinks he needs it.

"I am going to have you practice a few mundane exercises. Let's see how skilled you are at feeding me grapes."

"What?" Jonathan is totally perplexed. "How will this dial me down?"

"Come over here. This is an exercise in patience and doing something monotonous and not seeming bored to your partner."

Maia leads Jonathan to the bench. She puts the bowl at the right end, and then she seats him beside it. "You must always be one hundred and ten percent attentive." She holds his face in her hands so he is looking into hers. "You have to be aware of her body language and 'how' she says whatever she says. So you can better anticipate, and be one step ahead of her as often as possible." Maia lies along the bench on her back; putting her head on Jonathans left leg. "So, how do you feel is the best way to feed me grapes?"

Jonathan is accessing the situation. He doesn't want to be domineering or over masculine, but how to do this without seeming so? He also doesn't want to be clumsy or oafish in his delivery. He decides to hold Maia's head in his hand as he brings his body down with one knee on the ground. He then cradles her head in the crook of his left arm, lifting her a little so she won't choke on a grape. Now he brings the bowl closer to them so he can take the fruit out with his right hand.

"Would my lady care to partake in some fruit of the Gods?" He asks before ever attempting to pick anything from the bowl.

"Oh, you are good." Maia is quite pleased with his first choices. "Yes, please, I would love some." She responds coyishly, as a guest may do.

He grabs a grape. As she opens her mouth he lightly rubs the grape along her bottom lip then holds it in her mouth til she closes it over his fingers. He slowly pulls them out. He doesn't want her choking on it, but the move is very sexy.

Maia can already see why Veronica spent three hours with this one. He is like a cat, paying attention to every little detail before pouncing. He speaks softly but not in a whisper, "Would you care for more?"

"Oky doke!" Maia says as she turns to face him. She is quite chipper. She wants him to think about how she responds so he doesn't get lost in a routine.

This time he gently pops the grape into her mouth.

"Mmmmm" Maia chews on the grape unceremoniously. "These are really good!" Jonathan can't help but chuckle at her reaction. He smiles and places the next grape a little closer this time. Maia chews vigorously. "Mmm hmm." She is enjoying the fruit. He goes to place another grape in her mouth. She stops his hand and says

"You really have a great smile!" He has to think. What is he supposed to do here? She is ever so slightly leaning towards him. He decides to take the chance. He leans in for a tender kiss on the lips. Maia accepts it then pulls back. "Well played Mr. Shipton, very well done. Now, onto another mundane scenario."

Maia gets up and sits at the table. "Many of our guests are under the impression that champagne and strawberries are a good aphrodisiac. So it's always good to know how to pour a good glass of champagne and how to put a strawberry in a glass of champagne." Maia takes a bottle out of the holder. She wraps a cloth around it. She places the bottle under one arm and twists the cork back and forth with a pulling motion until it pops. She throws the cork in the bucket and picks up a glass. She tilts the glass and begins to pour. "This will keep the head from being too high in the glass." She then puts both the bottle and glass down. She picks up a strawberry and removes the greenery with a small knife that she had on the table. She cuts a slice into the bottom of the fruit and splays the fruit on the rim of the glass. "Voila! And now you!" She says then takes a sip of the champagne she just poured.

First Jonathan reaches for the cloth. He places it on his arm. He pulls the bottle out and lays it on the cloth face up. "Does the lady approve?" Maia nods positively and smiles. He then places the bottle just below his chest and pops the cork between his two thumbs stopping it from getting away with his thumbs. He does the rest as Maia did but, he adds a small strawberry to the bottom of the glass before pouring. He presents her with the fruit laden glass. Maia nods her head for him to take the drink. She sits down at the table.

"The next thing we need to address is focus. But I have a feeling you are already good at this. I will give you my shpeel regardless. You need to make your partner feel like she is the only woman in the world. You are with her and no one else. No distractions. <u>Truly listen</u> and <u>be interested</u>. Most women can tell if you feign interest. Your eyes do not wander." As she is saying this Jonathan is fixed on her. "But you also don't want her to be uncomfortable in your gaze." Maia smiles, she can see the wheels turning in his head as he tries to figure out 'how do I pay attention without being fixated?' "Now we are getting into uncharted territory for me." Jonathan admits. "I'm not sure how to pay attention but not too much attention."

"I take it you're a bit obsessive compulsive."

"I don't think so."

"Trust me, if you aren't, you are very close to. I know because I have a best friend who is and you remind me of the male version of her."

"Miss West doesn't seem the type."

"Oh no, not Miss West." Maia pauses. She has to think of how to make sure their new pony doesn't assume too often. It is a bad habit that is difficult to break. She is shaking her index finger at Jonathan. "and watch out for that assuming thing, it's a real ass biter!" Jonathan is laughing again. He has never heard anything said quite as these women do. He is definitely in a whole new world. "I will try to keep that in mind."

"Now, back to focus." Maia puts her hand on Jonathan's. "A move like this, ever so light as you pay attention, listen and show true interest, evokes trust from your partner. This is a very, very important aspect to every relationship." She slowly takes her hand away from his. "However, if she backs off you know…" Jonathan sits back. He brings his hands closer to him. "I know to lay off."

Peter walks around the corner. He has a smirk on his face. Not the same as the smile he had yesterday. He approaches the table when he is sure the coast is clear.

"Excuse me Miss Hanlin." Maia looks up. She is surprised Peter is there. "Peter, you know I shouldn't be interrupted during these sessions."

"I know, I am sorry, but you are the only one who can handle this. It's Toby."

"Is he alright?" Maia asks as she stands her concern apparent. Jonathan also stands. This does not go unnoticed.

"Yes, but the bulbs we planted a few weeks ago are not." Peter is walking away already, trying now not to crack up at Toby's error.

It is obvious Maia is torn because there is more she needs to cover with Jonathan.

"I will be right back Mr. Shipton." Maybe you can do a few sit ups while I am gone."

"Can I help?"

"No, thank you, Toby just needs a little more guidance than others sometimes." She starts to leave. Then she looks at Jonathan and smiles. "Forget the sit ups, enjoy some champagne before your first meeting with the doctor. You may need it." She gives him a wave and is off. He likes this idea much better. He plucks the berry from his glass and tosses it in his mouth.

♋

The west side of the grounds where some of the bungalows are located has some of the most beautiful gardens. As Maia follows Peter she can see why he came for her. Toby has pulled out almost all of the bulbs they had planted less than a month ago. Apparently anything Peter said to Toby hasn't sunk in.

Forcing herself to stay calm Maia walks towards Toby with open arms. "Toby darlin' come." Toby is smaller of stature than most of the men on staff. He is Korean but brought up in England so it is always a surprise when he begins to speak. "I'm just getting ready for the shipment coming in Miss."

"What shipment?" Maia continues to get closer to him.

"The one for the bungalow area." Maia is now next to Toby putting her arm around him. "The next shipment is for Tarzans tree house no Toby?"

"Ah, oh, yes Miss, I... "Maia starts walking Toby away.

She looks back at Peter and mouths 'fix this'. He looks at her with a 'why me?' face while lifting his shoulders to his ears, but he can't help the smile and shaking of his head as he radios Hawk and Bull for a hand.

Toby's head is hung low as they are walking. Maia knows this is not like him and can't let it go. "Toby."

"Yes."

"What's up?"

Toby doesn't answer right away. He knows he isn't old enough yet, but why do they need another guy? Don't they have enough already? He still has his head down when he asks. "Have you seen the new guy?"

"Yah."

"And?"

"And?"

"Well, what do you think?"

"Toby, he just got here yesterday. It is much too soon to tell, but you know if one gets this far they usually stay for a while."

"I know; I was just wondering." Toby is still sad in thought.

They are almost at the green house now. Maia is just coming to the realization that Toby is worried about his chances because someone new has arrived. " Look my young one, there is always plenty of room at The Garden for good men." She leans into him with her side. "In time you will have a better understanding."

"I know I need to be patient."
You are learning my apprentice."

"Thanks Mistress Yoda." Toby leans into Maia.

"Hey! I kinda like that. Now let's go to Tarzans place and see what needs to be done. Shall we?"
Toby's smile returns tenfold. Getting to spend time with Maia is a plus to him.

Walking along the pathway lost in her own thoughts, Veronica doesn't notice Virginia sitting on a bench at first. As she steps past her, Veronica feels some ones' presence. She stops and looks around seeing Virginia for the first time. "Ah, Virginia, is that you? Love the hair! Sorry I didn't see you sooner, I was… " she is moving her hands as she searches for the words. " Preoccupied." Now she can see Virginia has been crying.

"That's O.K. Miss West, I am used to going unnoticed."

Veronica walks back to the bench and sits down.

"Are you? Let's see what we can do to change that. What's the matter?"

"Oh, I'm fine." Veronica takes Virginia's chin in her hand and lifts it so she can see her face. When Virginia actually looks up, there is something different from this morning. She must have had her time with Chauncey and he has done a beautiful make over on her. The makeup is light, her hair is trimmed and the color is just richer. Veronica reaches for a tissue in her pocket. "Yeah, this does not look like fine." She hands Virginia the tissue. "What has you so upset?"

"Oh, it's nothing really." Virginia is on the verge of more tears.

"If it were nothing you wouldn't be crying. Come on, this is why I'm here." Virginia starts crying. Veronica takes her in a hug. Between her tears Virginia tries to get it out. "Everyone here is being so wonderful."

This is not the first time Veronica has been in this position. Some women go their whole lives never knowing they are appreciated because their parents wanted them to marry someone else who they thought was more worthy. The husband who thinks, 'well I married her, she knows I love her.' The children who just have expectations and you are their Mom you are supposed to do everything for them. Of course they love you, but it's too embarrassing to say so. Then there is the boss who only wants more for less. It is a sad but true state of too many womens lives. (Think about it, when was the last time you let the women in your life know how important they are to you? When was the last time you felt unappreciated?)

Veronica gives Virginia a squeeze, letting the tears fall. When she opens the hug so she can look at her tearful guest she hopes her words sink in. "This is how it is supposed to be honey. If everyone shared their appreciation of the slightest thing someone did for them the world would be a much better place." Virginia nods in agreement and is given another tissue to blow into.

"Virginia, this is why I opened The Garden. I want every woman who comes here to know how they should be treated."

"You need to know that you deserve to be respected and appreciated by yourself most of all, but also by anyone you come in contact with."

"So many women don't understand their own self-worth."

Virginia falls into tears again. "How do I know I deserve any of this?" Virginia asks.

"Every person deserves to be treated

like a human being."

Not even realizing she is doing so, Veronica joins Virginia in her tears. "You deserve whatever 'this' is. You deserve to be treated with love, respect and worth every day, but," Veronica lifts Virginia's chin again.

"But, it's up to you to make the changes you need so you can make yourself happy regardless of what others do or say."

Virginia lifts her head a little higher. Her mascara is almost nonexistent, but she is feeling better about the day already. "Thank you, Miss West."

"Thank you, Virginia, you've taken that first step." Virginia jumps up suddenly realizing the time must have slipped by. "Oh no, I have to go, I have..." Virginia looks around to remember which way she needs to go. When she has it, she grabs Veronica's hands. "Thank you."

"See you tomorrow!" Veronica smiles as she heads back to her office.

Striking a Nerve

It is time for Jonathan to have his first session with the Doctor. He has no idea what's in store for him and is actually curious after Miss Hanlin's comment about having a little champagne before meeting the Doctor, can he be that bad?

As he heads for the back entrance of the mansion Jonathan sees Veronica walking up from the Garden paths. He notices her eyes are a little red. "Are you O.K.?"

"I'm fine, why?" She has totally forgotten that she joined Virginia in her tears. Jonathan just thinks she doesn't want to talk about it. "Enjoying the sun while we still have some?" He asks her in an attempt to make conversation. "Is there rain coming?" She asks wondering what his switch in conversation means.

"Possibly in the morning, I heard." 'I heard?' he is thinking in his head, 'How stupid I sound. What the fuck is the matter with me?' They both arrive at the back door at the same time. Jonathan opens the door for Veronica.

"Thanks!" she says all perky like. "Miss Hanlin had a perky moment like that in our lesson today, she made me laugh!"

Veronica chuckles. "Good, she got to see your lighter side too then. Just remember, we have guests who use that perkiness to hide insecurity too. It can be difficult to decipher sometimes. I'm sorry, didn't mean to fall into instruction mode."

"That's o.k. I never thought of perky in that way until I started reading the training material. I never thought I would one day be part shrink."

"I prefer to call it being…" Jonathan says it with her… "A human compass"

"Ah, you are reading." Veronica says pointing a finger at him.

"So, were you just being perky, or is something else going on?"

"Oh! You are a sneaky thing." Veronica isn't sure herself so she declines to answer. "Off to the Doctors?"

"Yes. Any tips?" He asks as Veronica veers off towards her office, "Don't be late." Jonathan looks at his watch and begins to pick up his pace in the other direction.

When he reaches Michael's desk he is still a good five minutes early. Michael doesn't even look up from his computer. "Still in a tizzy are we?"

Jonathan is sure he has the wrong guy. "Excuse me?"

"Blimey! Sorry laddie, I thought you were the Doctor. You must be Shipton?" Michael stands to shake hands.

"Yes."

"I'm Nurse Cox."

"Cocks."

"Yes, with an x. I do believe they hired me jes becawse ah the name. But I'm all right with that."

"The accent doesn't hurt either I'm sure."

"Ye think so? Nah. Follow me." Michael brings him into Sienna's office. "The doctor will be in momentarily. Take er seat there." He points to the chair in front of her desk. Michael leaves Jonathan and heads back to his desk. He can't believe he just told a stranger he must still be in a tizzy. He hopes nothing is mentioned to the doctor. She will not be amused.

As Jonathan takes in his surroundings he hears footsteps coming towards him. It's not the nurse; this is a lighter foot, a small heel. He stands and turns thinking it is going to be Veronica, but no, the petite dark haired well put together pretty woman coming his way is the Doctor. 'I should have known the Doctor would be a woman.' He thinks to himself.

Sienna looks at her watch then reaches out her hand to shake his. "Hello, Mr. Shipton, I am Dr. Praddon. Nice to see you're on time." Sienna motions to the chair he was sitting in. "Shall we begin?"

"Sure." Jonathan sits down. Sienna grabs the books and papers she wants Jonathan to read. She puts them on the desk, she then moves a few things on the desk to their proper place, then turns to lean on the front of the desk and face him.

Jonathans mind goes immediately to Maia's comment about her friends' obsessive behavior. 'So this is the female version of me?' he thinks. He smiles not even realizing it. "Something funny Mr. Shipton?" Jonathan tries to be more professional.

"Oh, no, I just noticed all that paper work on your desk thinking I'm not done reading yet am I?"

"It may not look like it, but it's really not much compared to what you have already been through."

Sienna turns to reach for another book she has on her desk. "Let me know if I go too fast or if you have any questions as we go along. If you don't speak up, I can't help you understand." Jonathan nods, so Sienna continues. She is looking for a specific page in her book. She finds the page and opens it turning it to face Jonathan. The picture is a diagram of a woman's genital area. "Can you tell me what this is?"

Jonathan looks at the photo. He thinks it is self-explanatory but answers regardless. "Female genitalia?

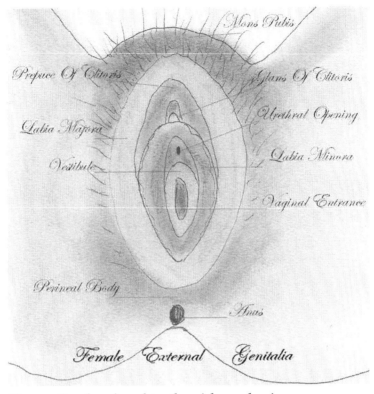

Mons Pubis

Prepuce Of Clitoris

Glans Of Clitoris

Urethral Opening

Labia Majora

Vestibule

Labia Minora

Vaginal Entrance

Perineal Body

Anus

Female External Genitalia

Sienna tips her head to the side and raises a brow. "Good, you can read captions." Jonathan smiles shyly. He's not sure how this is going. Sienna continues, "At least you didn't say it's where babies come from. What I am looking for is your impression, your thoughts." As she is talking Sienna grabs another book. She finds the page she is looking for. "What does it remind you of?"

She opens the second book and flips the book around for Jonathan to see. It is an artist's depiction of the female reproductive system as a flower in bloom.

Jonathan leans in. "That is beautiful!" He says so softly you can barely hear him. The corner of Sienna's mouth turns into a smile.

She reaches for the first book and puts the two pictures next to each other. "Here is your medical straight forward version and the artist rendition of a woman in all her natural beauty and glory."

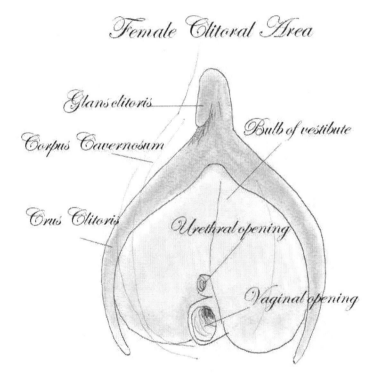

Female Clitoral Area

Glans clitoris

Corpus Cavernosum

Bulb of vestibute

Crus Clitoris

Urethral opening

Vaginal opening

"Rarely are the two cited as one in the same." Jonathan looks at Sienna, not sure where she is going with this. Sienna sighs. "This is what you are here to learn. How the female body functions. How her senses react to stimulation, to pleasure. Why the female body is what it is. I want you to be able to make the connection of who a woman is and the beauty of her." Jonathan sits up a bit. "I am going to like this class."

"You say that now Mr. Shipton. Let's see how you feel in a few weeks." Sienna opens another page of the medical book. She continues her lesson. The clitoris has 8000 nerve endings." "And there are 15,000 nerve endings in the pelvic area. Before you ask, a penis has 4000 nerve endings. If a man still has his foreskin there are 20000 nerves to excite."
"Damn!" Jonathan is a bit dumbfounded.
"You must be circumcised."
"Damn."
"If only people knew the truth."

"Damn." Jonathan is just staring at the picture. "Did you know this looks like an upside-down heart wrapped in a penis octopus?"

"What?" Sienna looks at the picture again.

"You did want me to tell you how I see things right?"

"Oh my God it does." They both start cracking up.

Sienna tries to straighten up but the laughter has taken over. They are both just laughing. Sienna finally stops long enough to breathe. "O.K., now I think we need a break to break this vision. Let's go to the coffee lounge."

"That's a great idea! The pressure has been a little trying so I think I could use some fuel."

"Right" Sienna stands to lead the way. As they pass Michaels desk Sienna looks to him. "Want something from the lounge?"

"How 'bout an Irish coffee?"

"Negative." She keeps walking.

"Coffee then" They are disappearing so he yells "Dark, but sweet, like mah boss!"

Julia Bishop makes her way down the stairs to the front desk. She has her hands full with her outfit from the night before. When she gets there Victor can't tell who it is behind all the green. "Excuse me Mr. Tanner." Julia muffles out from behind the mass of fabric. "Miss Julia, is that you?"

"Yes" she groans as she places the mound on Victor's neat counter top. "I was wondering if you could lead me to Chauncey so I can return his lovely, well, what was a lovely dress and shoes to him."

"Not to worry Madam, I will have someone take it for you." He begins to clear the mass of green off his counter top. "No!, No. No. If I may, I would like to return it myself. I would like to thank him in person."

"Very well." Victor stops trying to vacate the counter of clutter. "Go back towards the coffee lounge you will see a sign 'Queens closet' on a door to the right. If he is in, it will be unlocked."

"Thank you" Julia starts to pick up her mass of fabric."

Victor reaches for a recyclable "Garden" bag. "Here Madam, use this, and keep it for yourself once you have made your delivery to Chauncey."

"Huh, thank you Mr. Tanner! What woman doesn't appreciate a free gift?" She gets everything in the bag and heads off.

Julia meets Sienna and Jonathan on her way to Chauncey's. She notices Sienna's lab coat. "Hello Dr.?" She asks. Sienna responds "Yes, I'm Dr. Praddon may I help you?" Julia looks at Jonathan and smiles and blushes. "Uhm, may I ask you a question Dr. Praddon?"

"Sure" Sienna leans in a little.

"Uh, privately?" Julia asks taking a few steps back.

"Certainly" Sienna turns to Jonathan. "Can you find your way?" Jonathan nods and heads for the lounge.

"What can I do for you Miss….?"

"Oh, I'm sorry, Julia would be fine. Dr. can I set up time with you to talk about…" She looks around then leans in to whisper. Sienna leans towards Julia as well. "Vibrators?" Sienna is about to answer her, but a thought comes to mind.

"Actually Julia, my nurse is very well versed in the history and use of vibrators. He can help you so much more than I could."

"Really?" Julia is excited.

"Yes, his name is Nurse Cox. His office is just down that hall to the left. You can't miss it. There is a medical symbol on the wall next to the door and a clinic sign as well."

Julia can barely contain her excitement. She reaches for Sienna and gives her a big hug. Sienna pats her lightly on the back. "O.K., is there is anything else?" Sienna asks trying to make her exit.

"Oh no, that is just wonderful, thank you Dr." Julia leaves looking for the queens closet door.

"Tizzy that my dark and sweet." Sienna feels revenge in her near future. She turns back to head for the lounge. Julia waves to her before walking into Chauncey's "office".

When Julia turns to actually face where she is going, she stops dead in her tracks. Chauncey's 'closet' is a multitude of rooms. There are clothes hanging from the ceiling height then again at the mid wall height. There are rows and rows of clothes, shoes and accessories as far as the eye can see and beyond.

Julia begins walking amongst all of this in wonder. She then whispers "Hello? Hellooooo." She finds Chauncey pinning fabric onto a form of a female figure. His mouth is full of pins, he is wearing a tape measure around his neck. There is a wax pencil stuck behind his ear.

Chauncey is average in height and weight with a wild blonde head of curls. His bright blue eyes dance with mischief. He is wearing dark red velvet jean style pants and a basic white dress shirt that has hand painted swirls of color accenting here and there. His shoes are old style black wing tips. He turns to see where the whispering is coming from and his face lights up when he sees Julia! He takes the pins from his mouth and opens his arms as they approach each other.

"Aha, my garden goddess of love!" Julia returns his enthusiasm and hugs him tight. "My savior! Thank you so much!" As they come apart Chauncey looks her over. "Julia, you must stay longer. I need to update your wardrobe. Look at you, back to Cinderfuckinrella after the ball!"

"I knoooow!" Julia looks down at her frumpy attire. She never thought about it before, but she did love wearing the dress Chauncey let her borrow. " I am staying an extra night."

"Two, must be two. I can't work my magic that quickly!" He says as he brings her to a chair so they can sit and chat.
"I'm stretching it at one!" She sits and takes the bag off her shoulder. "I'm sorry for the state of your beautiful creation. It was soo lovely."

"Ah, let me see." He takes the bag from her. He looks inside. When his face comes up he has a shocked look on his face. "Girlfriend! It looks like somebody had a good time last night!" He puts a hand on her shoulder. Julia blushes bright red immediately. "Chaunceeeey..."

"Don't Chauncey me missy! Look at this jumble!"

" I know, I am so sorry."

"Did you have a good night?"

Julia hesitates then sighs a "Yesssss." "Then don't be one bit of sorry. The dress helped get the job done."

Chauncey is looking at Julia's outfit. "Now what will you wear for the rest of the day?"

"I'm fine." Julia shyly responds.

"Woman, you are not fine!" Chauncy snaps a z at Julia. "… And if you are going to be here for even just one more hour you need to feel fanfuckingtabulous!" Julia paws her hand at him.

"But first." Chauncey pauses. "How about a cup of tea, or would you prefer something a little stronger?"

"Maybe something a little stronger." Julia is thinking of her next stop. "I am going to learn about vibrators next."

"Learn, you mean, you, you have never?..." Chauncey is truly surprised now.

Julia is blushing again. "Never before last night, it was like..." She trails off.

"Well, don't stop now!"

"Oh, I couldn't."

An elaborate wooden cabinet that is full of shoes and jewelry is where Chauncey goes to pull out two glasses and a bottle of Eve's shameless red. He shows the bottle label to Julia. "Mm! That looks good."

He begins to pour. "Who is giving you this lesson?" He hands Julia a glass. Julia has to think about this for a moment. "The nurse? I think she said Cox."

"Ah, Michael will break it all down for you. You'll be fine. A toast to firsts my young lady." They lift their glasses and clink.

"Young at heart today anyway." Julia's a million miles away in her thoughts. First the hot bath, then a romantic dinner, how good it felt to kiss and have sex again. They both included her first orgasms.

'Guess one is never too old for something new.'

♋

A Lesson in Good Vibrations

It is getting late and Michael hasn't seen hide nor hair of the doctor in a while so he has decided to kick it a little early and go to Pandoras for a beer before calling it a night.

As he is shutting down his computer there is a knock at the door. When he looks up he sees an older woman peeking in. He figures she is looking for directions. "Can I help you?"

Julia has had a glass of wine and is feeling a little braver than she did an hour ago. She is also wearing a 'Chauncey original'; a copper colored shiny skirt with a slight slit up the front. The shirt is black with flecks of copper in it. It flares out at the hips. "Are you the nurse?" She begins to enter the office.

Michael is still oblivious to the oncoming attack.

"Yes."

"Cox?"

"Yes"

Julia's sigh of relief has Michael confused. 'Why would she know me?'

"I need some help with vibrators and Dr. Praddon sent me here to talk with you about it." Julia sits down in the chair in front of his desk.

The bomb has just exploded in Michaels head. 'How do I get out of this subtly?' His mind is racing, but nothing is coming to mind. He is usually pretty good at coming up with excuses, but right now he can't find one.

"O.K., what exactly would you like to know?"

Julia almost jumps up in her seat. "Everything! I don't know anything about them. All I know is how good the one Chevalier put… Uhm… uh." Julia is not only embarrassed, but she has also just let slip too much information and now isn't sure what to say.

Michael can't help but smile. This woman obviously needs some assistance. He comes around to the front of the desk. "It's alright, come on fire cracker, I am going to give ye the best vibrator lesson ye ever had!" Julia is absolutely giddy. She follows Michael to the exam room. "I like that; fire cracker!" She smiles feeling like the new world she has entered is just about to get bigger.

"And you can be calling me Michael if ya please." He brings an extra chair and makes sure she is settled next to the exam table. "Just give me a wee moment love."

"O.K."

Julia is looking at all the charts in the room. The walls are a warm blue. There is a chart of human muscles, one of the bones and one mapping all the nerves. Directly at the end of the exam table is a chart of the male and female genital areas. Julia is fascinated. She never looked at her womanhood in this light before.

You weren't supposed to ask questions. You don't talk about sex. You just let him do his thing and kiss him goodbye in the morning and hello at night. Even though she and Roger love, well loved each other and they were very close, she never learned about being open about what she wanted or needed. He never asked or explored so she just thought sex was supposed to be one way.

How could having an orgasm and feeling good about it be wrong? How could it be sinful? Julia is blushing just thinking about it. She is brought back to reality hearing Michael coming back to the room.

His hands are full of a box. When he enters the room he is apologizing. "Sorry it took me so long, had to recover a few items and..." As he puts the box on the exam table he pulls out a bottle of red wine for Julia. "I made a quick call so we can have food and drink during our vibrator discovery!"

"How do you all do it? You seem to be ready for anything here." Julia takes the glass he offers.

"That is the goal love." He opens her wine and pours some in her glass. After he puts the bottle down he reaches into the box again. He takes a bottle of beer from the box. "Do ye mind?" he asks Julia.

"Pfft, if I can, it would be silly to say no. Please, join me. Are you Irish?"

Michael grins; he opens his bottle and pours it in a mug. "What gives it away?"

"When you said wee, it didn't sound French."

"Ah, you've been spending time with Chevy eh?" Julia nods and grins.
"Lucky man. Now, while we wait for food we shall begin?" Michael begins placing vibrators on the exam table. He starts with a small hand vibrator like the one Chevalier used with Julia. "This is called a bullet." He hands it to Julia. "It is very popular because it is battery operated and very portable. Go ahead, turn it on." As she is doing so Michael places a few different types of vibrators on the exam table and puts the box on the wood floor.

"What does one do with this other than place it between your legs?" Julia is staring at the small device in her hand. Michael walks over to the chart on the wall. He points to the clitoris on the female genital chart. "First of all, make sure ye have plenty o' lube. A dry vibrator is only for hard cores. Ye want to lubricate yourself in the genital area and lube the bullet a bit as well. Ye want to press the vibrator against your clitoris." Michael is rubbing his finger back and forth on the picture on the wall to demonstrate.

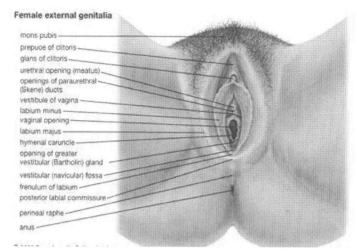

Female external genitalia

mons pubis
prepuce of clitoris
glans of clitoris
urethral opening (meatus)
openings of paraurethral
(Skene) ducts
vestibule of vagina
labium minus
vaginal opening
labium majus
hymenal caruncle
opening of greater
vestibular (Bartholin) gland
vestibular (navicular) fossa
frenulum of labium
posterior labial commissure
perineal raphe
anus

"Ye will have to experiment with the movement fire cracker. Do ye go up and down, or in circular motion, side by side, or all of the above?"

Michael walks back to Julia. He holds out his hand for the vibrator. Julia places it in his hand. He turns her hand palm up and demonstrates the movements on her hand, between her fingers and up her inner arm. "Ye can feel what it's like here, so jes imagine when ye put it on your clitoris." He walks over to get his beer and lifts his glass to Julia. "To good vibrations love!"

Julia lifts her glass. "To good vibrations."

There is noise from the front office and then they hear a deep voice, "Hello? Dinner has arrived!"

Michael calls "In the exam room man." Samson walks into the room. He fills the doorway. A big "Ooo!" escapes Julia's mouth.

"Thanks Samson, 'ave ye met, ah, I call her fire cracker."

"I was so excited I forgot! I'm Julia, nice to meet you Samson."

"Hello Julia fire cracker! Enjoy your meal and the rest of your," He looks at the vibrators, as he puts dinner on the exam table, "Evening." Samson smiles at Julia and turns to exit.

"Thanks man." Michael walks over to the tray of food. It is all finger foods. There are fresh carrot sticks, slices of green pepper, celery, cheese, dipping sauce for the veggies, bread bites stuffed with chicken ambrosia, some cold cooked shrimp shorn of their tails, and chocolate dipped strawberries to add a touch of sweet.

"Where shall we begin fire cracker?" Michael is scanning the tray for his first bite. Julia is looking at the remaining vibrators on the table. She takes a sip of wine then tilts her head as she is trying to figure out what she is looking at. Is that supposed to be a butter… fly?"

"Aye, will be getting' ta that in a moment. First some fuel ta fan the fire."

He grabs a shrimp. He walks over to Julia to feed her. "Shrimp?" He asks quite chipper. Julia grins and nods approvingly, so Michael pops the delicacy into her mouth. "I have been so busy today, I forgot about food." Julia walks over to the tray. She picks up a carrot stick and dips it into some sauce. She crunches into it with vigor as she picks up another carrot, dips it and gestures to Michael for him to open his mouth. He does. When she attempts to put the carrot in his mouth she misses slightly and sauce ends up on his cheek. "Ooo, I'm sorry nurse Cox!"

Michael finds the carrot with his mouth. While chomping on it he says' "No worries, my skin needs the masking ta be sure. Come now, try again." This time Julia picks up a bread bite sandwich. She is much more attentive to her aim, yet she stuffs the whole thing in his mouth.

They are now both giggling at Julia's alcohol influenced lack of aim. As Michael finishes his morsel he grabs for his beer and washes it down so he can get Julia back with a bit of his own food targeting.

Julia is enjoying a sandwich. Michael takes a piece of celery and dips it. He reaches over to Julia. She looks up and opens her mouth. He leads in and the celery dip hits her in the nose. "You!" she snaps for the celery and bites off the end of it. "You are lucky I am a lady young man!" Michael laughs and picks up a napkin to wipe off her nose.

"Now, before I am too full to pay attention, what does that butterfly do?" Julia picks up the vibrator in question.

"The wings flutter and the antennae's wiggle ta give you a blanket of stimulation." Michael is trying to be informative and formal enough so Julia remains comfortable with her session. He takes a sip of his beer.

"Why is the penis so small?" Julia asks in true curiosity. Michael almost spits out his beer. He can't help but chuckle.

"That love is a g spot stimulator. Your g spot is not far inside the channel of your vagina. It is anywhere from two ta three inches in and up like this." He is showing her with the model he takes from the counter. "The thought is ye should experience a better g spot orgasm with this shorter penile extension creating a constant friction action in the area."

Julia is turning this vibrator around and around in her hands the whole time he is describing its function. "Here love, turn it on." As soon as it starts fluttering and pulsing all over the place, Julia screams an "Oh!" and drops it on the floor. "It's like it's alive, and I would be smothering the poor thing into my va jay jay. I just don't know Michael."

It takes a few seconds for Michael to pick up the fluttering vibrator. He can't help but laugh at his pursuit. When he does catch the butterfly he walks over to Julia. "Here love, close yer eyes." She looks at him a little distrusting. "Come on now, you have to get a sense of it without looking at it." She closes her eyes. "Now open yer legs a wee bit." She does. He chuckles again. "O.K. a wee bit more." She does. He places the butterfly which is still turned on between her legs. She jumps up in her seat whispering

"Oh my!" then settles forward to get a better feel for what the vibrator can do.

"See Love, if ye don't look at it, you can enjoy it. Sort of like Joe Cocker; his singin' voice is amazin', but he looks like he is avin' a seizure when ye watch em. So ye don't." Michael takes the vibrator out from between Julia's legs. He places it on the exam table and heads for the food tray again.

Julia is fascinated by this young man. He is good looking, and it's easy to talk about such personal things with him. His accent is to die for. Julia knows she can't see Chevalier til tomorrow if at all. She wonders. "Michael, are you a companion as well as a nurse?" Michael is eating a chocolate covered strawberry. He stops at mid bite. 'Grreat, what am I supposed to say te that?' He is looking for the most politically correct response so he doesn't offend Julia. "Sadly fire cracker, it's not in my job description, and it's against policy." He is enjoying Julia's company, but he doesn't want her to get him confused with a well trained companion.

"Policy shmolicy, it's a shame really." Julia is disappointed but not surprised.

"If you can't be a companion, then tell me about this monstrosity!" Julia is holding a deluxe rabbit vibrator.

"Ahhhh." Michael knows this one will just take her over the edge if the butterfly bothered her so much, but he still wants her to know her options. "This bugger is a deluxe rabbit."

"A rabbit? First a butterfly, now a rabbit?" Julia is finding it difficult wrapping her mind around putting animal toys around her private parts. "Remember that close yer eyes thing I was telling you about?" Julia closes her eyes. "No, no, fire cracker, not yet. But should ye choose ta buy one of these babies ye can close yer eyes before usin' it."

Michael clears his throat as he prepares to tell Julia why these vibrators look like they do. "In many of the countries that make these adult toys, it is illegal to make them or have them there, so the companies have camouflaged these wondrous devices as action figures like animals, bugs, people, flowers and such." Michael shows Julia the dolphin vibrator, the turtle, and the rubber duck.

Julia shakes her head. "I know I'm old fashioned, but I'd rather see something foreign to my eye rather than something familiar. Is there anything that just looks mechanical?"

"Really? Most women seem to be drawn to these."

"Well, guess this being so new to me and all, it's kind of freakin' me out as my granddaughter would say." She takes another sip from her wine.

"O.K., O.K." Michael puts his hands up in surrender. "I do have a something in here." He stresses on the 'here' as he leans over to reach into the box for something else. When he returns his hands to the height of the exam table

266

he has something that looks kind of like a thick purple scepter. "This" he says as he stands up to let Julia feel it "is a version of a magic wand." He turns it on and places the head of the scepter inside Julia's elbow.

"Oh my! That has some kick to it!" Julia is surprised.

"And it is shaped to easily put where you want it to go." Michael maneuvers it back and forth to show Julia. "So does this all make more sense to you?" Michael sits across from Julia again.

"Michael, you are a life saver! I mean it. My husband just isn't interested anymore, and I still need something." Michael puts a hand on Julia's hand across the exam table. "A firecracker like you and he's not up for the wave? What's the matter with him?"

"You are adorable. Are you suuure you won't?"
Michael pats Julia's hand with his. "I'm sorry fire cracker, it's policy. My boss would have my you know what, you know where if I broke it."

Julia pats his hand back. "What a shame, a pity really, but you have been a tremendous help Michael, thank you so much!"

As Julia's last words are coming out of her mouth they hear Sienna's footsteps coming into the clinic. They both turn their heads towards the door. Sienna walks in thinking no one is there and that Michael left the lights on in the exam room. When she sees them she is startled. "Oh! I'm sorry I didn't know anyone was in here. I didn't mean to interrupt."

Julia gets up to hug Sienna. "Dr. Praddon, thank you so much for directing me to Nurse Cox, he has been a huge help and he is such a love!"

"Really. Good, I'm glad to hear that." Sienna is not surprised but doesn't want Michael to know that.

Julia walks back to stand behind Michael who is still sitting and puts her hand on his shoulder for emphasis. "It's just a shame that 'policy' (she uses her hands in quotes for emphasis.) doesn't allow Michael to enjoy more of the guest experience."

Hoping he can get a word in before Sienna rats him out. Michael quickly speaks up. "I told fire cracker, I mean Julia that policy doesn't allow me to act on a more intimate level."

Sienna is listening intently then she slowly says, "We have been known to make exceptions from time to time." Michael is looking at her pleading with his eyes.

"Really?" Julia is tightening her grip on his shoulders.

"We have had a few occasions, but unfortunately not with the medical staff." Julia's shoulders drop.

"I'm sorry Julia." Sienna turns and walks out.

"My loss fire cracker" Michael puts a hand on one of Julia's over his shoulder. He turns to face her.

"Mine too Michael, but so it goes. I better find my way to Pandoras for at least one tango before the night is through.

"If ye decide to buy a vibrator, let me know, I will help ye decide." Julia pats him on the shoulder and kisses him on the cheek.

"Thank you dear, I just may take you up on that." Michael gets up to walk her out of the clinic. "Go on, off with ye then."

As soon as Michael is sure Julia is out of hearing distance he goes back to Sienna's office and puts his head in the doorway. "I can't believe yew made me sweat!"

Sienna is collecting a few things from the desk. She walks up to him. "Did I fire cracker?"

"Miss Tizzy." Michael taunts her with it. Sienna back hands him across the chest.

"Ow!" Michael collapses his torso inward.

"Pussy." Sienna continues out the door. See you tomorrow 'love.'" She doesn't even look back at Michael who is grinning at her as she makes her exit. "Thanks for sending me little miss fire cracker." He starts turning out lights and his thoughts go to a beer at Pandoras before calling it a night. "Maybe this time I will make it out of the office."

♋

Self Preservation

After having one of the most amazing
conversations with a guest ever, Dominic;
bartender extraordinaire is feeling a little high
on 'like'. He is ready for the next step. His
break isn't that long and he just has to find the
Madam so she can give him the O.K. for some
flowers for him to give to her.

There is noise behind some bushes along
the path. It sounds like a woman moaning. He
goes to investigate but a man pops his head up
and puts his finger to his lips shushing Dominic,
so he figures the guy must have it covered.

Now he is almost tip toeing down the
path so he doesn't disturb the love birds
enjoying 'nature'. He spots Veronica up ahead
and quickens his quiet step.

Veronica is walking along the path to her
bungalow. She is supposed to be thinking about
her notes for tomorrows' class, but her mind
keeps going back to her first lesson with
Jonathan. "He certainly isn't going to need more
training in stamina." While she is lost in

thought she doesn't hear the footsteps behind her. When a hand touches her shoulder she jumps a mile, but grabs hold of the hand and turns to face her attacker bending their arm forcing them to their knees. "Uncle, uncle!" Dominic whispers loudly in his New York accent. He doesn't realize he startled Veronica, he just thinks he has annoyed her.

"Jesus Dominic, you scared the daylights out of me! Why didn't you call my name or something?" She releases his hand. He shakes it a bit and inspects it for damage.

"Damn! I was going to but I think there is someone going at it back there in the bushes. I didn't want to disturb 'em." He is still rubbing his arm. "Where were you when I was growin' up in Brooklyn?"

"Probably taking self-defense classes." Veronica's heart is beating a mile a minute, but finding Dominic at the end of that arm certainly is a relief. "What's up? Shouldn't you be liquoring up the masses?"

Dominic suddenly remembers why he is there. "I'm on a break and I was wondering if I could ask you a favor."

Veronica is hesitant when it comes to Dominic asking for a favor. He has a habit of bad outcomes. She looks at him suspiciously. "Ohhhh, K."

"It's not what you think. There is this sweet girl at the bar."

"Domenici."

"I just want to send some flowers to her room before she gets there."

"Flowers" Veronica holds her files to her chest.

"Yeah"

"That's it?"

"Please" Dominic puts his hands in a prayer to his boss. "I'll work late, I'll polish silver, I'll do whatever you want me to." Veronica waves him off. "Okay, Okay."

"So, what do you want me to do?" He asks trying to be sexy. He walks closer to her. "You know you want me."

Veronica gives it right back to him. She cups one hand across his cheek. "You're right Dom, I want you so badly, so badly that I want you, to get back to work!" She taps his face and turns to walk away.

"But, the flowers?"

Veronica keeps walking. "Tell Victor what you want; he will take care of it for you." Dominic turns bringing his fist down through the air. "Yes!"

When Veronica reaches her bungalow she gets an uneasy feeling; something isn't right. She blows it off thinking it's just from the lesson she gave this morning. She puts her paperwork down and goes to the tea kettle putting it on the stove. She grabs her files again and heads for the bedroom. She lays the files on her bed then strips down and puts on the robe she wore yesterday. It still has the scent of Jonathan and The Gardens custom body splash on it. She gets a chill up her spine remembering him pulling his fingers up through her hair. "Nice touch that was." She says to herself.

She sits on the bed and picks up the phone to call Victor. "Hello Victor, how did I know you would still be at your desk?"

"Where else would I be Madam?"

"Oh, I don't know, maybe enjoying a brandy and a book in your own place?"

"There's more action to watch across the way; by the fireplace."

" Oh, Really? Do tell. Oh, but first. Dominic is on his way to ask for flowers. Would you have someone bring them to the guest room he needs them to go to and send him back to Pandoras?"

"As you wish."

Victor is watching the scene unfold in the sitting room across from him. "Well, right now Trent is reading poetry to a young lady who has requested a session. He makes it look so easy. She is lying on her back with her head in his lap. He must have grabbed a poet's shirt from Chauncey on his way in. Ah, here comes the man you speak of. Talk to you later?"

"Actually, how about no calls until morning if that is possible. I'm beat."

"Not a problem. Sleep well."

"You too." Veronica hangs up the phone. She searches for her reading glasses on the bedside table to no avail. She slides the palm of her hand along her bed and under a pillow pulling out the culprit glasses from underneath. "Aha!"

The tea kettle begins whistling wildly. She gets herself up and goes into the living room. The front door is open ajar. She looks outside then glances around the room and closes it without giving it a second thought. She heads for the kitchen to make her tea. She turns the kettle off then pulls out her ceramic dragon cookie jar. She reaches in and grabs a tea bag. The tall mug she gets out of the cabinet has Michelangelo's David on it. She pours her tea and puts a bit of maple syrup in it and some milk.

Veronica takes the spoon out of her tea and brings the mug back to the bedroom. Her plan is to go over the notes from class this morning and figure out the best tactics to use for the best results for each woman in the group. She knows Stephanie is going to be the difficult one to get to. She hears a shuffle from the front of the bungalow. "Dominic this better not be you." She warns as she gets out of bed. She only takes a few steps before her ex; Erik Lockhart enters the bedroom. "Surprised to see me?"

Her initial reaction is exasperation. "What do you want Erik?" He continues to walk into the room. "You know what I want."

Veronica walks up to meet him. "That's not going to happen, just let it go."

Erik decides he better use a little intimidation. He is right in her face. "You have made a fool of me for the last time miss high and mighty."

Veronica turns and walks away from him. "You're perfectly capable of doing that all on your own." Erik is a manipulator and a user, but something about him is different tonight. 'What has brought him to me now?'

Erik just follows her. "You think you are so smart! I am the brains behind you."

She turns to face him. Her temper is starting to rise. "What are you talking about?"

"There'd be no you, if it wasn't for me."

"Hm, I guess you can say that." Veronica is now standing with her hands on her hips waiting for his next jab.
This leaves Erick confused. He expected more confrontation from her. He looks around the room for something he could confront her about. There is nothing in sight.

"Looks like you are doing fine for yourself Miss Madam." He decides to try a more romantic approach. "Can't you spare some for your husband?" He goes to put his hands to her face. Veronica pushes him away and steps back raising her hands to keep him at bay. "You keep forgetting the ex part Erik." Veronica is nervous now but doesn't want him to know it.

He is running out of ways to get her to give him what he feels is his 'fair share' of her business. "You treat your whores better than you ever treated me!" He whines. Veronica has had enough she walks right up to him. "Are you fucking kidding me?"

Erik feels he is striking a nerve. "Now that's the spirit!"

Veronica starts jabbing him in the chest with her finger. "You lost our money. You lost My Grandmother's house. You had no interest in me unless there was money involved. You are the most expensive whore I have ever met and I couldn't even get you to have sex with me! Now I'm supposed to let you take any of what I have worked so hard for since I got you out of my life? Fuck you!"

She has Erik pinned at the footboard of the bed. He looks like he is going to lose his balance and Veronica turns to walk away. He grabs her and turns her so she is the one who ends up on her back on the bed. Erik does fall but on top of her. Veronica is trying to get his sweaty smelly body off of her. "Get off of me!" She yells.

♋

Dominic has reached the front desk. He turns to see what Victor is looking at across the way. "Trent has it goin' on eh?"

"You could say that. I understand you wish to purchase some flowers?"

"How do you know?... "He stops to think and the realization hits him. "Oooh, she is a quick one that Miss West." Dominic leans on the counter. "I just want to put them by her room door. I'm not startin' trouble."

Victor pulls out some Garden Stationary and an envelope. "You shall write a note. I will deliver the note and the flowers to the name of the guest you specify."

"Fair enough Victor." Dominic leans to write his note. He taps the pen on a printout lying on the counter. "Hey, is this the new guy?"

"Why do you ask?" Victor is curious now.

"I just saw him in the bushes, I think he was with a guest if ya know what I mean?" Victor picks up the picture. "Are you sure this is the man you saw?"

Dominic stands up straight. "I'm pretty good with faces and this one is pretty distinct."

Before he can finish responding, Victor is on the hand radio. "Security." Anders responds immediately. "Yes Victor."

"Wolf sighting! Madams bungalow, now!"

"On it"

The crackling of the radio adds to the tension that has just changed the whole atmosphere. Trent has stopped reading and the guest is sitting up looking at Victor. Dominic thinks he is in trouble. "Hey, what's going on?" Victor tells Dominic to go to the Madams' bungalow in case Anders needs help. Dominic is off like a shot.

Trent stands up and offers his keep a change of scenery to the coffee lounge. She reluctantly agrees. Victor makes a few more radio calls then stands in wait.

♋

Erik gets into her face again. "Where are all of your little lover boys now?" He tears her robe open. He now has her pinned down and is trying to kiss her while one of his hands is reaching between her legs.

"Erik, don't do this."

"I will show you how it should be done, then you will mean nothing to them Veronica." He leans in and whispers in her ear. "Nothing."

His close proximity gives Veronica the chance to head butt him with the side of her head. Erik howls and loses his grip long enough for her to push him away and get herself off the bed.

She is looking for anything she can use as a weapon. She can see her tea and glasses on the bedside table. She makes a run for them. Erik has regained his senses and lunges towards her. Unfortunately he reaches her and they both land on the floor. Erik is trying to get a good grip on her. He tears her robe. "You could make it easier." Veronica is kicking at him, trying to get him away.

"Fuck you!" She is yelling now. He is crawling up her.

"I only want half the business." He doesn't understand why this would be such a hardship for her. He is back on top of Veronica. She looks him in the eyes and whispers with venom. "Over my- cold- dead- body."

Erik didn't notice Veronica had reached her glasses. She broke the arms off the frames while he was struggling to grab her. Veronica takes one of those arms and punches it down onto the fleshy part between his neck and shoulder pulling it down towards his chest once it punctures him. He rolls over screaming. "You fucking bitch!" Veronica gets on top of him and slams her knee between his legs. Erik immediately folds into a fetal position. He can't move. Veronica climbs on top of him and begins punching his face between words. "You... will... never... own... me... again!"

Sienna runs into the room followed by Maia, Anders, Dominic and Julia Bishop. Sienna reaches Veronica. "Veronica!" she yells, "Veronica, stop, stop!"

Anders comes to help the doctor get Veronica off the mangled mess of Lockhart. Veronica stands up struggling to get back on him as they force her to stay back. She is stiff with rage. She is still glaring at Lockhart as if she can kill him with her look.

Sienna hands Veronica to Anders. "I need to get my medical bag. "Don't let her go."

"Yes Doctor." he replies.

Sienna leans towards him speaking softly. "She might kill him."

Maia is walking over to Veronica and she remarks to Sienna "And that would be a bad thing?" Maia puts her arm around Veronica. "It's o.k. honey."

Julia is standing in shock seeing Veronica's clothing torn, the blood on her hand and on Erik's shoulder. Dominic walks over to Erik who has yet to move although his moans are audible. "Maybe we should call an ambulance." The bartender says looking at Lockhart's injuries. In unison he hears "No!" from Veronica, Maia and Anders.

When Anders finally gets Dominic's attention he nods towards Julia, silently telling him to get her out of there. Dominic gets the hint and takes her by the arm.

"Maybe we should go tell Mr. Tanner Miss West is o.k."

"Oh, O.K." Julia says softly as he leads her back out the door. Julia's head is swimming with what she just saw. This is not a first she was looking to experience during her stay. As they reach the front door Sienna is already back with her bag.

When Sienna enters the bedroom there is almost a communal sigh of relief. She first goes over to Veronica. "Maia, get some ice from the freezer and bag it for her head." Maia silently follows orders. Sienna is feeling Veronica for any lacerations she may not see. "Are you o.k.?" Veronica is shivering but she nods her head yes, not taking her eyes off Erik.

Sienna finds a gouge in her forearm. She gets some peroxide from her bag and dowses it in a cotton ball. "This is going to hurt honey." She dabs it into the wound. Veronica doesn't budge. Her icy stare is steady on Lockhart. Sienna takes the throw from the bottom of the bed to wrap around her friend's shoulders.

Sienna puts her best professional face on in order to deal with Lockhart and not make things worse. She leans over him and ungracefully pulls out the piece of Veronica's eyeglasses that was protruding from above his chest. Erik yells but goes back to being rather incoherent immediately. She then puts antiseptic on the wounds causing him to yell again. "Don't be such a baby, you're lucky I'm doing anything."

Reggie comes running in, stopping as he sees the scene in front of him. Anders looks at him. "Get a couple of guys. We need a hand." Reggie shakes his head in disbelief and walks out the door while radioing for assistance. Maia comes back with ice covered in a towel in hand. She looks at Anders. "Thanks Anders, we can take it from here."

"Are you sure?" He asks not wanting to leave Veronica's side.

"For now." Maia reassures him.

Reggie returns with Samson and Leandro. Anders walks over to Lockhart and the other three join him. They lift him up unceremoniously and take him out of the bungalow and head to the side of the main house.

The girls are left to themselves in Veronica's bedroom. Sienna and Maia bring Veronica to the bed. "Maybe a shower?" Maia asks. Sienna nods and reaches to help her friend up.

Veronica stands. "I got it." She begins walking towards the bathroom. Both Maia and Sienna jump a mile when Veronica yells "God damn mother fucker! Why the hell am I being punished?"

Recovery

The lobby is dimly lit but Victor, Dominic and Julia are standing at the front desk. Dominic has his arm around Julia. He is trying to console her. "It's O.K. Miss Bish."

"It's not O.K., poor thing. I've never seen anything like that. How could someone do such a thing?" Julia is shaking. She has never witnessed such an aftermath of an attack. Dominic continues to hold her under her arm. "Well Julia, it seems we always have to put up with small minded goomba's from time to time." She pats his arm. "She's lucky to have you all to react so quickly to such an emergency."

"Ah," Victor interjects. "We are lucky to have her Madam. She is like a mother hen." Julia cracks a smile. "You are like a family aren't you?"

"We are a family." Victor is trying to make sense of how Lockhart found a way in again unnoticed.

The night's events seem to be suddenly hitting Victor. He presses his hands on the counter bending his arms with the weight of his body. Giving himself a moment to breathe before the next thing he has to deal with.

"Isn't there something I can do?" Julia asks. She is beside herself.

"It will be taken care of Miss Julia, don't worry." Victor walks around to the front of the desk. Dominic, will you escort Miss Julia to her room please?"
Dominic nods his head.

"Thank you Mr. Tanner, but I think I need to be around people for a while. Maybe we can go back to Pandoras for a bit."

"Sure, we can do that." Dominic slips his arm around Julia's.

"Thank you." Julia follows Dominic as he leads her towards the back door.

With that out of the way, Victor heads outside to talk with Anders who has brought Lockhart to the side of the house where his car is parked. "The Madams' only directive was to not include the authorities." Victor is quietly talking to Anders while Erik lies rather still on the ground surrounded by Reggie, Leandro and Samson.

Looking over his shoulder upon hearing the news Reggie throws in his thoughts. "So clearly we can do what we want with the bastard then."

"Does that mean we can just make him disappear?" Anders asks.

"No" Victor wants to be sure they do not go too far. Every man here has a stake in The Garden and in the woman who treats each and every one of them with love and respect. "Samson, you take him in his car, and leave him in town. Someone follow and bring Samson back." Victor starts heading back to the main house. "All I ask is that he isn't dead, nothing more, nothing less."

There is a faint "No" mumbled from the mass lying on the ground. The men lift Lockhart up and toss him in the trunk of his car. Samson is walking around to get in the driver's seat. "Reg, go with him please. Leandro or Jake will pick you both up in about ten minutes."

"That should give us enough time." Reggie heads for the car.

Anders speaks up to Reggie. "Hey!" Reggie heads back toward Anders who is walking towards him. He whispers to Reggie. "Try to find out how he got in and make sure he remembers tonight."

Reggie nods in understanding and grins with thought of the fun ahead. He climbs into the passenger seat of the car. Samson starts the engine and slowly pulls out without turning the lights on.

Anders can feel the anger rise in him. How could he be so stupid? How could he miss this? What link is missing in this scenario? How did he get in again? 'For fuck sake, how did he do it?' Anders is heading back to Veronica's bungalow. He has to make sure she is alright.

♋

The shower has been going for quite some time. Sienna and Maia sit quietly until Maia can take no more. "How the hell did he get in here Si?"

Sienna gets up and begins pacing. "We don't have fencing around the whole property. Not everyone employed knows all the does and don'ts. This is just the slap in the face we needed to be realistic about security measures."

Veronica enters the room towel drying her hair. She is wearing a Garden robe since hers was torn in the struggle. "More like a slam in the head than a slap in the face. Maybe now we can have the moat I always dreamed of."
Sienna walks over to her lifting her hand to Veronica's head. "That bad huh?"

The side of Veronica's forehead is already swollen and the bruise is coming to the surface. Sienna touches it with her hand.
"Owwww!" Veronica jumps back and starts rubbing the side of her forehead with her hand. "Fine," Sienna walks up to her again. Veronica looks at her with suspicion. "Just let me look at it." Veronica lets her defenses down.

"I'm going to have a great headache tomorrow aren't I?" She looks at Sienna. Maia walks over to them. "Well, at least you won't look like him! You pummel very well Miss West."

The tension is broken as the three women enjoy a bit of laughter at the expense of Lockhart's damaged body. "That's what he gets for trying to bully me into giving him half of my dream." Veronica plops herself on the bed. "That's what he wanted?" Sienna asks as she and Maia join Veronica on her soft as a cloud bed.

"At first, then he just got stupid and pinned me on the bed. Henceforth my swollen noggin'."

"Honey, he didn't 'hurt' you more than you are letting on did he?" Sienna is looking at her with even more concern.

"Ha, oh no. I would have squeezed his balls between my knees before I let that happen."

"Damn!" Maia's face is all scrunched up. "Thanks for that vivid picture missy."

"Whatever works." Sienna sighs.

Sienna gets up to get something from her medical bag. She pulls out a bottle of two buck chuck wine. She twists the cap off and hands it to Veronica. Maia huffs "We have a cellar full of fine wines and you give her that?"

"Doctors orders." Sienna is pointing at Veronica. "Go ahead." Veronica takes a swig. Sienna sits back down. "Remember when this was all we could afford? I think we need a reminder tonight."

The look on Maia's face as Veronica hands her the bottle. It's like someone just silently farted in the room! "Fine. I believe you two need a reminder that it shouldn't take something like this for us to spend time together." The other two nod their heads in agreement.

"I'm sorry Mai." Veronica puts her hand on her friends' leg.

"Me too, it's just..." The other two look at Sienna and she rolls her eyes. "I know!" Maia takes a sip from the bottle. "Chicken". Sienna eggs her on. "Come on, you can do better than that!" Maia takes a bigger gulp. "Ahhhhhh. O.K. It's not horrible." She hands the bottle to Sienna. Maia scolds. "I was beginning to take your absences personally."

"What?" Sienna looks surprised.

"Our confident little Amazon was concerned?" The sarcasm in Veronica's voice proving she is O.K.

The bottle has made its way back to Veronica. She drinks, hands the bottle to Maia and gets up. She loses her balance as she does so. "Thanks for the wine Si, but I think I need the tea I never got to earlier."

"Wait a minute there missy." Maia has hold of her arm.

"Roni, you may have a concussion." Sienna is trying to look at her eyes.

"I'm fine, just stood up too quick." Veronica shakes off her worry warts.

"How many fingers do you see?" Sienna asks giving her the finger.

"My favorite one!" Veronica continues out of the room.

"Do I have to break you two up?" Maia's jovial demeanor is returning.

"No. Tea." Veronica heads for the kitchen.

The other two rally up. "No, no no."

"If you're so worried you can get off your asses and follow me." Veronica continues in her direction. The other two choose to follow, just to be sure.

When the ladies come into the living area, Anders is just entering through the front door. There is a chorus of screams and swears from the three women who didn't expect anyone to be returning. Poor Anders just puts his arms in front of him to protect himself from the projectiles of arms flailing in his direction.

"Anders! I've had the shit scared out of me twice already, I really didn't need the icing on the cake!" Veronica is slamming him in the side of his arm.

"I'm sorry! I didn't want to knock in case you were sleeping. I just wanted to check in to make sure you were o.k.!" Anders is slow to let his arms down. Just as he does Veronica hits him one more time for good measure. "Thank you." She whispers rubbing his arm where she just smacked it.

Maia walks over to the kettle and brings it to the sink to add water. "We are going have a cup of tea, care to join us?" Sienna holds up the cheap bottle of wine still in her hand. Sienna can't help but offer. "Or you can have some of this."

"I'm fine thank you." Anders puts his hands on Veronica's shoulders. When he looks into her face she can see the worry in his. "I am so sorry."

"Don't be silly, it's fine." She doesn't understand why he is so upset over a simple little fright.

"No, I'm sorry. None of this should have happened. I should have been more on top of things." Veronica can't help herself she puts Anders face between her hands.

"Hey, it's no one's fault. O.K.? Like Sienna just said before you got here, we just need to make some changes we didn't think about before." Anders puts his hands over Veronica's and brings her arms down. "No, but O.K. Just to be safe I'm staying on the couch here tonight if that's o.k. with you." Veronica pats him on the chest. "If it will make you feel better."

The thought of not keeping an eye on Veronica tonight has Sienna a little worried. "We can stay Anders, you don't have to worry." Maia doesn't see the dynamic in front of her and she chimes in. "Let's make a party of it!" Anders is about to speak but Veronica beats him to it. "Don't worry Si, if there is a problem Anders can call you."

"If you have a concussion you..."

"I'm fine. Come on drink your, what is that, strawberry wine, while we have a cup of tea." The four of them sit at the table finding subjects that don't include the evening's events in their conversation. Eventually they are able to find some light heartedness in the air again.

Intimate Healing

The cups and glasses are sitting on Veronica's kitchen table. There is a small tea cup night light above the counter by the stove. It was a gift from Veronica's mom when her little bungalow was ready for moving in. Veronica put it there so she could see the clock if she came out in the middle of the night. It always made her think of her mom.

Anders is lying on the couch with a homemade afghan that barely covers his mid section thrown across him. Veronica talked him into taking off his shoes and shirt but he wanted to be prepared for any other surprise. He can't sleep. There is just too much going through his head. What he missed, what he needs to do to fix it, whose ass is going to be in a sling for letting Lockhart passed the front drive.

It is dead quiet which is unusual at the Garden. There is usually some noise coming from somewhere. Then Anders can hear soft moans. There is a sound of movement as well. He hears it again. He gets up to check Veronica.

She is dreaming, making small movements with her body. He doesn't know if he should wake her or not. Just when he decides he should, she jumps and wakes. She doesn't see him in the dark. She gets out of bed. By her silhouette he can tell she is naked. He didn't expect that. Why he didn't is beyond him. He knows she doesn't like wearing clothes. He can feel his pants begin to tighten in the crotch. 'Not now damn it!' he reprimands his own body. He watches her as she reaches for a robe and throws it on while walking into the bathroom. Anders feels so lost. He's not sure what he should do so he whispers her name.

"Veronica?" He very rarely calls her that, it's usually Madam or Miss West so it feels odd coming out of his mouth. She doesn't answer so he walks to the bathroom. There is water running, but no light is on. Veronica is letting the sink water run over her hands and brings the water to her face. He knows that she knows he is there.

He walks behind her and puts his hands on her waist. "You O.K.?" Veronica leans back against him. Her eyes are closed, her robe is open. She sighs and turns her head to one side leaning on him. Her body is so warm against him. He is not even sure if she is awake. Then she turns to face him. Her eyes are still closed. She puts her head on his chest and the tears begin to fall.

He wraps his arms around her just shhhhing her, trying to find the best way to comfort her. He is still thinking 'this is all my fault.' As if she can hear his thoughts Veronica looks up to his face. "This is no one's fault." She reaches up to kiss him on the cheek but he turns to catch her on the lips. "Anders" she whispers. He thinks she is refusing him and that is fine. He apologizes. "No, apology, I just don't want you to pity me."

"Pity you? I'm standing here trying to be professional and you are mostly naked in front of me." He doesn't get to finish his thoughts. Veronica reaches for his crotch with her hand to see if he is lying. He moans immediately because he is already hard and ready. "Does this feel like pity?"

There is no more awkward silence, but Anders is very gentle and caring because he doesn't know exactly what transpired just hours earlier. He has Veronica's hair in his fingers as he leans in to kiss her. She feels a wave of tingles go through her.

Although she knows this may be one of many bad ideas in her lifetime she wants to forget her dream of Erik taking everything important to her, away from her. Anders is a man who gets her most of the time and intimacy always works for her. She tells her mind to shut up and begins undoing Anders pants.

They make their way through the dark back to Veronica's bed. Anders has walked out of his pants and has taken her robe off in the process. Veronica hasn't let go of his penis since she got his boxers down. She begins to kneel, Anders isn't sure if she is falling or if she is ok. He goes to catch her and she puts one hand up to say 'I'm ok'.

She wraps her mouth around the head of his penis while squeezing the lower half of it with one hand and moving her hand up and down in sync with her mouths movements. Her other hand is caressing his balls. He welcomes the wet tightness and sucking around his penis and the feel of the pull and caress of his sack is just intensifying the moment.

Wanting to keep this going in the direction Veronica wants, Anders leads her up and lays her on her back on the bed. He brings himself to her lower half but she catches under his arms with her legs and leads him back up. "Let me suck on you at the same time." He hesitates and she whispers "are you really going to make me beg?" He climbs on top of her and brings his penis to her face as he spreads her legs so he can bury his face there.

Veronica waits for him to begin licking and sucking her clit before sliding his penis into her mouth. She puts her hands on his lower back and guides his hips towards her so she can take more of him in.

While trying to pay attention to what he is doing Anders finds himself lost in the moment as Veronica pulls him towards her. He can feel his penis pulsing in beat with her movements.

He continues to tongue and suck on her clit and labia. He finds he is keeping pace with Veronica. He brings his tongue into her opening and slowly brings it in and out while sucking her into his mouth. He moves back to her clit and begins to suck hard and fast as she is doing to him. He pauses and sucks on a middle and index finger so he can enter her with his middle finger letting his index finger slide back and forth across the multitude of nerve endings along her anus. Once he feels he has a rhythm going he brings his mouth back over her clit sucking, tonguing and gently biting. His pace is matching hers again.

Veronica suddenly stops sucking on him for fear that she may bite him because of the intensity of her body's reactions making her clench in the kegel area, and the abdomen. She just wants to scream each time her body does so. She cannot help the gasps of "Oh, yes, oh God, and fuck" in a mixed pattern while continuing to glide her hands over his shaft. This encourages him to keep sucking. He can feel her stretch underneath him. "Anders" she breathes. He turns around. She must have reached for the lube because it was in her hand and she was lubing them both up as soon as he got close enough.

The feeling of her hand gliding up and down his shaft with the lube only makes him harder. Veronica puts her hands to his sides and leads him into her. He is already in her when he realizes he isn't wearing a condom. "Veronica, I don't have…" she just pulls him deeper. He knows he is safe, so he goes with her lead.

She lifts her head to suck on his nipples so he comes closer to make it easier for her. She somehow knows how to bite hard enough without pinching. He feels jolts of electricity run through him. This makes him move a little faster, which she seems to follow without a problem. He is thrusting his hips into her. She softly says "Harder". This is a good bad thing, harder will get them both more excited.

This is exactly what Veronica needs. Anders is an amazing partner. He just consumes her with his touches, his hold on her, his mouth everywhere. He is pushing his hips into her harder and faster but lowers his torso to hold her close. She can feel his breath in her ear with each push into her. His chest is close enough to feel the heat but he isn't crushing her. Veronica wraps her legs around him. This slows him a little but puts more pressure in his thrust every time he moves towards her.

"Anders" Veronica's lips are searching for his. Her hands are where his neck and head meet, holding him in the kiss while he continues to slam his hips into her. She feels his penis pulse and get larger so she frees him of the kiss just in time for him to cum. He tries not to be too loud, but even keeping his mouth closed his verbal release does not go unnoticed by Veronica. She brings him down to lie on top of her. He brings his arms under her shoulders.

She brings her legs down and they hold onto each other for a few minutes. Veronica begins to nibble on his ear. "Thank you." Anders kisses her cheek and rolls off her pulling her to his side. "No. I needed this just as much. Are you sure O.K.?"

"Thanks, you tell me."

Anders rolls his eyes. Why do women always have to make things difficult? "Damn it, you know what I mean." He doesn't know why he is still whispering.

"I know, and I don't know." Veronica whispers back, laying her head in the crook of his arm. Anders kisses her forehead holding her closer. Veronica lifts her head momentarily. She pulls the blanket up first with her toes, then with her hand. She lays her arm over his chest and puts her head back down. They fall asleep almost immediately.

♋

Life Goes On

The sun rises on a new day. Lockhart's car is parked in an alley. The trunk is open, the hood is open and all the tires are missing. A stray dog wanders down towards the car sniffing for some scrap of something to enjoy for breakfast. He comes upon a lump of a man lying in front of the car. He sniffs around him and decides this is a good place to relieve himself before moving on to find food somewhere else.

Erik is running. He isn't usually big on running but it feels good right now so he continues for a while. He is getting tired and feeling a little beat up so he stops and decides to pour his drinking water into his face. The only problem is the water isn't cold and it smells like piss! Erik is startled awake as the dog is using him as a fire hydrant. "What the ...! No!!!!" Erik's voice scares the dog who didn't realize the lump would move or talk. He takes off for the entrance to the alley.

"Shit!" Erik goes to get up but he finds he is in no shape to do so and he is dripping in dog urine. He looks around to see where he is. He sees his car. "Fucking bitch. You just wait." He is trying to get up when a police car stops at the end of the alley. The two cops get out. The first one asks "Are you O.K. sir?"

"I" Erik can't seem to get anything else out.

"Sir, is this your car?" Erik slowly nods his head yes.
The officers come closer. They both have their hands on their guns. They realize Erik isn't a threat so they walk over to him. "What happened to you?" the first officer asks. Before Erik can answer the second officer peaks his head out from the open trunk. "Are you sure this vehicle is yours sir?" Erik nods yes again.

The officer pulls a brown bag out from the trunk. He looks in the bag. "Well I guess that means you are under arrest sir."

Erik is suddenly alert. "What?! No! Wait, I can explain!" He still can't get himself up. The first officer sniffs. "Shit I hate these perps. Did you piss on yourself?"

"No, there was a dog."

"Right, a dog." The officer lifts Erik by his shirt. It's the last hour of their shift and they have to come across this loser. "Now I'm going to have to have my car cleaned so it doesn't smell like piss for a week!"

The two officers drag Erik to their car. Erik is trying his best to stay calm. "You don't understand."

"Oh, we understand alright." The second officer unceremoniously pushes Erik into the car. "You were trying to get the money and keep the goods and then they didn't trust your goods." Erik lowers his head in defeat trying to figure out how to get out if this. There is no sense in fighting the obvious. He was fucking set up by those animals she calls her staff. She may have won this round but he wants what is rightfully his. He will find a way.

♋

The sprinklers are already turned on this morning. They are watering the thirsty vines. Maia is walking along one of her gardens looking out at the spray of water causing a rainbow reflection in the sun's rays. She is thinking about last night's happenings. How lucky it wasn't worse, yet what could be done about this menace? How people can be so vile, entitled and vengeful. She is a being of peace but she will do whatever it takes to defend her 'happy little life' as she calls it.

'Why do so many people treat others as if they are above them?' She just doesn't understand those types of people. Veronica keeps telling her they may have their troubles, but they are just people of a lower vibration and haven't learned their lessons in life. What Maia doesn't understand is why they want to take as many others with them down their path of misery? She much prefers being around plants and animals. She understands their thinking. There is no gray area, for animals things are pretty black and white. You know where you stand. With plants it's a colorful life until they are at the end of their time or get killed by ignorance.

She will have to talk with Anders and Reggie about how to fix this. She sees a butterfly land on a blooming morning glory nearby. She walks closer for a better look. What kind can it be? She is distracted back into 'her world' as she loves to see it.

♋

The quiet of the early morning is Jonathan's favorite time to work out. He made his way to the workout area and was surprised to see Leandro and Reggie already there. They were sitting head to head in discussion. When they heard him coming they looked up. "Morning Shipton!" Leandro sounded awake, but didn't look it.

"Morning. Everything O.K.?" Jonathan asks, noticing both men looking sleep deprived.

"Just a little wolf hunting last night." Reggie grumbles.

Jonathan feels his stomach turn to knots. "Is Ver, I mean is Miss West O.K.?"

The two men look at him. They don't know what he knows and he almost called the Madam Veronica.

"Apparently she has already told you something." Reggie looks at him suspiciously.

"Only that her ex showed up and she had to deal with it." Jonathan walks closer to the men then repeats more firmly. "Is she O.K.?"

"She's alright man, a little shaken up I'm sure, but okay." Reggie assures him.

"O.K. Did anyone else get hurt?" Jonathan goes into his old work mode.

"Well, she beat the shit out of the wolf and then let us have a turn before we dropped him off in town." Reggie grins as he folds his arms over his chest with pride.

Leandro looks at Reggie and laughs. "Shipton, meet Reggie, he is part of the security team if you haven't guessed it already." The two shake hands and exchange pleasantries.

"Don't let us get in the way of your work out. I have to get to a meeting anyway."

Leandro gets up to leave. "We can finish this later Reg."

"Right" Reggie agrees. Then he gets up. "I'm sure I'll see you around Shipton."

"Later" Jonathan calls back as he begins his first round of leg lifts. 'Definitely never a dull moment around here.' Jonathan thinks. Then his mind wanders to Veronica. He will have to make sure for himself she is O.K.

Samson hadn't planned on being at Sienna's this late in the morning, but it was so late when they finished staging Lockhart's drug deal gone wrong and got the information they needed from him. When he returned he saw her lights on and just wanted to see how the Madam was doing. That was his excuse anyway. Sienna was up and welcomed the company because she knew she was going to get little sleep regardless of company or not.

Sleeping in was not usual for either of them, but apparently they needed it.

"Sienna its 9:30. Do you have anywhere you need to be?"

"It's what?" Sienna is slowly coming to.

"9:30 I have to..." Samson doesn't get to finish.

"9:30? Shit!" Sienna starts to get up. Samson grabs her arm. "Hold on there, not so fast."

"But it's 9:30!" Sienna sits back on the bed.

"And you have to be where?"

"I don't know, but not in bed." Samson leans over Sienna. "You never give yourself a break. Today you are giving yourself a break. Get a massage, eat a muffin, watch a horror movie in bed, whatever it takes. You are running yourself crazy."

"Who made you the boss of me?" Sienna's halfhearted attempt at indignance doesn't phase Samson.

"I know better than to assume that post Dr." Samson is getting dressed. "Do you have any classes today?"

"No, but I have exams."

"That can't wait a day?" Samson sits next to Sienna on the bed. Her hair is morning flippedtacular*. "Give yourself a break. Check in on your friend, but take it easy for one day."

Even though it makes her uncomfortable that Samson seems to know what she needs better than she does, it is also a relief. He just made her realize why her brain was having such trouble focusing. "Thanks. Guess I needed that."

Samson bends over to kiss her. It is a gentle 'loving' kiss on the lips. This takes her by surprise. They have sex, but this feels different. This is another uncomfortable moment for Sienna. It surprises Samson as well. He feels Sienna stiffen after his gesture of trying to show he cares. The awkward moment pushes him to make his exit.

"I'm going to stop by Anders office."

"O.K." Sienna sinks back in her pillow. "Samson!" she calls before he gets out of her bungalow. He comes back to stick his head in the doorway. "Yeah?"

"Thanks."

Samson smiles. "No problem. See you later?"

"Later." Sienna brings her knees up to her chin. What to do, what to do?

Meanwhile, Samson peeks his head out from Sienna's bungalow hoping no one sees him 'exiting the premises'.

♋

The Weekly Meeting

A group of Garden men are sitting around a table on a patio behind their living quarters. There is coffee and food available for them on the table. A beautiful fruit bowl is sitting in the center. There are a couple of patio umbrellas throwing shade over the tables to keep the glare of the morning sun from getting in the way of the meeting they are about to take part in.

There is much joking and laughter as Leandro recounts his surprise when Jonathan told him of his three hours 'plus' with the Madam. "Better look out gentleman, we have a bucking stallion entering the ranks."

Chevalier seems unruffled by the news. His French accent is gone and his usual British accent has taken over for the morning. "We all have our specialties Leo. Stamina or no."

"And how is your guest enjoying herself Mr. frenchay suavay?" Jake; the resident Australian couldn't resist asking. He had heard

Chevalier was going to have his hands full with a more mature pash* for a couple of days.

"She must have been happy; after all she is still here. As a matter of fact, I am off to see her when I am done with this nonsense." Chevaliers nose is in the air feigning disgust. All the men laugh.

Veronica and Will walk around the corner to the patio. She makes herself comfortable at the head of the table and Will heads to the other end passing out folders to each of the men containing job assignments for the next week. Veronica is taking account of who is there. The men are still talking amongst themselves until they notice the bruise on her forehead which leads them to look further. There is a gash on her left forearm.

"What the hell happened to you?" Terrance asks.
Veronica sighs. She knows she has to tell them, she just doesn't know how to word it.

"Had a little tangle with my ex last night." The questions start flying in.

"Are you alright?" Chevalier hates to see a woman hurt.

"I'm, O.K."

"How the hell did he get in here?" Jake can't believe he did.

"We don't know yet."

"Trust me fella's he looks a lot worse than she does." Leandro is beaming.

"Thanks Leo. Enough about me," She looks at all the men around the table. "Let's talk about what you have been up to." Veronica wants to get the attention away from her. She feels foolish enough for not being more aware, and doesn't want the men to dwell on it longer than necessary.

"Ms. Hanlin seems to think some of you must have gotten lost during the full moon celebrations the other night."

Trent looks guilty immediately. "Maybe it was some squirrels."

Jake goes with Trent and his alibi. "Yeah, I'm sure the raccoons saw the fire and wanted to warm up!"

"Anyone else?" Veronica looks around the table. "Guys, you know you're not supposed to be peeping Toms watching women during a very intense personal growth spurt."

Trent can't help himself. "But, it's such a beautiful sight!"

Others put their two cents in.

"Yes, I'm sure you are looking for the beauty of the transformation, but if you get caught...." Veronica pauses lowering her head she shakes her head softly. "You just need to be cautious, considerate and quiet. If one of those women feels someone is watching them you could lose more than just that ceremony for us. Got it?"

All heads are down except for Will and Chevalier, and the men are now quiet. "See how good you can be at being quiet?" They all chuckle at that.

Will is looking a bit cross. His arms are folded over his chest as he leans on a nearby table. "Thanks for telling me guys." The excuses then start. "Sorry man." "I thought we told you." "We'll get you next time."

Terrance speaks up, he wants the Madam to forget about the voyeurism and share some info on their newest family member. "I know it hasn't been long, but how is the new guy settling in?" Terrance is the local mixologist and Veronica's hot chocolate from the Bahamas.

"Too soon to tell gentlemen." The men are chuckling. Veronica realizes they know something so she decides to bait them. "But, he has already broken some records. So you all better be at your best my angels."
There is a variety of "Oh, man." "shit" "What records?"
Veronica smiles. "Seriously? You know I wouldn't hire anyone who couldn't handle themselves right? Let's see what's on the agenda for next week. Dugan, my Irish Rogue, you have a few days with a first time medieval wench."

"Aye." Dugan smiles.

"Trent, you lucky dog Velma has decided to come see Shaggy again." The men howl and rutt ro at Trent. Leandro gives him a pat on the back.

"Jake and Leandro have a group of ladies who are ready for basic car care."

"At least I'll be getting some." Trent reminds Jake and Leandro.

"It includes dog hair though man!" Jake counters. The men laugh again.

Veronica seems to ignore the jibes. "And Chevalier, you are on hold until Julia Bishop leaves."

"Do you really think she will be here next week?" Chevalier asks proudly. He would gladly spend more time with his mid-west woman!

"If you keep up whatever you are doing, yes." Veronica teases.

"I will do my best. May I go then? I have a surprise for Julia."

"Go for it." Veronica waves him off.

"Give it to her man!" Jake gives him a thumb up.

"Don't forget your accent." Leandro offers.

Chevalier is walking away. "Juveniles."

Even though Veronica doesn't want the men focusing on her, she also wants to cut this meeting short. She has too much going on today to hang out this morning.

"Hey, some of you could learn something from Chevalier's dedication to his pash. She is stating at least one extra day, and I am willing to bet she will be back. Any questions before I carry on with the day?" Everyone seems to be on the same page with Veronica and no one has a question. She is relieved. "Good, carry on with your bad selves then." She makes her exit with Will by her side. The men watch til she is out of sight. All of them quiet in their own thoughts of what happened to the mother hen. Fortunately Leandro feels he can relay enough of the story to put his friends' minds at ease.

Swimming Lesson

Julia Bishop is grateful the pools at the garden are heated otherwise she would have never even attempted to put her big toe into the clear depths. Julia only planned on being at the garden for two days; it has been three so far.

Chevalier left her a message to meet him at the pool. She decided to come over a little early so she could get into the water and not have him watch her get into the water. There is nothing worse than watching a woman inch into the water for a half an hour, other than having someone watch you as you do it.

She is wearing a one-piece navy blue bathing suit with white stripes up the sides. It looks like it was made in the 50's. Chevalier had it sent to her room. She never had a bathing suit that had snaps in the crotch like a leotard. She has covered her hair with a colorful shower cap; for lack of a better word.

Easing into the water, she swims across the pool. She stops at the opposite side turning around while holding the wall. She begins kicking her feet and twisting her hips to exercise the morning kinks out of her body. While she does this she closes her eyes and leans her head back to the ledge.

Chevalier makes his way from the main house to the pool. He planned on meeting Julia before she left her room for the day but missed the early riser by more than a few minutes.

The grounds are full of beautiful plants and art. A mixture of natural and human made eye candy everywhere you look. The pool is a master piece of stone and glass surrounded by tropical plants. Chevalier comes around the corner of the pool and spots Julia. He slows down and begins a stealthy walk like a cat ready to pounce on its prey.

As Chevalier slowly enters the water Julia sighs as if remembering something. He stops, hoping she doesn't open her eyes. She doesn't. He quietly swims up to Julia. As he approaches her he reaches his arms down wrapping her legs around his waist.

"Zhere you are mon cherie." Julia is startled opening her eyes. "Ave you been waiting long?" he asks.

"You have perfect timing. I was just thinking about you." She claims blushing a little as Chevalier walks her away from the wall turning her in the water.

He looks her over. "This suit looks magnifique on you. Why are you wearing le cap?"

"Oh this? Just trying to keep the color in the old mane." "Come now mon petite fleur" he says as he begins to take the cap from her head. "Live a little. I will wash your hair in z shower later."

"That's the best offer I've had yet today! Ooo, what is that?" Chevalier cocks his head before answering. "Zhat, oh Zhat is nothing."

"I know what nothing feels like", Julia glances below the water, "and that my man is not nothing."

"Just a little excitement to start the day mon fleur." He has brought a water proof vibrator and is leading it up to her crotch and begins moving it over the bathing suit. He wants to make sure she is stimulated before finding himself inside her. He quickly prepped and put his condom on before coming to the pool 'just in case'. It would be difficult to do it in the water holding her at the same time.

Looking around to make sure no one is watching Julia looks at Chevalier. "Are you sure this is O.K.? What if someone else comes in the pool?"

"Ow did your time with Nurse Cox go?"

"You know about that?" Julia feels suddenly guilty like she cheated on him. She loses concentration as Chevalier unsnaps her bathing suit. "Huh!" Julia gasps. "Chevalier!" He puts a finger over her lips.

"Trust me."

Chevalier moves the vibrator into place and is tickling her clit. "Oh" Julia is shocked, but is also enjoying yet another first for her visit.

"I think it is a good thing you are not afraid of something new."

He begins to finger Julia with the vibrator still in his hand. Julia's breathing changes as she tries holding back from gasping with each sensation. When Chevalier feels she is ready he brings Julia down a little. Hearing Julia's "Ah" He knows she is O.K. He is in. He gently moves Julia up and down in the water. Julia sighs again.

"And this has no calories." Julia brings herself closer to Chevalier as he continues to move her in the water.

"If we just ave a normal conversation, oooo will be zee wiser?" Chevalier isn't moving Julia so much now, but his hips are moving under the surface. Julia begins to laugh. "You expect me to have, ohhhhh, a normal conversation when you are, ohhhhh, I don't think so." Julia bows her head.

"See, I told you it would be a good swim." He kisses her forehead. "Maybe this iz another first?"

"Ha ha ha, how did you know? Ohhhh." Julia is so glad she made the choice to come here, yet knowing all good things must end already brings her a little sadness in this remarkable new chapter in her life.

Friendly Advice

The breakfast crowd at Pandoras is a buzz. Some people saw a man get thrown into the trunk of a car. Was he dead? Was he an intruder? Dominic is busy trying to keep everyone calm saying it was an employee who didn't live up to expectations.

Jonathan is sitting alone at a table on the patio. He has the high protein breakfast plate of orange roughy, fruit and a small spinach salad. His guilty pleasure is café mocha.

He is almost finished with his breakfast when a man comes up to his table. "Hey, I'm Dugan, are you Shipton?"

"Yeah, Jonathan" he puts his hand out to offer the seat across from him. "Why doesn't anyone call me by my first name?"

Dugan takes the seat. "Because ye aren't gonna ave it long laddie. Once you get thrrrough your trainin' ere you will get a workin' name to go by."

"Really?" It hadn't even occurred to Jonathan that he would need to change his name.

"Ye really don't want the ladies ta be able ta find ye, nor de ye want the men in their lives ta find ye either."

Trent comes over to the table. "Hey Dugan, want some coffee?"

"Would ye mind Trent?"

"Comin' up!" Trent heads back to the station for the coffee.

Dugan sits back. He is taking in the new arrival. "So, ye think this is the life for you?" Jonathan looks at Dugan. He lets the words hang in the air for a moment while he thinks how to best answer this challenge.

"It's not as easy as I thought it was going to be. But it's much more interesting than I thought it was going to be."

Dugan knows Jonathan is letting him know he is planning on sticking around for a while. "You are still in training laddie. You haven't even touched the tip of the proverbial iceberg. Wait til you are actually in the trenches.

332

Oh ye will ave some amazin' experiences. When a woman knows she can trrrust you, everything works like a well-oiled machine. It's getting ta that point that's a whole different ball game. All da trainin' in da world cannot prepare ye for what may appen."

Leaning back in his chair Jonathan is listening intently, but he wants to look non chalant. Doesn't want Dugan to know he wants all the information he can digest. The better he is the better chance he has of being taken on. "So tell me, are you the one who has been sent to scare me off?"

"Not likely. I would rather see ye add to the reputation of The Garden."

"Not worried about the competition?" Jonathan wants Dugan to know he is confident although he isn't one hundred percent yet. The last couple of days have been a bigger eye opener than the months of reading and homework he has already done.

Trying to feel this guy out is a bit of a challenge for Dugan. Usually the new pony is just eager to please and outright insecure of the 'competition'. This one has a very cool demeanor. He is not so easy to read. "Nah, I'm jes ere to help you with the reality my friend. There are the slappers, the scrrratchers, the scereamers, the punchers, oh yes, and let's not forget the actreeess's." Dugan's hands are flying in gesture with each description. Then he leans in. His face softens. "Then there are the angels with serious fears and emotional challenges."

"There is a fine line between being the man they are hoping for, and being sensitive enough ta know when or if ta stop, and how ta help them through whatever they are dealing with. On the rare occasion they ave a breakthrough and not a break down, there is nothin' like that feelin'." Dugan stops for dramatic Irish pause then picks up his cup for a swig of coffee.

Not realizing he has been drawn in by Dugan's speech, Jonathan's mind is going back to the first training manuals. "Where were you when I was buried in chapters 5,6, and 7 months ago?"

"Ah, baby steps my friend." Dugan's hands are going again. "If we jes throw ya inta da fire you'd be sorry, the Madam would be upset, the guest would never come back. It would be quite a catastrophe really." Dugan settles back into his chair for more coffee.

"Ha, nothing like putting the pressure on Dugan. Is this the way you greet all the new guys?"

"Aye, pretty much."

Trent comes back to refill Dugan's coffee. "Need anything else gentlemen?" Dugan puts his hand over his cup. Jonathan thinks about it a minute then says "No thanks."

"Trent" Dugan stops him from leaving. "Ave ye met our latest lad Mr. Shipton?"

"Hey man" Trent takes the coffee pot out of his right hand extends his hand to Jonathan. "Welcome to the sanity."

"Thanks, the sanity?"

"Yeah, if you fit here it will make more sense than anything else you've ever done. Good luck." He heads over to another table with his coffee in hand.

Jonathan gets up from his chair. He slides it under the table. "Thanks Dugan. You've given me something to think about. Better get some studying in before my next session."

"No worries laddie, I think you will fit in jest fine." Dugan stands up. The two shake hands. Jonathan takes the lead in leaving. As Dugan is heading out he catches Trent's eye. He gives him a wink. Reassuring him that Jonathan has potential and hopefully is not an ass.

Recognizing Demons

The ladies from the change your mind, change your life class are all sitting around the fire pit in the coffee lounge again. They don't look quite like they did yesterday. They have all spent time with Chauncey and today they are looking fresh, a little more put together and they are excitedly talking about their challenges from the day before.

Veronica walks in the door with a travel mug in hand. As she reaches the ladies they quiet down, first because they want to see what she is going to say, then they are even quieter because they see her face. Veronica looks them all over. "This is more like it! You all look fantabulous! I can't wait to hear all about your days yesterday." She sits down with her mug of tea in hand.

Stephanie is almost smirking. "What'd you do walk into a door?" Veronica smiles. "You haven't learned yet? Guess I can't really say anything. I was so good at telling you all to follow your own gut instincts and then I did exactly what I told you not to do."

"And that would be?" Penny asks with honest concern.

"I knew I should have been more careful, more cautious, because someone threatened me. I blew it off thinking I was over reacting. Then he made good on his threats."

There are gasps all around the couch. Even from Stephanie who seems to dislike Veronica. "Fortunately I am here as an example that you should listen to your little voice, but when you don't you can sometimes still survive it."

Virginia happens to be sitting closest to Veronica. She puts her hand on Veronica's knee. "Are you sure you are up for this today?"
"Ha, I believe I'm doing better than he is and that leads me to talking to you all about learning some self-defense. Hopefully you will never have to use it, but if you do, it's always good to have the confidence and the ability. But that is for you to keep in mind for another time. Now, I want to hear about your days yesterday."

No one is in a rush to be first. The ladies shuffle uncomfortably in their seats.

"Really, not one volunteer? Guess we'll have to start with one end and go down the line."

Everyone looks at Virginia because she is the closest to Veronica, but Veronica's head turns to the other end where Stephanie is sitting. "So where did you find yourself yesterday Stephanie?"

"I don't want to go first."

"There are many things in life we don't want to do aren't there? I can have Jen go first, and then I can have Terrance come in and talk about his experience with you, if you would prefer that."

"Why are you picking on me?"

"If I was picking on you, you would know it. But now that you mention it, you are the only person in this room who is negative, who doesn't accept responsibility for their actions and who doesn't seem to really want to be here. How fair is that to those who do want to be here?"

After a few seconds of silence Stephanie gets up and heads for the door. As she reaches it she turns back to face the group. "You must have deserved that bash in the head bitch!" She leaves the room in a huff. Most of the ladies are sitting in stunned silence.

"Hm, that went well." Veronica releases a big sigh. "Now Jen, care to share?"

"Before I do, that was harsh, brilliant, but harsh." Veronica pauses, not sure if she should share her strategy with everyone, then decides she should and get feedback from them as well. "Sometimes we need a little tough love. We don't always see how we affect other people through our own actions or by what we say. If no one brings it to our attention we go on thinking either its o.k., no one notices, or that no one cares."

Some of the ladies are nodding their heads in understanding. Others are still looking uncomfortable and unsure of how to react.

"Let me ask you this, how many of you have dealt with someone like Stephanie and you talked about that person behind their back, but never said anything to them about their offensiveness because it made you uncomfortable?" Now everyone is on the same page. "They carry on and you suffer in silence or you get them out of your life. That is the easier path, but is it the better one?"

"We just have to let it play out and see what happens. All I really want to know about what you did yesterday is how you felt about it. Was it a good experience? Did you come out of it feeling better?"

Now all the women are more at ease because not only has Veronica moved on, but she isn't interested in particulars of their experiences, just the results. That is much easier to relay than having to admit you can't sing, or your painting wasn't intended to be a Picasso look alike but it is. There are those who are proud of their overcoming of a fear though and are ready to talk about it.

Jen is the first to speak up. "Well, I have always had a fear of guns. My Dad has guns. The first memory I have of them is my Dad target shooting at squirrels in the back yard. I loved watching those squirrels collecting nuts, chasing each other around trees, then he comes out in the yard saying 'Gotta get those varmints outta my yard.' Four loud shots later and all the squirrels were lying dead everywhere." There are 'ohs', and 'poor baby' being said all around the group.

After a short pause Jen is able to continue her story. "From that time on gun shots scared the crap out of me. So yesterday I decided to meet Houston. He looks like they took him right off the Marlboro billboard. He is all cowboy, and all gentleman. He walked me through the safety factors of the gun three times. I'm not kidding, three times! I was so nervous I was even shaking. Then he showed me how to hold it and we took practice shots with an empty gun. He even put blanks in so I could hear the sound without being afraid of hitting something."

Now Jen is standing using her hands to show how she was holding the gun. Every one could see the excitement in her body language. "After what seemed like five minutes to me and was actually two hours he had me shooting live ammunition at a target the size of the side of a bus; thank goodness. But I did it and hopefully I can get rid of those dreams of dead squirrels in my yard."

"That is wonderful!" Virginia is happy for her.

"So cool!" Penny is sitting on the edge of her seat.

Jen is grinning ear to ear.

"Who's next?" Veronica asks. She is pleased to see Jen got the ball rolling because a few hands are raised.

♋

Working With Friends

Veronica is in her office. She is sitting in her desk chair looking out the window as the sun is setting at one corner of the window. Maia walks in. She sees Veronica staring out the window. "Hey!" She says with as much cheer as she can muster.

"Hey." Veronica barely replies back.

"Roni, what's going on?" Maia continues into the room to see her friend face to face.

"Hm?" Veronica continues to look outside.

Maia looks out the window. "Exactly, what's going on?"

Sienna walks in. Maia waves her in to her and Veronica's direction. "Good, maybe you can tell me what's going on with her."

"Is this a trick question? Sienna asks as she comes around to face Veronica. Once she sees her, she snaps her fingers. "Hey, Ron, what's the matter?"

"I'm tired, it's been a long few days and it's not over yet. One of my students hates me, I fucked the head of security, bad timing on my part and I don't know when Erik is going to either show up again or have me arrested for assault."

Maia is concerned now. She hadn't thought of that. "You really think he would do that?"

Veronica looks at Maia. "In a heartbeat."

Sienna heads for the phone. "We just beat him to the punch then. We call the police and tell him what happened."

"Oh yeah, just tell them that I beat the shit out of him and then my staff followed up with their own methods and possibly planted drugs laced with oregano in his car."

"Oregano?" Maia is totally confused now. "What good would that do?"

"Trying to sell poor quality drugs and keep the money therefore he gets beaten to be taught a lesson." Sienna answers before Veronica does. Veronica looks at her knowing this means Sienna must have spoken to Samson. She decides not to mention that right now after Sienna's being upset the other day over their teasing. Maia on the other hand doesn't feel it's a sensitive subject. "Fine, you two both suck."

This was not what either of the others expected her to say.

"What are you talking about?" Sienna is looking at her like she is a little crazy.

"You wouldn't know anything about oregano in drugs if you hadn't already talked to someone 'involved' in last night's events." Maia spreads he arms in front of her. "Obviously you two are getting laid, and are in the know, and I am neither."

"I didn't mean for it to happen..." Veronica starts to explain. Sienna also starts. "He just showed up at my door."

"You two are pathetic." Maia has now crossed her arms to pout in frustration.

"Wait a minute miss high and mighty!" Veronica is beginning to see the humor in Maia's disappointment. She doesn't want to start cracking up without her friends following though. "Who abducted an unsuspecting laborer less than two weeks ago, tethered a hot air balloon and had her six foot tall way with him two hundred feet above the ground?"

"That doesn't count!" Maia continues to pout.

"And why not?" Sienna asks accusingly.

"Because, well, it just doesn't." Maia has nothing.

It only takes a few seconds to sink in, and then all three women start giggling.

"I didn't abduct him!" Maia doesn't want her friends to think anyone would possibly refuse her.

"Whore." Sienna jibes her.

Maia hits back with, "Takes one to know one."

"Ooo, come on you two can do better than that!" Veronica eggs them on.

The giggling and loud voices draw Will into the office. He walks in with the false pretense of seeing what is wrong, but honestly ever since he got the news of last night he has been upset. Why no one called him to let him know what was going on, why did he only hear about it this morning? He needs to make sure they see he is important enough to be on the A list.

"What is going on in here?" Will makes his presence known.

"William!" Maia greets him with a huge hug. "Save me from these harpies!"

"Harpies? Look whose talkin' kidnapper!" Sienna smirks.

Maia continues, "Seriously, maybe William can help us. We need a restraining order, something to keep that dick head from getting back in here unchecked."

"Dick head?" Veronica is taken by surprise once again by Maia's choice of words.

"What do you want me to call him?"

"Dick head will do just fine."

This opens the door for Will. "By the way, thanks for not calling me last night. Maybe I could have done something?"

Sienna doesn't want him feeling slighted. "Will it all happened so fast, we were just reacting." She walks up and puts her hand on his shoulder.

Making quotations with his fingers Will responds. "I understand I'm not part of the inner circle."

Maia is now on Wills other side putting her hand on his shoulder. "Come now, our main concern was getting to Veronica."

"I know, but I would never act without calling one of you first." Will has his arms crossed now. Veronica walks up behind him. "Feeling slighted my genius?"

"Don't try to smooth this over Veronica." Will is trying to stay annoyed but he is rather enjoying the attention. Sienna starts playing with his hair. "How can we make it up to you William?"

Will moves his head into Sienna's hand. "I am not a push over ladies." Veronica puts her hands on his waist and Maia rubs his arm with her hand. Maia teases, "Come now, there must be something."

Suddenly Will sees himself in his bedroom. The three women are dressed in lingerie. They are leading him to his bed. Sienna takes his glasses off and throws them to the side. Maia turns his head to face her. She begins kissing him while Veronica is undoing his shirt from behind.

In quick secession his clothes come off. Veronica is rubbing his shoulders. Maia hasn't released him from her kiss. Sienna is rubbing his chest and brings her hand down to his…

"Will?" Veronica's voice is in the distance. "Will?" She is speaking a little louder now. Sienna is snapping her fingers. Will is sucked back to reality.

Sienna is concerned. "Are you O.K.?" It takes a flash of a few seconds for Will to re acclimate to reality. He takes in a deep breath. "Just thinking of how you three can make up for this faux paux.

Tapping him on the chest Sienna is reassuring. "Good! Tell Veronica and Maia all about it, I've got some things to take care of." She leaves before anyone can say anything. Maia follows her lead. "I think you two should figure this out. Roni, you know where to find me."

"Cowards!" Veronica throws the accusation loudly in her best French accent. She leans back on her desk looking at Will who hasn't quite grasped that the other two have flown the coup. "O.K., so what is it this really about?"

Will looks over his glasses at her. "That bastard could have killed you." Veronica puts her hands on Wills cheeks and lightly taps one. "But he didn't." Will puts her hands in his, brings her hands down and lets go. He walks away. "You were lucky." He turns back to face her. "Veronica you aren't just my boss. You know you mean more to me than that."

"And you know I wouldn't know what to do without you. Will someone would have called you if they knew what was going on." Will walks back to her and sits next to her. "Veronica, it's not that no one called me. You didn't call me."

Veronica puts her hand on his leg. "I wasn't calling anyone. It was a fluke that Dominic saw Erik then saw his picture on Victor's desk."
He takes her hand off his leg. "Veronica, you never called."

"Will."

"Instead you called Anders."

"I didn't call anyone." Veronica is feeling her heart drop. Why doesn't he understand? It's not like she was having a party and didn't invite him. How can I make him understand?

Will gets up. "But I'm not the first one you call." Veronica takes his hand.

"For some things you are. For some things I call Victor, for others I call Sienna."

"And how does Anders rank above me in a call?"

It dawns on Veronica that Will is feeling threatened by her being close to Anders. "Will, my relationship with Anders is very different than my relationship with you."

He is walking out of the office. "Obviously."

"Don't you walk…!" He is gone. Veronica follows him.

"What is your problem?" Will is sitting at his desk, he doesn't say anything. Veronica leans over his desk. "I can't fix this if you don't tell me what's wrong."

Will looks up at her. "Fine! I feel like the oldest son of a divorced Mom. I've been the man of the house in every way 'but one'." He emphasizes this. "Then Mom starts dating a biker, a questionable character that I don't know if I can trust. Now I'm thrown aside. I'm not needed anymore." Veronica falls back into the chair in front of Wills desk. "Jesus Will! My mind was reeling with a hundred different scenarios, you as my son was not one of them."

She smiles and she gets up and walks around to get behind Will. She hugs him from behind putting her head on his shoulder. "You are my man Friday. You are one of my best friends, and I will never throw you aside. Now imagine me being upset because you find a woman you have a connection with that I could never have with you? You would laugh at me."

Will puts his hand on veronica's hug. "You are the one always telling me...

> *"There are times when your emotions just say fuck you rationality! I'm going to hold onto this*

for as long as I like."

Will continues "I didn't say what I am feeling makes sense. I just want you to have faith in me, to count on me."

Veronica turns Will's chair to face her. She kneels in front of him. "If you left me tomorrow, this place would close in a month. How much more can I rely on you?"

Will drops his head and shrugs his shoulders.

Sometimes There Is No Reason

Veronica is back in her office. She is rather relieved Will's dilemma wasn't as complicated as she was anticipating. Her son ha! If she ever had a son she could only hope he would be as wonderful as William Chambers. He is smart, funny, cute as a button and very attentive. Hopefully he will make some girl happy one day.

As much as Veronica loves other people's children, she never had the urge to have her own family once she was old enough to do so. As a child she thought she would have many children. She loved playing with children younger than she was. In high school she spent time working with autistic children and foster care children. She realized there were enough people in the world that needed help. She didn't need to add to that. Besides she always has enough people to take care of in her life.

Her phone rings. She picks it up. "Hello, yes Victor, thank you." She gets up and heads out of her office. When she passes Will's desk he is on the phone. She motions she will be right back. He nods o.k.

When she gets down the hall Stephanie is coming down the stairs. Veronica comes to the bottom of the stairs just as the young lady reaches the bottom.

"Mind if we talk?" Veronica asks.

"I don't think there is anything left to talk about."

"So, you think I will be wasting my breath again."

"Wasting my time again is more like it."

"What exactly did you expect when you came here?"

"What?" Stephanie doesn't understand why Veronica is asking this question. Veronica repeats her question. "What were you expecting when you came here?"

"Maybe some help, some understanding."

"Why don't we have a cup of tea and talk about that."

"You haven't done anything so far." Stephanie proclaims while standing her ground at the bottom of the stairs.

"Stephanie, your walls are so high, I am not going to get over them unless you let me in. Give me ten minutes of no walls and I can guarantee you won't leave today."

"How much you want to bet?"

"Walls, down?"

"Fine, ten minutes."

The two women head for the coffee lounge in silence. Once they get there and order their drinks of choice Veronica leads Stephanie outside to a small bistro table off to the side of the main house. It is surrounded by beautiful gardens.

Stephanie looks around. "What, you don't want anyone hearing our conversation?" Veronica sits. "We can go back to the lounge if you prefer." Stephanie woodenly takes the other seat.

"Stephanie, the sooner you realize that not everyone is out to get you, not everyone is out to hurt you, the sooner you can find your own happiness regardless of what others do and say." Stephanie defiantly takes a sip of her decaf soy latte. She thinks this 'Miss West' is full of hot air.

Veronica sighs and joins her in a sip of breakfast tea before she continues. "I don't know what you've been through. I don't know who has squashed you emotionally into your anger at the world, but I do know that"

"Choosing love, happiness, compassion, and support heals you much quicker than the road of hate, anger, ridicule and resentment."

Stephanie rolls her eyes. "That's helpful." Veronica is still searching for that one key that will open Stephanie's trust. Her aha moment. Veronica decides to try another route. "Stephanie, we are all here dealing with our own struggles, our own insecurities, if we don't let others help us as well as helping others it is much more difficult to get beyond the past, or to get through a rough time today."

"You talk like you know everything. You don't know anything about me."

"Then tell me."

"Right, so you can use me as an 'example' in one of your seminars?"

"You're making a good case for one already."

Stephanie huffs and crosses her arms again.

"Look, if you never trust one person, at some point, you are going to go through the rest of what life you have left like this. Is that what 'you' want? You have given someone else the power to make you miserable. And they most likely don't even know they have it nor do they know how you feel. If they did, would they care? Why not take 'your' power back? Let that person and everyone else know you are better than fine, and that you don't need them to be happy."

Stephanie looks at Veronica with hatred, but her expression changes for a mere millisecond as if something just made sense. Stephanie stands up. "I can't do this." She starts to walk away. Before she gets to the edge of the garden she stops. When she turns to face Veronica again her eyes are filled with tears. Veronica stands up but doesn't move right away. Then Stephanie blurts out. "You are such a bitch! Why do you have to fix everything?

Why can't you just let it be?" Veronica takes a step towards Stephanie, but Stephanie runs towards the back door of the house and disappears inside. Veronica sits down and takes a deep breath. She can only hope something she said makes sense to Stephanie, if not today, one day.

A Mysterious Note

The following morning Jonathan is lying in bed reading a paper on how some women need to be emotionally comfortable before they can be sexually aroused. Dr. Praddon has assigned him to have some knowledge of this by their next meeting. There is a knock at his door. He yells "Coming!" throws his shorts on and heads for the door. When he opens it no one is in sight. He looks down the hall; still no one. He looks down at the floor and there is an envelope with 'Shipton' written on it. "Hmm." He picks up the note and closes the door behind him.

Before opening the envelope he sniffs it, nothing. He tries looking through it, nothing. He shakes it, nothing. He shrugs. It must be safe to open. When he does flip the envelope over the flap was never sealed. 'Wonder why that is.' He thinks to himself. Once he gets the contents out he finds there are two pages. The first page is hand written, it reads;

Dear Jonathan,

Looking forward to our next session. Please shower and shave. Please wear a button down shirt. No other clothing in particular required.

Just follow the map on the next page. If you could be at your destination by 3pm, that would be grand.

Do enjoy the rest of your morning, and if I know you yet, enjoy your studying for Dr. Praddon.

All my best,

Veronica

Jonathan looks at the map on the second page it has a dotted line from the men's quarters to a door under the stairs by the coffee lounge in the main house. "That's curious" he says aloud. There are written instructions under the map.

When you arrive at the door marked "PANTRY" open it and walk inside. Turn the light on then close the door behind you. Walk to the far end of the pantry and look to your right. There will be a very nondescript jar of pickled herring on the third shelf from the top. Lift the jar and follow the instructions you find below.

"Hm" Now he has something else to look forward to today.

Resolutions

It's early in the morning for The Garden. Victor is just opening the daily paper at his desk behind the front counter. There are staff members walking through with different duties on their minds. No one says 'good morning' to Victor when he has the paper in his hands. Young Toby has even left a hot cup of coffee on the counter for him without a word.

Victor is so involved in his reading he doesn't even hear Julia Bishop walk up to the counter. She watches him for a few moments before making her presence known. She is struggling with her own inner dialogue. She really doesn't want to leave, but even spending more time with Chevalier didn't get the vision of seeing what Miss West went through out of Julia's head. She feels the need to get back to her family. Finally she clears her throat in order to get Victors attention away from the stock section of the paper.

At first Victor thinks he is just hearing things. Then another "Ahem" reaches his ears.

He is about to reprimand the intruder for the interruption. His annoyed look softens as soon as he sees Julia at the counter. "Ah, Miss Bishop." Immediately Victor begins folding the paper and standing up to help her with whatever she needs.

Putting her hand up to stop him from getting up Julia apologizes for bothering him so early. "I was just hoping you could call for a ride to the airport." She says calmly.

"A ride?" Victor is confused. He thought she had decided to stay longer.

"Yes, after seeing Miss West the other night, I realize my family needs me. As much as I have thoroughly loved my time here, I have to go."

Leandro walks in carrying Julia's luggage. "Well Mrs. B! I think this is it. Are you sure you're ready?" Julia turns to see what Leandro has placed on the floor.
She smiles. "Thank you Leandro, you are a doll. Yes, I do hope to come back, but I am ready."

Turning back to face Victor Julia opens her purse. "Time to settle my account Mr.

Tanner, I can only imagine the damage." Victor hasn't even turned on the computer yet. No one checks out this early.

"Give me a moment Madam. The computer will need to wake up and catch up to us."

The rumblings of morning activity is beginning to sound as people come down the stairs heading for the coffee lounge or for a bigger breakfast possibly including mimosas at Pandoras. Leandro has already left with her bags to the front drive. Reggie has arrived looking for print outs that he needs for security's day. The silence between Victor and Julia as he is waiting for the computer is awkward. Julia doesn't like quiet. "Mr. Tanner?"

"Yes?"

"Are you also part of the other staff here?" Victor raises a brow to look at Julia with a feigned sense of shock. "Surely I don't know what you mean Madam."

"I mean like Chevalier." Julia is busy looking in her purse not really paying attention to how Victor is reacting.

"Hardly Miss Julia." He is typing his password into the computer hoping it boots up quickly.

"That is a shame. Your gentleman like persona would be perfect,"

"Are you suggesting?"

"I'm just saying there is something alluring about you." She looks at him with an innocent smile. Victor walks over to the printer to retrieve her bill.

"I don't believe anyone has used that term to describe me before, but thank you." He returns with her bill.

There is a look of confusion on Julia's face as she looks the bill over. "I think you have under charged me Mr. Tanner. I spent much more time than this receiving Chevalier's butler services, and there is no mention of my swimming lesson in here."

Merely as a formality Victor looks at the bill. "Julia." He says softly but very matter of factly. "The staff gives me their hours as they see fit. Mr. French was very adamant about this number."

"But… "Julia begins to tear up.

"No, no. No crying at the front desk. I am not good with teary eyed women." He reaches down for a box of tissues under the counter. Julia graciously accepts a couple and dabs her watery eyes.

"I can't believe… " She pauses. " I can't believe I wasn't going to come here. I don't think you know how much these last few days will get me through in the next few months."

"Our door is always open." Victor uncharacteristically places his hand on hers. "Now, why don't you get yourself some breakfast? It will be at least twenty-five to thirty minutes before the car is ready."

"Thank you Mr. Tanner I will do that."

Julia is gathering her purse to leave. Suddenly it begins to vibrate. She turns bright red and Victor raises a brow. "You may want to take the batteries out of that before going through security at the airport." Julia turns bright pink as she reaches to shut off her recent purchase inside her purse.

By the way, it's Victor." Victor gives her a wink and walks back to his desk. Her grin breaks into a wide smile feeling ever so special to be on a first name basis with the dry witted, handsome and refined gentleman.

♋

The green house sprinklers have just turned on. The rumblings of the pipes underneath ease as the water pressure reaches the separate nozzles and drip hoses along the rows of infant plants and those who are too fragile to endure the elements of central California's winds and chill.

The phone in Maia's office begins to ring. After a few rings Peter makes his way in the door to answer it. "Yeah?" He begins looking hopelessly for a pen. There must be one somewhere in the pile of papers, seeds and gloves on Maia's desk. "Hold on". He puts the phone down and opens the top drawer of her desk.

While searching for a pen he notices a photo of Maia and her brother Luca dressed in ski wear standing on a beautiful mountain with snow-capped peaks behind them. He puts it down and reaches for a pen. "Sorry 'bout that. O.K., go ahead. You need it by next Monday? Got it. Thanks Dr. Edwards. I will make sure she gets this.

After hanging up the phone he picks up the picture again. He sits in the desk chair which creaks with age under his weight . He turns the photo over. On the reverse side there is a note. "To my sister, my salvation, I will love you always. Maio." Peter finally has his aha moment after reading this note.

The relationship Peter has with his siblings has always been one of competition. His father was proud to push his children into always striving to be better than each other. However, he forgot to show them how to love and appreciate one another. This hits Peter like a ton of bricks. So many things begin making sense to him. Why he pushes so hard for perfection. Why he didn't understand Maia's need to do 'something' for her brother even though he is gone. "Fuck! Now what?" Peter says aloud to himself. Now that he recognises this what is he supposed to do with it?

There are footsteps outside the door. Peter puts the photo back in the drawer and slides it closed. He sits back in the chair. He knows it is Maia. He thinks to himself. 'How can I make it up to her?'

Maia walks in the door. She is already dirty from digging somewhere on the property, but that didn't stop her from picking up a couple of coffees for her and Peter. She knew he would be ready for their pow wow before the crew meeting this morning. "Good morning my grinmeister!" Maia announces when she sees she is right and Peter is there. She puts her hand out to him with his coffee in it.

"Mornin'" He takes the cup from her. Maia is looking into the green house to make sure all the watering is going on as it should. "Good, it looks like everything is in order this morning!"

Peter goes to take a sip of his coffee. "Not so fast!" Maia snaps. "I almost burnt my lips off! See?" Holding her lower lip between two fingers, she shows him the swollen inner pinkness. He chuckles. "Thanks, just what I needed to see first thing in the morning."

"First thing? You are way behind #1. I've been at it for hours already! Taught a Yoga class this morning then weed hunting in the back 40 and..." Peter interrupts her.

"Oh! Before I forget Dr. Edwards called. He needs more supplies."

"Did he say when?" Maia is calculating in her head when the latest batch will be dry enough.

"He was hoping for Monday."

"Alright, that should be enough time."

Peter lifts his coffee cup to her. "Think its o.k. Now blister lip?"

"That's not funny. It still hurts!" They both take a sip. "Oooo." Maia is having a little more trouble than he is.

Now that they've both had a chance to smell, taste and feel the rejuvenating process of their morning coffee sink in, Maia feels now is her opportunity to talk with Peter about his odd behaviour. Peter is ready to apologize to Maia for not understanding. They both begin to speak at the same time.

Maia starts with "I'm ..."
As Peter begins with "About the whole..." they both laugh.
Maia starts. "O.K. You first."

"No, ladies first, I may be a jerk but I am a gentleman."

"O.K." Maia puts Peter back in her chair and sits back on her desk. "You've been acting a bit odd lately Peter. Don't misunderstand me, the happyish demeanour has been great! But it doesn't feel sincere. I'm sorry, I don't want to put you down if you are trying to forge a new path in your life. I just want to be sure whatever it is you 'are' doing, you are doing for the right reasons. Does that make sense to you?"
Peter cocks his head "Kind of."

"Let me put it to you this way. I didn't hire you for your charm or your witty attitude."

"Thanks"

"Now hear me out. I hired you because you are brilliant at what you do. You know your shit and you are a very good manager."

"O.K."

"Ah. Let me finish. However, if you are trying to make a shift to a lighter spirit in your life, I have only one request. Please do not lose your serious moody angst ridden side altogether. We have women who pay big bucks for your handsome sullen angst."

For the first time in a long time Peter bursts into laughter. Also a first for him; how glad he is that he has no clue where Maia's philosophy comes from but he is appreciating her so much right now, in this moment. How she can put him down and compliment him with the highest regard all in one breath. How the hell she does it is beyond him. Maia is laughing along with him, but she isn't sure why he is laughing. "You know I am very serious, right?"

"Oh, yes, I do, and thank you. No one has ever made me feel so good and so bad about myself in such a short amount of time."

Maia stands up and goes to Peter. She places a hand on his shoulder and one on his knee as she squats next to him. "No, no, no! I didn't want to make you feel bad."
Peter pats her hand with his. "I know, you just have a way of saying things sometimes that totally perplexes me."

"But you do understand what I am saying now right?"

"Yes, yes I do. Now stand up, you're making me nervous like you're gonna propose or something." He pulls her up. He stands and puts her in the chair. Maia's "Ha!" just makes him grin again.

"O.K., guess it's my turn." Now he leans back on her desk. "First I want to apologize for being such an uncompassionate jerk." Maia tries to interrupt.

"Eh, eh, my turn" he waves his finger at her. "My relationship with my family is much different than you with yours." He opens the drawer to her desk and pulls out the photo. He hands it to her. "My brothers and I would never write a note anywhere near what Luca wrote to you. I am sorry I didn't understand. I'm sorry I judged you."

Looking at her brother in this picture she knows he would be proud of Peter's epiphany and she is ever so grateful to have had the relationship she did with her brother. "Thank you."

"Now as far as the grinmeister goes; yes I am trying to make a change, and yes it was feeling awkward, but after today I believe it will possibly make more sense. It will be a work in progress, but I don't think you have to worry about me losing my dark moody side." He lifts his cup to her. She reciprocates. They toast and drink.

Maia is still having trouble. "Ooo, oo."

"Maybe you should have Dr. Praddon look at that."

"So she can taunt me about how stupid I am! I think not."

"O.K. then," Peter gets up and goes to the mini fridge. "Guess you will just have to trust me." He grabs a gel pack from the freezer. "Here, at least keep it from swelling." He hands it to her. "Come on, five minutes and then you don't have to explain the swollen lip to the boys. You know they are going to think I finally punched you in the face." They both laugh as she puts the ice pack on her lower lip. "Ooo, ooo."

More Than A Wine Cellar

It's 2:45 pm. Jonathan is standing in front of the door marked "PANTRY" with 'Personnel only' written below. He can't believe his hands are sweaty. Is he actually nervous? Or is it just anticipation of the unknown? 'His brain is yelling at him. Come on man! Open the door already!' He puts his hand on the handle. He turns it. At first it seems to be locked but a little more enthusiasm in the wrist wakes it up and the large country pantry door opens. He sees a string hanging in front of him. He looks up. It looks like it is attached to a light on the ceiling. He pulls on the string, the light flickers spastically for a few seconds then turns on.

Closing the door behind him, Jonathan starts to walk towards the back of the closet. It is filled to the brim with "stuff"! There is plenty of coffee, and you can smell the good and the flavored ones. Jonathan doesn't get the hype behind flavored coffee. Why would anyone put nut flavoring in a perfectly good cup of wake the fuck up? As he takes a few more steps there are cartons of creamers, sugar; real and fake. There are plenty of napkins, an assortment of cups, straws and huge one gallon cans of chocolate syrup.

A few more steps in there are cans of, bottles of, and boxes of all kinds of food. He must be on the right track. He gets to the end of the room. The wall in front of him has a fire extinguisher hanging on it and a rack with a broom, a mop and a dust pan. He looks to his right, and he counts the shelves from the top. 1, 2, 3… Lo and behold there is the boring jar of pickled herring just waiting to be lifted. He picks up the jar expecting to find another note beneath it. Instead he can see there is a button under the jar and the wall in front of him is opening away from him. He puts the jar down then looks to see what is behind the wall.

There is a small landing followed by a well-lit staircase going down. 'A basement in California' Who let them build this?' Jonathan starts to head down. As he is walking, he notices the pictures on the walls have the names of the different Hanlin Cellars Sensual wines.

First there is 'Eve's Shameless' Red. The full figured woman on the label is wearing a burgundy dress with a low back and a high slit in the skirt. 'Sticky fingers' merlot has a man in a kilt with no shirt on. His right hand is raised with the back of his hand facing out. His pinky and ring fingers are bent down, his other three fingers are up. He is smiling.

At the bottom of the stairs there is a huge poster of 'Entwined' Shiraz. The couple on the label is exactly that. It is difficult to tell where one ends and the other begins. Jonathan almost forgets he is on a time schedule. He looks around for a clue, a direction. There is a note tucked into the top corner of the entwined frame. It is a piece of paper folded in half. This is also hand written. 'Follow the hall to the door on your right. Knock twice.' Jonathan walks down the hall. The first few door s he comes across are on his left. Each marked with a make of wine. 'So this is where they keep the stock.' There is a sign next to the first door he comes to on the right. It is a bright yellow warning sign.

FOR THE SECURITY AND SAFE
KEEPING OF OUR GUESTS AND STAFF
THERE ARE CAMERAS IN OPERATION
EVERYWHERE IN THE DUNGEONS. IF YOU
HAVE A PROBLEM WITH THIS YOU DIDN'T
READ THE WAIVER YOU SIGNED BEFORE
SIGNING YOUR CONTRACT FOR YOUR
VISIT. PLEASE RETURN TO THE FRONT
DESK IF YOU DO NOT WISH TO PROCEED.

'Dungeon? This should be interesting.'
Jonathan knocks twice. There is no answer.
'Great, either I'm early or she is late.' Then the
door slowly opens.

The light in this room is dim in
comparison to the hallway. Jonathan's eyes are
taking a little time to acclimate to it. As he steps
in he can barely make out Veronicas face as she
steps out from behind the door.

He takes another step into the room so
she can close the heavy laden iron looking door.
It groans as she closes it. Jonathan isn't sure if
it's o.k. to speak so he just waits for Veronica.
He can see her better already. She is wearing a

simple pull over dress that hugs her body enough to show her curves, but it's not skin tight. The v neck plunges into her bosom accentuating her chest. She raises her right hand which is holding a 'riding crop'? Oh man. He did not expect this.

"Have you ever been blindfolded Jonathan?" His mouth is suddenly dry. He doesn't even know if he will be able to speak. He fills his mouth with spit in hopes that his voice won't crack when he tries to answer.

"No." The timber of his voice comes across low and sexy. No sign of nervousness.

"Ah, I love a virgin experience." She walks up to him and places a black silk scarf over his eyes.

"I need you to pay attention to how everything feels. "You are going to be leading women through many different blindfolded scenarios. If you don't know what it feels like, how are you going to know what to do? What pressure to use, how much force to use, how much… you get the picture right?"

He is guessing she is sliding her riding crop up his pants, then slowly across his crotch. It has now found its way under his shirt and she is sliding it like a windshield wiper over his chest. His nervousness has oddly melted away. He is paying attention to what he is feeling, while listening for her movements to give him a sign of where she is and what is next. He is also listening for her breathing to see if it gives any indication of what to expect. Unfortunately she is very quiet so it is hard to tell.

"There is no such thing as a safe word here. If your partner says stop, it means stop. If she says no, it means no. This way you don't have to try remembering some ones pets name or their favorite song." She is walking around him while she talks; sliding her crop with her. Jonathan is feeling a little dizzy from her movements. 'How can I feel dizzy? I can't see what she is doing.'

Veronica has taken his hands into her own. She is leading him forward. She stops him, turns him around and tells him to "Sit slowly." He finds himself on the edge of what feels like a bed.

The undressing begins. She starts with the top button. As she gets the shirt undone to just below his chest he can tell she is opening the shirt as she goes along. Suddenly he feels the warm suckling around his nipple. The surprise makes him jump a little. Already his penis begins to react.

He didn't even realize she had undone the rest of the buttons because he was too busy feeling the warm moisture of her tongue and mouth on his chest. She is biting into the side of his neck and tonguing down his torso, then pulling at his belt to expose more of his body.

There is the pressure of hands on his shoulders leading him to turn and lay on one side of the bed. His shoes, socks and pants are taken off. He still has his underwear to protect him 'for now'. There is nothing for a few seconds which feels like an eternity, then music begins to play. It is almost eerie, definitely in minor keys. Maybe it's supposed to keep one unsettled. It's working.

It sounds like a match has been struck and lit. What could that be for? Candles maybe? Then the aroma of incense strikes his nasal passages. It isn't flowery, but more masculine, if there is such a thing. He is still listening for where Veronica is and what she is doing. He hears her voice over the soft music. "Different aromas can cause different reactions. Make sure to check the guest's information on allergies likes and dislikes before choosing a scent."

He jumps again when he is touched ever so lightly. It must be feathers. They are being brought from the bottom of his foot up his leg and then chasing in circular motion on his abdomen. "It is very important to remember any circular movement on the mid-section needs to be done in clockwise motions. Your energy flows in a clockwise motion here. You don't want to do anything to back up someone's system.". ' back up what?' he is thinking, but is taken away as the feathers lightly touch and move around his body, Jonathan notices trigger points of sensation and how his excitement level keeps rising. Inside his elbows, behind his knees, behind his ears, all of these areas are more sensitive and he reacts even if it's slightly. He knows Veronica is paying attention to them as well.

When she takes the top band of his under wear in her grip, she slowly pulls them down and when they reach his mid-thigh the feathers graze across his penis. He wants to jump out of his skin. 'Is she holding them in her mouth?' They are not there for long because she is continuing the removal of his last bit of civility.

Again he is waiting for what is next. The aroma in the room is heady, the music is loud enough to hide the sound of her movements. His body is suddenly jolted to attention when out of nowhere Veronica's mouth is around his penis. She is sucking and tonguing firmly but not too intensely. Just as suddenly she stops. Jonathan's breathing has changed. He is so hard he feels like he must be 14 inches tall pointing at the ceiling right now! Her voice begins again. "Surprise your partner when you can. It is exhilarating to the brain, which in turn creates remarkable physical sensation."

Before he knows what is happening Veronica takes both of his arms and ties them in what feels like another scarf. She attaches it to something over his head. He is hesitant. "These bonds are never unbreakable." She shows him how easy it is to escape.

"You are never out of control. You are allowing someone to give you pleasure and allowing them to feel in control." He relaxes a little.

'Hence the cameras' he thinks to himself.

Next his legs are being spread apart. Each leg is being tied in turn. He feels her tongue along the bottom of his foot. She disappears. Then her tongue is moving along the inside of his arm. She suckles the inside of his elbow vigorously flowing electricity everywhere and causing him to twist and turn his body. At the same time he feels the scratch of her nails going up his torso and circling his chest. His breathing is even heavier now.

The next pull of her nails is along the inside of his arm. He can only imagine her stretching across his body causing her dress to lift accentuating her ass as she drags her nails up from his arm pit to his elbow. "You don't want your partner to know where you will be next. You want their senses to be on full alert."

Every time Veronica pauses and is away from his body he can still feel her presence. He can still taste her from their last session. He is holding onto the straps above his head but making sure he can loosen out of them because he is afraid of pulling down whatever they are attached to in one of his electrical pulses.

"I am asking your permission before I continue. May I drip warm liquid onto your chest?" Veronica wants to give her request time to sink in. She will not rush him.

"Yes." is his simple answer. He barely finishes the 's' when he feels the hot liquid perfectly aimed to a nipple. It isn't scorching, but it is effective enough. "Ahhh" escapes his lips. A second drop of hot liquid hits his other nipple. Next, her hands are massaging his chest, into the hair. It isn't drying, he thought it would be wax. It feels more like an oil.

Her absence this time is a little long. Then he feels her at his feet again. At first he can't tell what she is brushing along the inside of his leg, then he realizes it is her hair. She is crawling up the bed brushing his body with her hair. He is picturing what she looks like then her hair is tickling at his balls. She stops to suck on his ever hard penis again making him squirm a bit.

When she stops and he feels her brushing along his torso he also feels her naked breasts following. 'Fuck, she's naked!' Jonathans grip on the scarf tightens. At the same time he is getting his feet out from the bonds below. Veronica rubs her breasts into the oil already on his chest. The sensation is incredible. She then lowers herself to tongue his nipple while straddling his torso. He can feel her wetness against his penis as she slides up his body. She is pulsing as well.

When her mouth reaches his face he loses all restraint. His arms come loose, he wraps them around her. His mouth finds hers and he urgently begins to kiss her. He brings her to her back on the bed and brings himself between her legs. All this time he hasn't lost his blindfold. He puts his head into the crook of her neck using her to rub the black silk from his eyes. When he opens his, she is looking at him with as much desire as he feels. "This isn't supposed to happen." Veronica says softly, but she doesn't say 'stop'.

Jonathan buries himself in her once again. He has never felt so much sensation all over his body. He is usually focused and he usually has much more control. This is all new, and he thought there was nothing new to learn. He knows he has to find a condom. Veronica reaches to the side. Condom and lube are there.

This is not what Veronica expected, again. What is it about this one that she is all over him? "What is going on with me?' She forgets her fleeting thought and gets lost in their chaotic bonding.

Jonathan is kissing Veronica so deeply, it's as if a thirst cannot be satisfied. They are wrapped, entangled, and engulfed in each other.

Time has stopped. Jonathan brings his arms underneath Veronica pulling her as close to him as possible. She is feeling wanted in a way she never has before. She returns every action from Jonathan with sincere want in return.

When he is spent, they lie on their backs. For the first time he is noticing the room. It is a dungeon; complete with an iron maiden, a stretching rack, and there are leather and chain straps on the walls, rings of metal hanging. He can only imagine what has taken place in this room? Obviously he just had a hint of it today.

"Jonathan?" He turns to face Veronica. "You have to stay in control." This is not what he expected to hear. "You are going to be with some beautiful young women. Some of them will know what they want, most of them won't. You have to be sure it is all about them. The sex may not always happen."

"O.K." Once again she has him feeling unsure. "But was I wrong just now?"

"Yes and no. I was wrong for letting myself get lost in the moment of you taking over. I don't know what it is about you, but I am having trouble staying on track with you." Jonathan can't help but grin. Veronica smacks him. "Don't smile pony boy! It's not funny!"

"Funny isn't the word I would use, I'm just glad I'm not the only one. You make me a little crazy Miss West. I'm not used to losing control."

Veronica starts to get out of the bed. "Maybe I should have you work with someone else." Jonathan reaches for her arm.

"Please, don't. I will learn better with this challenge." He pulls her back onto the bed.

"The question is will I? At least you have made it easy for me to give you your working name."

"Really? What is it Trouble?" Veronica smiles and caresses his cheek with her hand.

"That would work, but for some reason I can't get Gaige out of my head. I think it fits you for some reason."

"Gaige, that could work." He kisses the inside of her hand.

'Fuck!' is in Veronica's head. 'Why am I not stopping him? Why am I not reprimanding him?' He pulls her close and lies on top of her and it all starts again.

When Monday is your Saturday

The day is winding down. Anders still isn't happy with the outcome of Lockhart finding his way into The Garden. Reggie got out of Veronica's ex that he was sleeping with a woman whose friend told her about The Garden and about the Madam; Miss West. When she told him where it was he knew Veronica's Uncle had owned a house in that area. He easily put it together.

Anders didn't buy his story. The women who come here don't like to talk about it with men. It is their private oasis away from reality.

How was he going to get rid of this thorn? He remembers a friend from his military days. Maybe he can help him out. He picks up the phone and dials. He is lucky enough to reach him right away. "Hey, Dutchman! Yeah, it's me. I know, it's been a while. Look, I need a favor."

After laying out the situation, Dutch is more than eager for the distraction from 'retirement'. As they are finishing their conversation Maia walks in. "That wouldn't have to do with our oregano bandit would it?"

"Well, if he goes for the bait and still comes back I will be sure to be ready, but I honestly doubt he will."

Victor, Reggie and Samson all seem to have had the same idea. They arrive in Anders office as he says, "I think winning a tropical vacation for two will suck him in nicely." Victor smiles, "Good to know we are on the same page."

"And the same team" Reggie chimes in. Maia looks at the clock on the wall. "Oh! Sorry gentlemen I need to test some wine!". All the men give her room to exit stating their goodbyes.

"And to what do I owe the pleasure gentlemen?" Anders asks the men filling up his office space.
Samson speaks up. "I was hoping we could find a way to keep Lockhart away from here and away from the Madam. But it sounds like you're already working on it."

"I don't think our trouble maker will be returning any time soon." Anders sits back in his chair. His hands are behind his head. His grin broadens. "Now maybe we should pretend you never heard any of my conversation and go unwind at Pandoras."

♋

Mondays are usually slow at The Garden. It is a night off for most of the staff so many of them gather at Pandoras on Monday nights if they are 'on the grounds'. There is a jukebox in the back dancing area playing some dance techno mix. The sound level isn't very loud at this time though. Maia is sitting at the bar chatting with Dominic about the latest batch of 'Sinfandel' wine they are uncorking. She has actually changed out of her usual cacky shorts and tank top and is wearing flared jeans and a flower print long sleeve scoop necked shirt. She is donning a very walk friendly sandal encased in so many bright colors you could never lose her in a crowd.

"The bottle has been breathing for about thirty minutes, are you ready to try a glass? Dominic asks the wine maker.

"Why not, since I seem to be the only one interested."
Maia sits herself up like a school girl who is about to be quizzed.

Dominic raises the bottle high above the glass for a long pour. He pours a mouthfuls' worth and hands the glass to Maia. She lifts the glass, looks at the color, swirls it around watching for the 'legs' of the wine. She breathes in the wine with a full nasal inhale. "Mmmmm" comes from her as she exhales. Then she closes her eyes and takes a sip. She swirls the deep garnet liquid in her mouth, letting the flavors ride over her tongue making 'mmm' noises here and there.

Dominic always finds this first taste the most fascinating. It's also rather sexy watching Maia do it. Some people look ridiculous, but somehow she makes it look hot! He can always tell when she and the Dr. are happy with a wine. When they swallow that first taste and bow their head and pull their whole body back almost like they just creamed themselves, he knows they are happy. If they swallow and open their eyes it is just o.k. If their eyes are open by the time they swallow they are not happy with the results. Today Maia bows her head in a grateful prayer to the grape gods.

Dominic is watching so intently that neither he nor Maia notice Sienna and Veronica as they walk up to the bar. Sienna puts her hand on Maia's back. "Couldn't wait two more minutes?" Maia opens her eyes.
"The timing of the first taste of an aired bottle is a precise science my friend. And those who dare to be late miss out." Maia puffs her chest in faux defiance. In her best stuck up voice she welcomes her friends. "Hello ladies."

There are already two glasses set on the bar next to Maia. Dominic raises the bottle. "May I ladies?"

"Thank you Dominic." Veronica nods in approval. He repeats the same high pour but this time he fills all three glasses one third up the glass. He is called away by a customer at the other end of the bar.

The ladies clink their glasses in a toast. Maia sits back as Sienna sits next to her. Veronica pulls a stool to sit between them a little behind. She doesn't like looking over Sienna to share in the conversation. Maia swallows her sip. "Man what a few days!"

Sienna finishes her first taste of the wine. "Oh, Me oh Maia, this is amazing! But yes I agree, the last few days have been stressful, including asshole alert."

"You mean dickhead?" Maia interjects.

"Let's not even go there, please?" Veronica raises her hand to stop the flow of conversation. "There are much better things to talk about, like our new addition to the family."

"Oh yes, I think he will do fine if he can lower his intensity a touch." Maia seems to like him too.

"Intensity, he just cracked me up. He said my diagram of the female clinical region looked like a penis octopus holding an upside down heart."

All three women laugh. "Really? Now I have to see it again." Veronica is trying to remember what the diagram looks like. She takes another sip of the wine. "Maia, this is incredible."

Maia sticks up her nose again. "Hmph" Don't care to question me about my methods again Miss West?"

"I believe I've learned my lesson maestria*."

"After spending some time with Mr. Shipton I think I have the perfect name for him. He seems to like it."

"You already talked with him about it?" Sienna is surprised. "You must really like this one."

Maia is practically jumping out of her seat. "So, come on, don't make us wait."

Veronica leans in like a quarter back in a huddle. "What do you think of... Gaige?"

"Hm, strong and to the point. I like it!" Maia approves.

"Gaige. I'll have to sleep on that one."

"Really Sienna?" Veronica's sarcasm pops up.

Sienna waves her off. "Oh, you know what I mean."

The music has gotten a little louder. There are more people dancing. When the guys have time off they still consider Pandoras a place to meet women and have a good time, which in turn makes it good for business.

The ladies just had their wine glasses refilled when Samson comes over to the bar. He stays a slight distance away trying to look like he isn't paying attention to Sienna who is closest to him. As if he heard them talking about him; Jonathan shows up at the bar. He taps Maia on the shoulder. "Care for a dance Miss Hanlin?" He puts his hand out waiting for a response. Maia leans towards Veronica and Sienna.

"Initiative, I like!" She gets up to take him up on that dance offer. "Let's go Sir Gaige!" Jonathan looks at Veronica gives her a nod of acknowledgment and smiles while taking Maia's arm. He looks at Maia. "Maybe you will let me lead this time?"

Sienna snorts, "Not likely." They head to the dance floor.

Taking another sip of wine in unison, Sienna and Veronica put their glasses down and both of them give a sideways look towards Samson. Sienna whispers to Veronica. "Does he seriously think he isn't being obvious?"

"He isn't. Only you know why he is standing there, so why don't you ask him to dance?"

"Right, just make it completely obvious."

"Sienna, you two have danced together before, it will only be obvious if you want it to be."

Sienna gets up from her chair. Without even looking at him she addresses Samson. "The least you could do is to ask me to dance Samson." Samson takes a chug of his beer. He turns to face Sienna. Without a word he takes a step to her, picks her up and carries her to the dance floor over his shoulder. All the while she is yelling at him.

"Put me down! What the hell are you doing?" Thus making it the perfect cover so no one will be the wiser.

It looks like it is going to be busy for a Monday night. The last few days must have affected more people than Veronica thought. As she is going over the most recent events Will comes up behind her. He places his head on her shoulder. She tilts her head to his. "I'm sorry" Will whispers.

"Are we O.K.?" She asks him.

"We're O.K."

"Forgiven then... son." Veronica starts giggling.

"Stop!" will stands up with his arms blocking the verbal blow.

"I'm so proud of you, son."

"O.K., now I need a drink." Will waves his hand trying to get Dominic's attention. Before the bartender extraordinaire makes it over Will feels a tap on his shoulder. "Veronica." He starts then stops because the tap was Jen from Veronica's change your life group who decided to stay a couple of extra days to work on a few more of her fears including approaching someone she is attracted to. She is shuffling "Excuse me Mr. Chambers, would you like to dance?" He looks at Veronica who is trying to be neutral and not do anything to make Jen feel this is a set up because it isn't. However, he notices the slight tilt of Veronica's head towards the dance floor and the raise of her eyebrow. "I would love a dance." Will smiles and reaches for Jens hand.

Looking at the stools on either side of her Veronica raises her glass into the nothingness in front of her. Dominic fist bumps her glass. "Salute boss!"

"Salute. Looks like it's just you and me Dom."

"That ain't so bad is it?"

"Of course not. So how did it end up going with the flowers?"

"The flowers? Oh yeah, I didn't get em' to her so she left before I could get her number."

"Dominic, this is The Garden you know... Where dreams can come true."

The worlds barely come out of her mouth when the woman he was talking about sits at the bar a few stools down from Veronica. Dominic is looking at Veronica and hasn't noticed yet. "Yeah but."

"But what?" Veronica asks.

"How am I supposed to call her?"

"Sometimes we just have to look for the unexpected."

"Excuse me, Dominic?" He turns to see who is calling for him. His face lights up like Christmas. He looks back at Veronica. "You devil."

She smiles. "A thank you for all you're help last night."

He pauses, "Do I look o.k.? My breath?"

"Oh God! Go On!" Veronica encourages him.

"Coming beautiful!" Dominic heads over to his crush with the excitement of a school boy.

Left once again to her own devices, Veronica closes her eyes and takes a deep breath. She hears Anders voice quietly in her ear.

"Mind if I join you Miss Kick Ass?" She doesn't open her eyes but her smile reappears.

"Not afraid I'm going to hurt you?" She turns to look at him.

"No, I hear you won't do that to men you kiss in front of your ex." He sits down and motions to Jake who is keeping an eye out for who needs what while Dominic is engrossed in conversation.

"I'm sorry, I can't thank you enough for playing along."

"I think you thanked me well enough. How are you?"

"I still don't know really. When I'm busy I'm fine, but then something creeps up on me out of nowhere and I just want to scream and punch."

"You know I'm available for sparring anytime you want it."

"Be careful what you offer sir, I may be one who takes advantage."

Jake has arrived with bourbon on the rocks knowing Anders usual drink. He places it on the bar in front of him.

"More wine Madam?" Jake asks as he lifts the bottle.

Veronica shakes her head. "No thanks Jake, maybe in a few. And thank you for covering while Dominic gets his *second chance*."

"No worries." He heads over to someone else calling for beverages.

Anders takes a sip of his drink. "Maybe I need to be taken advantage of a little. Besides, *it's all in one's perspective as to who is taking advantage of who right*?"

"Are you eaves dropping on my classes?"

"Doing rounds in security can be very educational Miss West. Shall we?" He puts his hand out for hers.

They make their way to the now crowded dance floor. "Livin' La Vida Loca" is playing. 'How fitting' Veronica thinks to herself as Anders brings her around for her first turn and they begin to dance. Veronica is happy to see her family of friends letting loose, and living in the moment.

"For who knows what tomorrow may bring?"

♋

The Garden Dictionary

* Sometimes words need to be invented or refound. If you have a question about a word with an * near it I hope to have remembered to put a description of said word here.

Active meditation –For us at The Garden it means meditating in motion. Whether it is in dance, swimming, walking or even during sex, you go deeper into yourself while your body is physically active. And a guided active meditation is when someone talks you through it.

Bordella – A whore house of men for women.

Flippedtacular- When hair is in total disarray after a restless night's sleep.

Maestria - female interpretation of maestro. Saying she is a mastress of what she does.

Pash – Short for passion. This is what the guys call their Janes so to speak. After all, this job is their passion.

Undescriptive- Vague, not easy to describe.

Va jay jay – slang for vagina aka hoo ha.

Whadiya- slang for "what do you"
Wariess- Like god has its' counterpart in goddess, warrior needs to have its' counterpart. When a woman cries in mourning it is a blood curdling sound it also needs a word worth its' weight in description.

Products on the shelf if The Garden store

Body Splashes
Eve scent – body splash made of vanilla, citrus, spice and as Veronica said, loaded with pheromones.

Wariess Blend – A stronger clove, orange and cinnamon blend.

♋ Hanlin Cellars Wine ♋
Sensual Line
Reds
Eve's Shameless   Sticky fingers
Sinfandel
Dark & Sweet Port   Popped cherry
Entwined

Whites
Adams Apple   Fig leaf White
White knight

Going Solo Dessert wine

Fun wines
Vampire Port
Virgin White

Don't forget The Garden Journals
and Goddess pens.

Our coffee mugs, key chains
and Goddess totems.

A Note from The Author

There is nothing in this book that hasn't been written before, nothing that hasn't been thought by someone else in the last couple of thousand of years. But not every thought has reached every person in the world. I can only hope I reach at least one person. Maybe one person will be lead to feeling better about themselves. Maybe someone will discover new possibilities in their life because of this book. If someone takes the steps to spiritual freedom, to leaving negative self destruction behind them, to having better sexual relations, I will be happy. I will be ever grateful.

I believe the world can find its way to being a better place when people face fears. Facing the unknown is difficult for most of us, but blindly accepting anything about yourself without searching to see what more you are capable of is a shame. I have done this myself, I am not immune. This book is not written by a psychology professor, it is not a gospel, it is hopefully thought provoking, fun, and encouraging.

This is a book of fiction, but it *could be real*. You just have to choose what works for you. Thank you for taking the time to discover The Garden of Eve. Hopefully you will find out more about them and meet some new extraordinarily ordinary folks to come.

To Kari and Claudia,

None of this would be possible without you. I appreciate your friendship, our sisterhood, our laughter and the fact that we are one another's rocks. Love you two ladies to the moon and back,

...and remember everyone *be you to full!*
In love with laughter,

Flo

Map of Hanlin Cellars vineyards and The Garden property

Maia's
Crop

stables

B6

B2   B5

Vines

B1   B4

B3
Tarzan's

pool   patio
Spa   Staff
Gym   Pandoras

Veronica   patio
Main
house   Vines

Sienna   Pond

Vines   garage   Green
house

Victor   tennis   Maia

Vines   Grand
Hall   Vines

Wine
gift shop

Made in the
USA
Lexington, KY